Dear Reader,

S0-AEA-685

Welcome to the fifth title in the series of *Great Lakes Romances*®, historical fiction full of love and adventure set in bygone days on North America's vast inland waters.

Like the other books in this series, *Aurora of North Manitou Island* relays the excitement and thrills of a tale skillfully told, but contains no explicit sex, offensive language, or gratuitous violence.

We invite you to tell us what you would like most to read about in *Great Lakes Romances*®. For your convenience, we have included a survey form at the back of the book. Please fill it out and send it to us.

At the back, you will also find descriptions of other romances in this series, stories that will sweep you away to an era of gentility and enchantment, and places of unparalleled beauty and wonder!

Thank you for being a part of *Great Lakes Romances*®!

Sincerely,
The Publishers

P.S. Author Donna Winters loves to hear from her readers. You can write her at P.O. Box 177, Caledonia, MI 49316.

*To Pam Chambers*
*for loaning me your* Cottage Physician.
*What would I have done without it?*

*P.S. I am completely confident that one day, my name*
*will appear in the dedication of your book!*

♥   ♥   ♥

### Notes

This novel is a work of fiction. Names, characters, places, and incidents are either the product of the author's imagination or, if real, are used fictitiously.

The North Manitou Island lightkeeping structures no longer exist, but illustrations have been included to enhance reader understanding of this novel. The interior diagram of one half of the keeper's quarters reflects a degree of accuracy in its detail, but is not intended to show precisely the two-family split dwelling.

### Acknowledgments

I would like to thank the following people for volunteering their assistance in preparation of this work:

Bill Herd of the National Park Service, Empire, Michigan, for historical information about lightkeeping on North Manitou Island including photos, diagrams, and maps from park archives

Hilda Stahl, award-winning author of over one hundred books for adults and children, for advice on plot and characters

Reverend Bobby Dale Whitlock of the United Methodist Church, Caledonia, for lending a copy of the Church Discipline 1888, and for advice regarding Preacher Mulder's character

Ron Hulst of Caledonia High School for the keeper's quarters interior diagram

*To Kerri,*

# Aurora of
# *North Manitou*
# *Island*

*The lights go on!*

## Donna Winters

*Donna Winters*

## Great Lakes Romances®

**Bigwater Publishing**
**Caledonia, Michigan**

Lyrics are from the following:
"Beautiful Isle of Somewhere" copyright 1897 and 1901 by E.O.Excell, words and music
"Oh Promise Me" copyright 1889 by G. Schirmer
"The Man Who Broke the Bank at Monte Carlo" copyright 1891 and 1892 by
Francis, Day & Hunter

Matrimony Ritual is from:
*The Doctrines & Discipline of the Methodist Episcopal Church*
copyright 1888, Phillips & Hunt, New York

Medical advice is from:
*The Cottage Physician* copyright 1892 C.King, Richardson & Co.

Bible quotations are from the King James version, copyright 1897

*Aurora of North Manitou Island*
Copyright c 1993 by Donna Winters

*Great Lakes Romances* is a registered trademark of Bigwater Publishing,
P.O. Box 177, Caledonia, MI 49316.

Library of Congress Catalog Card Number 93-70501
ISBN 0-923048-81-2

All rights reserved. No part of this publication may be reproduced, stored in a retrieval
system, or transmitted in any form or by any means--electronic, mechanical, photocopy,
recording, or any other--except for brief quotations in printed reviews, without the prior
permission of the publisher.

*Edited by Pamela Quint Chambers and Anne Severance*
*Cover art by Patrick Kelley*

Printed in the United States of America

93   94   95   96   97   98   99    /  CH  /   10   9   8   7   6   5   4   3   2   1

# Keeper's Quarters
## Upper Floor

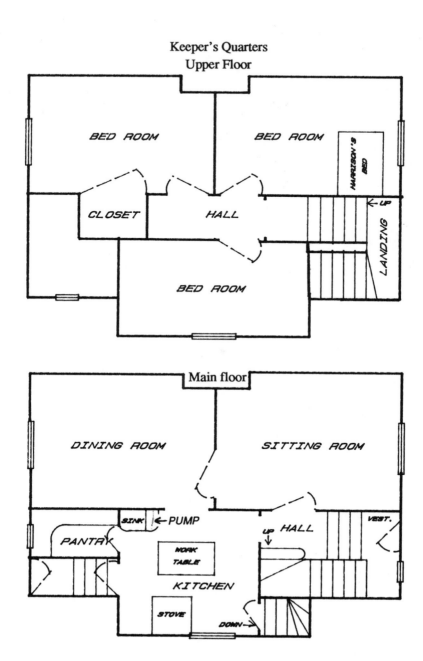

BED ROOM

BED ROOM

HARRISON'S BED

CLOSET

HALL

← UP

LANDING

BED ROOM

## Main floor

DINING ROOM

SITTING ROOM

SINK ← PUMP

PANTRY

WORK TABLE

UP HALL

VEST.

KITCHEN

STOVE

DOWN →

*North Manitou Island Light*

*North Manitou Island Keeper's Quarters*

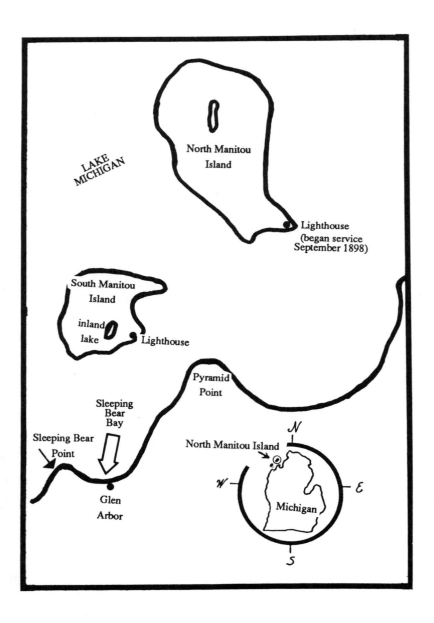

# CHAPTER

## 1

*Thanksgiving Day Evening, 1898*
*Lightkeeper's Quarters*
*South Manitou Island, Michigan*

"Harrison's gone! I just know it!" Aurora Richards released her pent-up fears in the solitude of her cold bedroom. "Nothing would have kept him from our wedding today. Nothing! Unless . . . " She squeezed her eyes shut, then opened them again in a vain attempt to block out a vision of Harrison's small sloop wrecked on the shoals of the Manitou Passage.

With fingers numbed by the chill of her unheated bedroom, she unhooked the bodice of her satin wedding dress while gloomy thoughts continued to taunt her. "Today should have been the happiest day of my life. Instead, it has been the most endless, anguishing . . . "

She placed the costume—one she had spent months

beading with a thousand seed pearls—on a rose-scented padded hanger, and hung it against the door of the wardrobe. The gesture was an admission that all her plans, all her dreams, the very purpose of her existence had come to an end, and she couldn't help thinking she never wanted to lay eyes on the gown again.

With a rumpling of muslin, she rid herself of petticoats and corset and kicked off her wedding slippers. Pulling on the thick flannel nightgown she had thought she would never wear again, she let the soft fabric fall down about her legs as she scurried across the cold hardwood floor and flipped back the covers of her bed.

Snuggling into the down mattress, she doused the kerosene lamp, leaving the room bathed in the spill of soft light coming from the lighthouse tower.

She lay her head on her pillow, pulling the feather comforter up over her ears, hoping to bury her fears beneath the covers and drift off to sleep. A few restless moments later, she threw off the comforter. Kneeling beside her bed, she searched underneath for her fur-lined slippers, then returned to the wardrobe for her heavy flannel wrapper and began to pace from window to door and back again.

Through the frosty glass, she tried to make out some vestige of Harrison's sloop approaching the lighthouse dock, but the turbulent waters of the crescent bay were ominously empty. Below her bedroom, in the parlor, more than a score of wedding guests still waited for news of her missing bridegroom and the search party that had been sent out over six hours ago. But she could not bear to hear more of their well-meaning reassurances.

Never in her wildest imaginings would she have

dreamed the ordeal that had become her wedding night. And never, in the five years she had known Harrison Stone, had he ever failed to present himself at the promised hour.

Now, after years of courting and planning and waiting for the perfect day on which to seal their union in holy matrimony, the only man she ever loved had left her a bride without a bridegroom. Not only that, but she was distraught with worry over what might have become of him on the freezing, storm-tossed waters of northern Lake Michigan.

Tears welled up, spilling down her cheeks. She retrieved the last of her dry handkerchiefs from her dresser. A glimpse in the faintly illumined beveled mirror above it reminded her she had forgotten to loose her hair. With fumbling fingers she managed to remove the hairpins from her Gibson Girl style, shook her head vigorously to free her waist-length golden-brown tresses, and pulled on the sleeping cap that hung on her bedpost. She would forego braiding her hair for tonight.

Staring at her tear-stained face, she addressed herself. "Thanksgiving Day, and what have I to be thankful for? A ruined wedding? A dead bridegroom? I feel as though I've been widowed even before I've become a wife!"

As she resumed her pacing, she thought of her betrothed, the tall, quiet, intrepid man who had courted her with dignity and persistence from the day she had turned fifteen. Oh, the plans they had made over the years! They'd marry and live as lightkeepers on a Lake Michigan island. They'd have four children—two boys and two girls—and teach them the traditions of keeping the light, and the ingenuity necessary for running a steam-powered fog signal.

*He* wanted the girls to be just like *her*, with bright smiles and laughing blue eyes, and brown hair shimmering with highlights the color of the noonday sun. *She* wanted the boys to be just like *him*. She loved his strong chin and soft gray eyes, and each one of the ten freckles across the bridge of his distinguished nose!

No one on earth could ever understand her the way Harrison did. He knew when she needed him near for comfort. Then, he would take her hand in his and sit close beside her. It was almost as if his own strength was imparted to her by the firm, yet gentle contact.

He knew, too, when she needed to be alone. At those times, when she would bury herself in her sewing, he would sit quietly across the room and read, refraining from interrupting or demanding her attention. In his considerate and thoughtful ways, he reminded her of her father.

How she had loved her papa, but he had been taken from her when she was only thirteen. Mr. Trevelyn, the head lightkeeper on South Manitou, and his sons, Nat and Seth, had been steadfast friends, helping to see her and her mother and sisters through the loss, but they couldn't take the place of her papa.

Two years later, Harrison had been hired as second assistant keeper, and from the moment they had first met, it was as if they were made for each other. Besides her papa, he was the only man she had ever loved. He meant the world to her!

*But Harrison is gone!*

The thought pierced her heart with a cruel and merciless stab. She was trying desperately to staunch a new flow of tears when she heard someone running up the stairs.

"Aurora!" Her eighteen-year-old sister, Charlotte,

shouted to her even before she reached the bedroom.

Aurora arrived at the door just as Charlotte charged into the room, nearly knocking her over when they collided.

"Aurora, Harrison is safe!"

"Is he here?"

"No, not yet, but he's all right!"

"How do you know?"

"I've been watching the North Manitou light from the tower . . . I saw . . ."

Though Aurora realized her sister was breathless from the exertion of running down more than a hundred twenty spiral steps in the lighthouse tower, through the long passageway, then up a flight of stairs to the second floor of the keeper's quarters, she could summon no patience for word of her beloved.

"For pity sake, Charlotte, tell me what you saw!"

"The OK signal . . . from the North Manitou light. Three long flashes, then a long-short-long, just like Mr. Trevelyn taught us!" She referred to the Morse Code used by the head keep' whenever he had gone out in the light service vessel on a rescue mission and was coming home safely.

Aurora threw her arms about her younger sister. "He's alive! Harrison's alive!" she repeated, as if the news were too good to believe. "He's coming home to me!"

# CHAPTER

## 2

Aboard the seventy-five-foot steamer, *Manitou Lady*, Aurora wanted nothing more than to be with Harrison once again. She watched the approach to North Manitou from the window of the deck cabin. In the gray light of an overcast day, its sandy shore looked foreboding, lying across the steel-blue waters of Lake Michigan four miles northeast of South Manitou. As the *Manitou Lady* left the protection of the crescent harbor, the icy wind picked up, leaking into the cabin, causing her to draw her Mackintosh coat closer about her.

For three days, storms had whipped up, abated, then come again. On Friday, during a break in the weather, the search party consisting of Mr. Trevelyn's sons, Nat and Seth, and Nat's brother-in-law, Fritz Schroeder, had come back from their successful attempt to locate the missing bridegroom and the minister. Unfortunately, they had not brought Harrison and Preacher Mulder with them, arriving instead with a bit of bad news. Harrison had been injured during the Thanksgiving Day storm, and was unable to come to South Manitou for the wedding as planned.

Another two days of bad weather passed before Nat and Seth were finally able to take Aurora and all of the

Richards family to North Manitou Island for the wedding. Charlotte, nineteen-year-old Bridget, their two younger brothers, and their widowed mother were traveling together aboard the steamer for the wintry excursion. Regrettably, Mr. Trevelyn and his wife had to stay behind on South Manitou to tend lightkeeping chores.

As the *Manitou Lady* drew closer to her destination, the fifty-foot lighthouse tower on the corner of North Manitou Island grew more distinct. Behind it stood the roomy, three-story red brick keeper's quarters. Aurora's pulse quickened at the knowledge she would soon reside with Harrison in one-half of the split house where he had recently been promoted from his South Manitou job to assistant keeper of the new North Manitou light.

Adding to Aurora's nervous anticipation of the postponed nuptials was the fact that Nat and Seth had been willing to say little about Harrison's injury, telling her only that he had twisted his leg badly and would need some time to get back on his feet.

Aurora brushed the bothersome notion aside. Harrison was a healthy, strapping, twenty-five-year-old man, or at least he had been until the Thanksgiving Day storm. No matter what had happened, he would soon mend, she was sure of it. After all, if he were too badly hurt, the Trevelyn brothers would not have been willing to take her across to North Manitou for the wedding.

In her mind's eye she imagined Harrison in good health beside her now, looking down from his six-foot-two-inch height, making all five feet of her melt inside with the look of adoration in his warm, gray eyes.

An unwelcomed blast of cold air breezed through the cabin door, abruptly whisking away her comforting reverie, bringing her quickly back to the present as Eli and Dorin, her eight- and nine-year-old brothers entered with a rush.

"We're almost there, Aurora! Will Keeper Dixon let us go up in the tower?" Dorin asked excitedly.

"Yeah. Can we go up in the tower?" Eli repeated.

Aurora couldn't help smiling at the two bright-eyed boys who were obviously far more enthralled with the prospect of visiting the recently completed lighthouse than in seeing their oldest sister get married. "If you behave like gentlemen, perhaps Mr. Dixon will take you up there."

"Oh, boy!" Eli exclaimed.

"Come on, Eli! Let's go up to the pilothouse and watch Nat bring the boat in!"

Aurora opened her mouth to caution her brothers against bothering Nat now, while he tended the tricky business of docking the boat, but the boys dashed out of the main deck cabin before she could get the words out.

Once ashore, Aurora didn't wait for the others, but picked up her skirt and ran along the sandy path to the two-hundred-foot boardwalk leading to the keeper's quarters. Bursting through the left front door, her feet carried her quickly through the vestibule and up the four steps into the kitchen where an unexpected encounter with Serilda Anders brought her to a quick halt.

Aurora had never cared much for Harrison's childhood friend, whom she had met a few times at baseball games between the teams of North and South Manitou. Her fierce loyalty to Harrison seemed to belie their so-called platonic relationship.

Besides, the twenty-five-year-old spinster gave every appearance of being a prideful, outspoken North Manitou

Islander, from the high color in her cheeks, to the shabby blouse waist and skirt she was wearing. The dingy white cotton waist with its frayed cuffs and worn collar offered blatant proof of her need for a seamstress's touch. Were they friends, Aurora would have tactfully volunteered to help Serilda make a new one cut from a simple but practical design. From the looks of her, she didn't know the first thing about sewing!

Harrison had said she had been hired on temporarily to help Keeper Dixon. With Mrs. Dixon away on the mainland for the winter to care for her ailing sister in Leland, the Dixons' household chores fell on Serilda. Evidently, Harrison's friend had now extended her domain to the assistant keeper's half of the house as well.

"Serilda, I wasn't expecting to see you here." Aurora managed to infuse the words with more congeniality than she felt.

"For goodness sake, call me Spunky. The name Serilda nettles me so much, I never could get on with anyone who persisted in callin' me by it," she insisted brusquely as she held the teakettle beneath the spout of the pump at the kitchen sink and filled it with well water. Putting it on the burner to heat, she added two sticks of wood to the fire in the cook stove, then turned to Aurora. "Harrison's upstairs in the first room on the right. Let me warn you though, he ain't feelin' too much like company. Can't blame him none. I ain't never seen a broken thigh bone stickin' out through the skin the way his was."

"Broken thigh bone? Sticking out through . . . " Aurora felt suddenly lightheaded and began to sway. Spunky's steadying arm guided her to a yellow spindle-back chair at the work table in the center of the kitchen.

"Settle yourself down, now. He'll get over it by spring. He's improved considerable since they brought him in here Thursday night." Spunky drew cold well water into a tin cup and offered it to Aurora.

Surprised by the Anders woman's accommodating gestures, Aurora sipped the cool liquid, trying to overcome her queasiness. "I knew Harrison had twisted his leg and would need time to get back on his feet, but I had no idea about his broken thigh."

Spunky finished setting an assortment of unmatched mugs and teacups from Harrison's cupboard onto a tray then paused to brush a dark blond strand of her unkempt hair from her forehead as she faced Aurora. "Can't blame them Trevelyn fellas for not givin' you the whole truth of the matter. They didn't want to worry you more than necessary."

The ruckus at the front entry told Aurora the others were coming through the foyer. She sprang to her feet. "I'd like to see Harrison alone. Please don't let anyone else upstairs for a few minutes."

Spunky nodded. "Mind what I said, now. Harrison ain't exactly receptive to visitors."

Aurora spun away, hurrying to the front hall and staircase, her eyes on the oak treads as she ran up the steps. Halfway there, she bumped into Preacher Mulder, whose steadying hands on her shoulders prevented her from losing her balance. "I'm so sorry, Pastor! I was in such a rush to see Harrison, I didn't notice you." She quickly sidestepped the portly man and continued her ascent.

"Miss Richards, perhaps I could have a word with you before—"

She smiled over her shoulder. "Forgive me for being

so hasty, but I must get upstairs. I trust you're ready to perform the ceremony. I'm planning to be wed as soon as I've spoken to Harrison and changed into my gown. Now, please excuse me."

The door to Harrison's room, the first one on the right, stood open. The residue of carbolic acid disinfectant mingled with the less offensive odor of a sweet-smelling alcohol—patent medicine, she presumed. She paused at the threshold to study him.

He lay on his back in the double bed, his head and shoulders propped against a mound of pillows. A sheet partially covered his left leg, but enough remained visible for her to see that strips of white muslin bound it to a heavily padded splint. With determination, Aurora moved forward to stand at the foot of his bed.

A scowl furrowed Harrison's sandy brows, and the moment his troubled gray eyes met hers, he shut them and winced, as if in pain.

Never had she seen him so helpless. The look of him, dependent and vulnerable, sent her heart to her throat. In that same moment, her love for him increased ten-fold, filling her with a powerful desire to nurse him back to health.

"Harrison?" She waited, but he made no attempt to respond. Despite the fact that he was a normally tacit man, his silence worried her. Stepping beside him, she spoke quietly. "Harrison, I came just as soon as I could so we can be married."

Harrison glanced at Aurora briefly, then turned away, looking out the window at the bleak clouds. But he barely noticed the steely gray canopy overspreading the Manitou Passage. The gentle scent of her apple blossom toilet water surrounded him, filling him with an awareness of her presence. The decision he had been forced to make due to his injury became more abhorrent to him by the second. How could he send away the young woman he loved beyond life itself, and had wanted more than anything else in the world to take as his wife?

Resolve came rolling back, recalling that fateful moment in Thursday's storm when the mast had snapped and he'd caught his foot, wrenching his leg and breaking his thigh in the scramble to avoid a blow to his back. In one agonizing moment, his most precious dream had been yanked from him, though he had been too stunned to realize it at first.

On Friday, in the immediate aftermath of the traumatic event, he had yearned more than anything for this moment—to be with Aurora and accept the comfort she could offer. When the Trevelyns had suggested taking him to the mainland to see the doctor in Glen Arbor, he had stubbornly denied the serious nature of his injury, confident he could overcome it by following the advice in Keeper Dixon's medical manual.

The Trevelyns reluctantly departed for South Manitou without him. In their absence, he had been forced to face the feebleness of his condition, and the likelihood that a leg as badly broken as his would probably leave him a cripple.

Haunted by memories of his grandfather who had walked on two canes during the last years before his death, only now could Harrison begin to empathize with Grandpa Harry's circumstances. Only now, after three days of helplessness filled with reflections on the past, had Harrison been capable of making decisions he considered necessary concerning his future—and Aurora's.

Too late, he realized bringing Aurora to North Manitou was a big mistake. Now, he reckoned with an agony far greater than his physical injury—the anguish of calling off the wedding. It was for her own good.

"Go away, Aurora."

Aurora felt certain Harrison's mumbled words were born of fatigue and pain, and not any real desire for her to leave. She reached out, gently pushing a wave of his light brown hair off his forehead, then briefly touched the back of her hand to him. At least he wasn't running a fever.

The blue flannel nightshirt he wore was rumpled at the collar, and she smoothed it down. "If you're tired, I'll come back later, after you've rested."

Aurora's momentary contact sent a warmth straight to Harrison's heart, making him want more than anything to seek solace in a shared embrace. Then he stared down at his broken leg bound between splints, a leg he could no longer depend on.

Until this accident, he had chosen a life free of strong drink, but the pain of the injury had so overwhelmed him, he would have done anything to dull it. When Cad Blackburn, the Chicago visitor at the nearby Anders farm, handed him a bottle of Spunky's cherry wine and stood over him insisting, "Drink!" he did just that. Since Thursday, he had relied on moderate amounts of alcohol during the day, and a small dose of opium each night just to make it through. Now, he wasn't at all sure he could manage without the medications.

Even more troubling was his conviction that no good could possibly come to a woman married to a cripple. His Grandmother Lacy's selfless care of Grandpa Harry, for whom Harrison had been named, had proved that beyond a

21

shadow of a doubt.

Harrison steeled himself to reply. "Go home where you belong, Aurora."

Harrison's directive, only a fraction more forceful than his last, seemed misbegotten to Aurora. She took his large hand in hers, giving it a squeeze. Troubled by his lack of response, she lay his limp hand carefully at his side. "I'll be back to see you again in a little while. Maybe then you'll feel strong enough to take your wedding vows. In the meanwhile, I'll change into my gown."

Before she could turn to go, he reached out to catch her by the wrist in a painful grip. Gazing into her eyes, his own penetrated her with a look she'd never seen from him before, a look so uncompromising it cut her to the quick.

"The wedding is *off!*" he asserted through clenched teeth. Then he threw her hand aside. "Now get out of here!"

Stunned, Aurora stood momentarily speechless. Then she quickly rallied her wits about her. "You need me to care for you!" she insisted with an impassioned plea. "It makes no difference to me how long it takes your leg to heal. I want to marry you *today.* I love you!" she professed, on the brink of tears.

He leaned forward, his cheeks hot with shame for the way he was forced to treat her. Nevertheless, he must sever ties, and he must do it now. Gathering willpower, he spoke clearly and distinctly, counting more on boldness than honesty to send her away.

"I don't need you! I don't want your help!" he declared, though lying tormented him almost beyond endurance. He braced himself to continue. "Spunky will care for me. Can't you understand? The marriage is off!"

"But Harrison, we love—"

"The only love I feel for you is brotherly love, not the kind to make a marriage! Now go away, Aurora!"

The impact of what Harrison had said, and the certainty with which he had said it, hit her like a gale storming up through the Manitou Passage. Five years of courtship, five years of plans all a mockery! Spunky was the one he had loved all along!

*What a fool I've been!*

Horrified, she whirled away. Nearly blind with despair, she flew from the room, her feet carrying her down the stairs with a power all their own.

She came to a stop just inside the living room where her mother, sisters, Preacher Mulder, and Spunky had gathered to warm themselves with tea. How she hated that Anders woman!

Then grief overcame hatred, and her shoulders shook uncontrollably with suppressed sobs. Her mother and sisters quickly surrounded her.

"Aurora, what is it?" her mother gently demanded.

"What's happened to upset you so?" Charlotte asked anxiously.

"You'd better sit down and tell us," Bridget suggested, pulling up a chair.

Aurora sat, and with a consummate effort, managed to respond. "Harrison said . . . he doesn't love me . . . that Spunky will care for him," she choked out. "Then he told me to go away!" Feeling as limp and useless as her damp handkerchief, she slumped against the back of the chair.

Spunky set her beverage on a table with a clank and rose. "He said that now, did he? Why, that lyin', pathetic excuse of a man! I'll give him a wiggin' he ain't likely to soon forget!" She shook her fist in the air, startling Aurora with the vehement outburst before stomping out of the room, the vibration of her heel against hardwood rattling the china cup she had left behind.

"Miss Anders, I should like a word with Harrison, as well," Preacher Mulder called after the earthy woman, pushing himself up from his chair with effort. On his way out of the room, he paused beside Aurora, placing a large, comforting hand on her shoulder. "Miss Richards, I had hoped to counsel with you before you saw your betrothed, to warn you about the change in his temperament since the accident. When he spoke to you, he spoke out of anger over what has become of him, not in truth."

Aurora lifted her chin determinedly. "I realize that now. I love him too much to give up on him," she said with quiet resolve, "but with his mind set as it is, I can think of no argument to convince him to marry me now."

A hint of a smile tipped the corner of Preacher Mulder's mouth. "Then you haven't reckoned with the likes of Miss Anders and Preacher Mulder, and neither has Harrison Stone."

Harrison could tell by the rhythm and force of boot leather on stair treads that Spunky was on her way up with a mission, no doubt because of what he had said to Aurora. No matter. He knew what lay in his future, doomed as he was to a life of uselessness. And there would be no Aurora in it.

Spunky stalked across the plank floor, halting within arm's length. Hands on waist, she bent over him. "You cruel, callous, cold-hearted clod . . ." She shook her finger in his face. "You went and broke Aurora's heart. The poor girl's downstairs right now cryin' her eyes out. And what for? 'Cause you're too proud to admit you need her! Seems to me you oughta count your lucky stars she still wants you. Instead, what do you do? You go castin' her aside like some flat rock skimmin' over the water, you mean, merciless—"

"Now, now, Miss Anders," Preacher Mulder scolded, puffing to catch his breath as he entered the room and dropped onto a chair on the opposite side of Harrison's bed. "It won't do to make matters any worse than they already are."

Spunky's hand dropped to her side. "Maybe so, Preacher. Tend to get carried away with myself sometimes. I'll take my leave and let the two of you talk man to man." She turned to go, pausing by the door to face Harrison again. "By the way, Stoney, there's one thing more I want you to understand. I agreed Thursday night to help out here, but the arrangement's only temporary. The job belongs to Aurora. She loves you. She wants to take care of you, and now that she's here, I'm movin' back to my quarters on Keeper Dixon's side of the house." Spunky paused for breath. "You can refuse to take Aurora as your wife if you want, but don't expect me to come rushin' to your side the next time you need somethin'. You can shout and holler and pound the walls and I won't budge. I got better ways to spend my time than caterin' to the likes of you, you ungrateful turncoat!"

As Spunky's footfalls faded away, Harrison wondered what he could say to convince the scrappy woman to change her mind and stay on.

Preacher Mulder cleared his throat. "Well. Miss Anders certainly has strong feelings about your circumstances."

Harrison leaned forward, adjusted his pillow slightly, then lay back, troubled by this new crisis. "She'll come around," he said with far more confidence than he felt.

"I shouldn't count on it. She sounded quite decided on the issue, and I can't say as I blame her. You can't expect Miss Anders to care for you indefinitely, in any case." The preacher paused to inspect his fingertips, recovering from a mild case of frostbite suffered during Thursday's storm. Without looking up, he continued. "Miss Anders is right about Miss Richards. As your wife—"

Harrison interrupted with a groan. When the preacher's eyes met his, Harrison's gaze remained steady as he stated with conviction, "I won't marry her."

"I don't believe you mean that."

Harrison sighed. Though the encounter with Aurora had taken a toll on him, he was more exasperated than exhausted. "I'm but half a man now. That's not near good enough for Aurora Richards."

"I can assure you that's not the way Miss Richards feels. Besides, you'll recover by spring."

"There's no guarantee of that!" he almost shouted, causing the preacher to sit back in surprise. With quiet disdain, Harrison added, "She feels sorry for me. That's all."

"The only one feeling sorry for Harrison Stone is *you!*" Preacher Mulder's voice rose in volume, taking on a pulpit resonance.

Harrison closed his eyes, unwilling to listen, but he could not shut out his pastor's sermon.

"I beseech you to heed God's word. He tells us, 'all things work together for good to them that love God, to them who are the called according to His purpose.' I'm confident you can recover the usefulness of your leg if you want, but even a man with only one good leg is capable of living a productive, meaningful life. You must accept what has happened, Harrison, and go on."

Though Harrison kept his silence, his mind was screaming. *I'll never accept what has happened, regardless of what you preach, Reverend! When you're done, you're going to stand up and walk out of here.* I'm *the one who's left to face tomorrow from a bed, dependent for every little thing on someone else.*

The preacher's familiar moan of exertion told Harrison he was pressing himself up from his chair. Harrison opened his eyes a slit, thankful he would soon be alone again. But when Preacher Mulder reached the end of the bed, he turned back, placing his hands against the footboard as if it were his pulpit lectern. Harrison opened his eyes wide and glared at him, eager to send him on his way.

"Whether you want to listen or not, Harrison, this is one sermon I am compelled to deliver. You must believe that good things will come out of your accident. You needn't worry about tomorrow, for God promises to supply your need, He promises to be with you always, and to hear your prayers in times of trouble.

"He knows that until now, you have been strong in a physical sense, and that some of that strength has been lost. Just as there is a time to plant and a time to reap, there is a time to be strong in the flesh, and a time to be strong in the spirit. Now is your time to be strong in spirit—strong as is Miss Richards in her love for you. Look toward the future! It holds blessings for you both!" Preacher Mulder leaned forward, gesturing in earnest. "Don't turn your back on life!" After a long silence, he left the room.

*Blessings?* Harrison wanted to shout. *How could a leg as badly broken as this one be called a blessing?*

He reflected on his grandfather's injury, and the back-breaking work it caused his grandmother, sending her early to her grave. He loved Aurora too much to do the same to her.

Harrison thought again about his pastor's words, and was still fuming over them when Nat and Seth Trevelyn entered the room, coming to stand on either side of him, a pair of grim faces.

Nat spoke first. "I've known you since I was fourteen and you were fifteen, Stoney," he recalled sentimentally. "You were my hero, the one I looked up to. Makes me feel mighty bad to say this, but for the first time since I've known you, I'm disappointed in you." He paused, his eyes steadfastly on Harrison's. "We left Friday for South Manitou, thinkin' you wanted Aurora here. At least that's what you'd said. Now that she's arrived, you're tellin' her to go away, you don't want to marry her. She's mighty upset, and I can't say as I blame her. I think Seth and I deserve an explanation."

Before Harrison replied, Seth spoke up.

"Aurora's like a sister to us, growing up at the light station together, and all. We didn't pull you out of the drink Thursday night to have you go and do this to her. Not when she cares for you like she does, and you need her like you do."

"That's right. It just don't make sense!" Nat concluded emphatically.

Following an uneasy silence, Harrison offered a terse explanation. "I just can't burden her with this." He nodded

28

at his broken leg. "It could be a problem for the rest of my life, and I couldn't ask her to—"

"You know Aurora better than that," Nat said bluntly. "If I were you, the one person I'd want helpin' me to get through a tough time like this is Aurora Richards. She's got a way of always lookin' on the best side. But you tellin' her you don't want her—that's different. I never thought you'd be so bullheaded!"

"You can't change what's happened," Seth said, "but with Aurora's help, you could make the best of it."

"That's right," Nat hastened to say. "What it comes down to, Stoney, is this. The weather's turnin' bad again. We're gonna have to leave real soon if we're gonna make it back to South Manitou today. When we go, we're not takin' Aurora with us, and we're not leaving until you make her your wife," he stated firmly.

"So buck up," Seth sternly advised, "because we'll be back in a few minutes with Preacher Mulder and Aurora and the rest of the Richards family, and you'd better take those wedding vows, or we'll break your other leg! Then where will you be?" With a parting chuckle, Seth and Nat left the room.

# CHAPTER

## 3

Aurora stood before the mirror in the sitting room, fussing with her gown and veil—infused with the soft scent of the rose sachet she had packed them in. Despite the comforting heat from the stove, her hands were as cold as a Manitou blizzard, and trembling from nerves.

Before the Trevelyn brothers had gone upstairs to speak with Harrison, they had told her to change for the wedding, offering the promise, "Stoney will come around by the time we're done with him."

Then Spunky had taken her to Keeper Dixon's side of the house to put on her gown. If her mother and sisters hadn't been there to give her confidence, she never would have taken off her gray wool shirtwaist.

Spunky had been a source of practical help and encouragement too, making sure the trunks Aurora had brought from South Manitou were put in the room across the hall from Harrison's—both the one with her clothing and the one filled with linens, lengths of yard goods, and skeins of yarn for sewing and knitting. Spunky had offered, as well, to unpack and make up the bed while Aurora was changing her clothes. Aurora was beginning to regret her earlier anger directed toward the woman who gave her such staunch support.

The Trevelyns entered the sitting room. Nat wore a modest smile, and Seth put on a subdued version of his crooked grin. As Nat approached her and offered his arm, she thought how much he deserved to be home on South Manitou with his wife, Meta, right now. Instead, he was playing the role of older brother for a bride in distress.

Arms linked, they faced Preacher Mulder. Spunky, Keeper Dixon and Aurora's younger brothers who had just come inside from a tour of the light tower, as well as her mother and sisters, Bridget and Charlotte, stood in attendance. Except for the soft whisper of wind pressing against the windows, the room fell silent, the atmosphere thick with expectation.

"If you all will go upstairs now and take your places at Stoney's side, the weddin' ceremony can begin," Nat told them.

Aurora and Nat waited for the room to empty, then moved to the bottom of the stairs. When the others had disappeared beyond the landing, Aurora whispered to him, "Are you sure Harrison is willing?"

Nat gave her hand a pat. "Everything will be fine."

As they started up the stairs, Aurora wondered whether Nat was right, or if she would suffer yet one more humiliating blow over her plans to wed. If Harrison wouldn't have her, she thought she would just run away to the mainland to live the life of a spinster seamstress—in Traverse City, perhaps, where no one knew her. There, she was sure to find plenty of customers who would appreciate her.

At the top of the stairs, her mother and sisters waited in the hallway. The bedroom door was closed! Aurora's throat constricted, and her face threatened to crumple in a new flow of tears at being shut out.

"It'll be just a minute," Charlotte assured her. "Spunky and the fellows are helping Harrison get ready."

While they waited, Charlotte helped Aurora arrange her veil over her face. The next few moments passed slowly. The door to Harrison's room opened at last, and Nat led her to Harrison's side. Even through her veil, she could tell Harrison had made a concerted effort to prepare for this moment. His sandy brown hair was neatly groomed, and no longer was he clad in the wrinkled flannel nightshirt. He had replaced it with a stiffly starched white shirt and collar with a striped tie, a vest, and a suit coat. The jacket to his new gray pinstripe suit—evidently the one he'd said he was having made especially for their wedding—set off his broad shoulders against the white bed linens. But the most welcome sight of all was the brief look of pleasure on his face when he saw her.

Harrison wondered whether he would ever be able to take his eyes off the lovely young woman he was about to take for his bride.

*I don't deserve her!* The single thought seemed to dominate all others. *Not now, not like I am. How can I possibly join myself to her for as long as we both shall live? I never should have listened to the Trevelyns. They were just bullying me for their own convenience, so they could leave North Manitou in good conscience.*

*That's a bucket of hog slop!* A different voice inside taunted him. *Aurora wants you, and you want Aurora. Take your wedding vows in good faith. Preacher Mulder is right. There is a time for everything, and now is your time to be strong in spirit. All will work out for the good for you both!*

While these thoughts battled in Harrison's mind, the preacher opened his book and began the ceremony, finishing the "Dearly Beloved" opening.

"I require and charge you both, that if either of you know any impediment why you may not be lawfully joined together in Matrimony, you do now confess it: for be ye well assured, that so many as are coupled together otherwise than God's Word doth allow, are not joined together by God, neither is their Matrimony lawful."

Aurora held her breath, keeping her eyes steadfastly on Harrison's. Though she knew neither of them had legal grounds to prevent marriage, she feared the opening might cause Harrison to argue against matrimony on an emotional basis.

A lifetime seemed to pass before Preacher Mulder continued. "Harrison, wilt thou have this woman to be thy wedded wife, to live together after God's ordinance in the holy estate of Matrimony? Wilt thou love her, comfort her, honor and keep her, in sickness and in health: and forsaking all other, keep thee only unto her, so long as ye both shall live?"

Harrison didn't have to look around to know all eyes were on him. He could feel them burning into him, scorching through his shell of resistance, melting his martyr's armor. He gathered what strength was left and gave his answer with more conviction than he felt. "I will."

Aurora rejoiced. Never had two sweeter words been uttered in her presence. Within a few fleeting moments, she heard herself making the same promise.

Then Preacher Mulder directed Harrison to take her right hand, and the warmth of his long fingers curling about hers began to chase away her jitters.

A phrase at a time, Harrison repeated after the minister, "I, Harrison, take thee, Aurora . . . to be my wedded wife . . . to have and to hold from this day forward . . . for better, for worse . . . for richer for poorer . . . in sickness and in health . . . to love and to cherish . . . till death us do part . . . according to God's holy ordinance . . . and thereto I plight thee my faith."

Then Harrison loosed his firm grip, and she took his huge hand in her small one. Would she be wife enough to see him through this time of sickness? She had to believe she would, she just *had* to! In as steady a voice as she could manage, Aurora, likewise, repeated after Preacher Mulder the promises, then he prayed.

"O eternal God, Creator and Preserver of all mankind, Giver of all spiritual grace, the author of everlasting life; send thy blessing upon these thy servants, this man and this woman, whom we bless in thy name; that as Isaac and Rebecca lived faithfully together, so these persons may surely perform and keep the vow and covenant between them made, and may ever remain in perfect love and peace together, and live according to thy laws, through Jesus Christ our Lord. Amen."

Harrison fished inside his vest pocket, producing a slim gold band. In handing it to Preacher Mulder, the ring dropped into the folds of bed linens. After an anxious moment, the pastor found it and returned it to Harrison with the words, "Place it on the third finger of Aurora's left hand."

As Harrison worked the ring over her knuckle, he spoke

the words Preacher Mulder read from the church discipline. "With this ring I thee wed, and with my worldly goods I thee endow, in the name of the Father, and of the Son, and of the Holy Ghost. Amen."

Taking their right hands and joining them together, Preacher Mulder continued. "Forasmuch as Harrison and Aurora have consented together in holy wedlock, and have witnessed the same before God and this company, and thereto have pledged their faith either to other, and have declared the same by joining of hands; I pronounce that they are husband and wife together, in the name of the Father, and of the Son, and of the Holy Ghost. Those whom God hath joined together, let no man put asunder. Amen."

As the pastor continued through a blessing and prayers, Aurora's spirit soared, lifted by her love for Harrison and her desire to care for him and please him in every way. Their marriage might not be complete in the physical sense until his leg healed, but in the meantime, they could build the foundation of a loving, affectionate relationship to last a lifetime.

By spring, he would recover from his injury, she was sure of it! With her loving attention, how could it be otherwise?

Now that Harrison had taken his vows, his love and desire for Aurora intensified, focusing into a beam brighter than that of the Third Order lamp atop the South Manitou light tower. At the same time, his fears of inadequacy loomed ever greater before him, a high mountain capable of blotting out the light, casting over him a dark shadow he might never escape. In the days to come, he couldn't help wondering which would prevail?

Preacher Mulder closed his book and smiled at Harrison. "You may kiss your bride."

With Bridget's help, Aurora lifted the layer of sheer silk from her face and bent down to Harrison. When their lips touched, the brief kiss sparked an answering desire. Startled, she shook it aside. Further intimacy would have to wait.

No sooner had the precious moment passed, than Nat stepped beside her. "Let me be the first to wish you and Stoney the best." He planted a brotherly kiss on her cheek, then his gaze shifted to the darkening slice of water and sky visible from the four-pane window. Huge snowflakes had begun to fill the air, swirling as the wind picked up, then falling on the layer of white already accumulated on the ground from the previous three days. "I hate to rush away, but from the looks of the weather, we'd best save the reception until a different time." His gaze on the preacher, he said, "You'd better come with us. We can't take you to Glen Arbor tonight, but you can stay with us on South Manitou until the lake calms down. God willing, it'll clear enough for us to get you home, then take the *Manitou Lady* to Frankfort before winter sets in for good."

Aurora's mother moved close. "Best wishes, daughter. I'll be thinking of you." When they embraced, a lump began to form in Aurora's throat. Until now, she hadn't reckoned with the fact that for the first time in her life, four miles of water and ice would separate them.

Charlotte offered a hug. "I can't believe we won't see one another until spring."

"Nor can I," Bridget said, touching her cheek to Aurora's.

"I'll miss you all," Aurora admitted shakily.

Her younger brothers kissed her cheeks, and suddenly they all were gone. As their voices drifted away, she struggled against tears.

Spunky was the last to leave. "I'll be over with dinner plates for you and Stoney later. No sense you tryin' to find your way around a new kitchen tonight."

Aurora mouthed a "thank you" and turned to her new husband.

Harrison took note of the glimmer in Aurora's blue eyes and knew it was not the outcome of happiness over their uncustomary nuptials. He knew, too, Aurora needed his emotional support at this difficult moment, but he seemed barely able to think of anything but the pain that was beginning to throb in his leg. He loosened his necktie.

"Let me help you," Aurora offered, but when she reached out to him, he shoved her hand away.

"My nightshirt. In the closet." His request was uncharacteristically terse.

She quickly found the garment, taking a moment to brush away a fresh tear. She'd never seen Harrison so abrupt—nor so ill. As his leg improved, perhaps his disposition would also.

When Aurora returned to Harrison, he was immediately aware of the dampness on her cheek, and the hurt look she tried to cover with a forced smile. Words of apology were on his tongue, but before he could utter them, a new wave of pain overtook him, and his jaw clenched.

While Harrison pulled on his nightshirt, Aurora busied herself putting away his tie, shirt, and suit coat, struggling to keep a grip on her emotions. Falling apart now would do neither of them any good.

By the time she had finished hanging his clothes, he

had repositioned himself beneath his covers, having discarded several pillows on the floor so he could lie flat. She picked them up and pulled a chair to his bedside, piling them there within his reach.

Though his eyes were shut, she was certain he couldn't be asleep yet. "Can I get you anything?" she asked softly, reluctant to leave without offering.

"No, thank you. Please go now," he replied without even a flicker of his closed eyelids.

His face was flushed. She wanted to feel his forehead again to see if he were running a fever, but she dared not touch him. "I'll be across the hall if you need me," she half whispered.

Her room was dim in the waning light of early evening. Outside her uncurtained window, the stiff breeze was even more evident, whirling the snow in circles, at times making it seem to fall upward. Despite the newness of the keeper's quarters, the glass rattled softly, allowing a cold draft to seep in.

Aurora lit the oil lamp, and saw that Spunky had unpacked linens from her trunk as she had said she would, and put one of the pillowcases Aurora had embroidered with apple blossoms on her pillow on the single, solitary bed.

The room was stark, even for a lighthouse station, with white plaster walls and ceiling, and hardwood floors. A washstand, low dresser with mirror, and vanity stool were the only furnishings in addition to her bed and trunks—except for one sheet-draped piece that stood in the corner like a table. Quickly, she removed her veil and crossed the bare floor to pull off the muslin.

She gasped. Before her stood the most beautifully

polished solid oak sewing machine cabinet she had ever seen! And on it lay a flowery, gold-embossed card penned in Harrison's meticulous handwriting.

*I've often wished to have a friend*
*With whom my choicest hours to spend*
*To whom I safely may impart*
*Each wish and weakness of my heart*
*Who would in every sorrow cheer*
*And mingle with my grief a tear*
*And to secure that bliss for life,*
*I'm blessed to make that friend my wife.*

*Harrison*

The sentimental words, so unlike Harrison's usual self, brought more tears. She read them again, cherishing each line, then ran her finger over the deep grain of the dark oak cover. Never had she imagined that she would have a sewing machine of her own so soon.

For years, she had been using her mother's machine. Knowing it must stay on South Manitou, Aurora had begun saving last year for her own, and had set aside half of the twenty-two dollars needed to order one from the Montgomery Ward Catalogue. On Harrison's meager salary, she knew he had to have saved long and hard to purchase such a costly item.

She glanced across the hall. Though Harrison's room was dark, she could tell he had drifted into a light sleep by the sound of his breathing, which was interspersed with soft noises of discomfort. She looked again at the machine and considered opening the cover to admire the inner workings.

After a moment, she put the card back where she had found it and replaced the drop cloth.

For now, her greatest desire was to keep her husband as comfortable as possible. She would have time for sewing later, when Harrison had improved. She was anxious to change out of her wedding gown so she would be ready to tend him when he needed something. Now that he was asleep, she could steal into his room and sit quietly by him, regardless that he had asked her to leave him alone.

From her closet, she pulled out the shirtwaist she had worn earlier that day. She was laying it on her bed when she heard an insistent knock on the door at the back of the house.

She assumed it was Spunky or Keeper Dixon, too polite to simply walk in. Carefully, she picked up her long skirt and train in one hand and the oil lamp in the other as she descended to the first floor and made her way through the kitchen and down the six steps to the rear entry.

"Spunky? Open up!" The loud male voice carried through the thick oak door.

Thinking it was Keeper Dixon, Aurora turned the brass knob, realizing too late the man on the other side of the door wasn't Keeper Dixon at all, but a total stranger!

# CHAPTER

## 4

Aurora stood face to face with a tall stranger who was dusted with snow from the tassel of his stocking cap to the toes of his gum boots.

Without invitation, he stepped inside out of the blustery wind, pulled off his hat, and smiled. "Pardon my intrusion. I was expecting to find Spunky. You must be Mrs. Stone." His voice was mellow enough to earn him the baritone position in a male quartet without singing a note.

"Yes." Although Aurora was delighted at being called by her married name for the very first time, she was not too enchanted to notice he was giving her a good looking over.

"I can see now why Stoney was willing to risk his life to get to his wedding. Just my luck, I've come too late for the nuptials. No matter. I'll just take off my boots and go on upstairs and offer my congratulations to the bridegroom."

"You'll do no such thing!" she countered, surprised at his pushiness, and her own short response. She attempted to be more diplomatic. "Harrison is sleeping. He badly needs his rest, and I can't allow him to be disturbed. Besides, you haven't even introduced yourself."

"My deepest apologies, Mrs. Stone. I seem to have taken leave of my manners. I'm a friend of your husband and Spunky, Cadwallader Blackburn, at your service." He bowed with a flourish. "Cad to my friends."

She raised the lantern for a closer look at the six-foot-tall stranger. The soft flame flickered off the handsome angles of his face, illuminating a broad smile that couldn't help but win hers in return. "As I said, Mr. Blackburn, Harrison is asleep right now, but I'm sure he'll be awake before long, if you care to wait in the sitting room."

Cad's easy entree into the new Mrs. Stone's good graces didn't surprise him any, accustomed as he was to having his way with the fairer sex. Right now, though, he was in need of a cup of Spunky's strong, hot coffee, and a hearty meal to go with it after his cold trek from her pa's farm. More than likely, she had dinner preparations well underway, but that obviously wasn't the case with Mrs. Stone. "Thanks for your kindness, ma'am, but I'd best make a call next door. Miss Anders is expecting me. I'll stop back here later, if that's all right."

"Certainly, Mr. Blackburn. If Harrison wakes up, I'll tell him you've come by, and plan to return."

Spunky was alone in the Dixon side of the house, hurrying to finish dinner preparations before Keeper Dixon returned from adjusting the light, when Cad's unmistakable pounding commenced on the door. Quickly, she tossed another piece of hardwood into the kitchen stove, slammed shut the cast iron door, and hastened to allow him entrance.

"What kept you? A gent could near freeze his ears off in this wind in the time it took you to answer." He slapped his cap free of snow, handed it to Spunky, and stooped to unlace his boots.

"Aw, quit your bellyachin', Cad Blackburn. It's about what I'd expect from a slick Chicago man like you. Too soft to stand up to a North Manitou wind."

He dropped his boots onto the entryway tiles with two thuds. "There, you're wrong. Chicago winds are as strong as any northern Michigan has to offer. I've suffered my share trudging along Lakeshore Drive, I'll have you know, *Miss Serilda.*"

"Don't call me that!"

To quell her protest, Cad pulled her quickly into his arms, aiming to steal a kiss. Oh, how she wanted that kiss! At the same time, she was angry with herself for such feelings and determined not to let Cad know of the pleasure she took in his affections.

Her hands against his chest, she forced him off, then stood back to shake a finger at him. "Mind your manners, Cadwallader Blackburn!  Keeper Dixon  will be comin' through that door any minute now." She ran up the few steps to the kitchen, leaving him to hang his coat and muffler on a wall peg.

He followed her to the stove, hovering close as she lifted the lid from a large iron pot. The aroma of turkey and gravy wafted up. "I'm so cold and hungry after the walk from your pa's, I do believe I  could polish off half that dinner all by myself."

"Well you're not gettin' half. Keeper Dixon and I are plenty hungry, too. Besides, I'm savin' two platefuls for Stoney and Aurora.  I mean to take it to them when we're done here."

"Aurora?  Are you speaking of the new Mrs. Stone?"

"None other."

"A right comely woman, in my estimation." He offered a sly smile.

"And how would you know?"

Cad chuckled at the hint of jealousy in Spunky's question. "I went looking for you next door, and she answered."

"I shoulda known. Seems no woman escapes your notice on this island. You should pay half as much attention to the chores y'r doin' at pa's farm in exchange for your room and board. You couldn't get our best milk cow to put so much as a drop in her bucket the first time you milked her back in September. Of course, that's about what I'd expect from someone who spent his summer and his money at the card tables in the Monte Carlo cottage."

"You severely underrate me. Since September, there's been a considerable increase in Bessie's output. Wish I could have had similar success at gambling."

"You never shoulda put up y'r ticket back to Chicago in a bet. I don't blame your pa one bit for makin' you stay on North Manitou until you've earned the fare back home. It oughta be a lesson to you. My pa only took you in to keep you from starvin' to death till you can get a payin' job when the cottage folks come back next summer. Lucky for you, nobody outside o' my family knows the truth of it, or you'd be too ashamed to step foot off of Pa's farm." She took out a mug, poured coffee from the pot she kept on the back burner, and offered it to Cad. "Here's somethin' to warm you while I get dinner onto the table. Take it into the sitting room. At least there, you'll be out from under foot, and I won't have to listen to you brag on yourself for a spell." Actually, she'd kind of missed Cad's bragging since she'd moved in to help Keeper Dixon.

When Cad had gone from the kitchen, she got out her tray and prepared it with sliced bread, small cups of applesauce, and a plate of pickles, then carried it to the dining room. There, she set the food on the table along with the plates, cups, and saucers from the built-in china cabinet and the silver from the velvet-lined drawer. As she reached for the rose-figured sugar bowl, the tea tin beside it which she had brought with her from the farm, reminded her of her special dream.

She set out the bowl, then reached for the tin. Coins rattled inside. She glanced into the sitting room, hoping Cad, with his keen ear for money, hadn't heard. Through the door connected to the sitting room, she could see he was engrossed in a book from the light service portable library about his favorite subject, horseless carriages. She turned her back to him and quietly opened the tin.

In it were a few folded bills, and several gold and silver coins she had earned this past spring and summer. With the pay from her work for Keeper Dixon this winter, she would have enough money come spring for the trip she had long dreamed about—a fancy cabin on a steamer to Chicago, and shopping in all the biggest stores!

How hard she had worked and saved, selling goods to Mr. Cherryman at the island's general store. There, summer visitors came to purchase the maple syrup she and her brothers had boiled and bottled, the eggs and butter from her pa's farm, the cherry and apple preserves from his orchards, and the fresh bread, cakes and pies she had baked in the wee hours of the morning and carried, still warm, to him for his glass display case.

Some of her earnings had also come from the hogs she had raised, slaughtered, and sold to the life-saving station near the village. The fellows there were particularly fond of her pork, and the special sausage she produced in her pa's kitchen.

In a family like hers, it wasn't easy to put money by. The extra jobs had made it possible for her to save a few dollars. Now she was glad she had dragged herself out of bed at four in the morning to do the baking, even if it had meant she didn't get to bed until after ten o'clock, when the summer sun had set and work had come to an end in the fields and orchards and barn.

Her household chores at the light station seemed easy by comparison. In a few more days, Keeper Dixon would pay her for her first month's work. This temporary job was the perfect way to pass the time until spring when her pa and brothers would need her again on the farm—the perfect way to earn the rest of the money for her trip. Without a sound, she set her money tin on the shelf and returned to the kitchen to finish supper preparations.

Aurora changed into her gray flannel dress, put away her wedding gown, and had been sitting with Harrison for half an hour, listening to the wind and icy snow against the windows, when a knock came again on the rear door. The sound woke Harrison from his troubled sleep, and when he saw her beside him, he looked displeased as well as pained.

"Spunky promised to bring dinner for us. I'll go let her in," Aurora explained, quickly taking her leave.

Even before she opened the door to Spunky and Cad, she could hear his laughter, and her good-natured scolding, making her look forward to the day when Harrison would be in good spirits again. Spunky handed Aurora a covered plate and began to remove her coat. "Here's your dinner, leastways all that I could keep from big jaws, here." She poked Cad in the ribs with her elbow. "He's got Stoney's portion."

"I'll set mine in the warming oven and prepare Harrison's tray right away," Aurora said, carrying her plate to the kitchen stove to keep it warm. She promptly arranged a tray for him with silver, a napkin, and a cup of water.

Cad set the plate for Harrison in the center and started to pick up the tray.

"I'll carry that up myself, Mr. Blackburn," Aurora quickly informed him. "Why don't you and Spunky make yourselves comfortable in the sitting room. I'll be down as soon as Harrison has eaten."

As she climbed the stairs, Cad's voice, in conversation with Spunky, floated up behind her. He mimicked her imperfect English, raising protest. Their congenial bickering made Aurora think a stronger current flowed beneath the gently rippling surface.

She paused when she reached Harrison's doorway. The hospital-like odor was even more offensive at mealtime, making her aware that her first dinner with her new husband wouldn't be romantic, but at least they would be together, just the two of them. His eyes were closed, but opened the moment she crossed the threshold.

She set the tray on his dresser. "Spunky and her friend, Mr. Blackburn, are both downstairs," she commented as she propped him up with the pillows and smoothed a place at the edge of the bed where she could set down the tray and not interfere with his splint. When she lifted the cover from his dinner, delicious steam rose from the meat-laden turkey gravy that smothered two buttermilk biscuits.

The aroma, laced with Spunky's special blend of poultry seasonings, would normally have made Harrison ravenously hungry, but tonight, the smell unsettled his stomach. Still, he opened his mouth and shoved in one bite, then set down his fork.

"Aren't you hungry?"

He ignored the question. "I'd like to talk with Cad. Alone."

Such a cold dismissal from the man who had always been eager to spend time with her cut her deeply, but she tried to ignore the hurt. "Do you want me to bring you something different to eat?"

"Just do as I asked," he said crossly.

On her descent to the first floor, she forced a pleasant smile in place to cover the pain she was feeling inside and went directly to the sitting room. In a cozy atmosphere tinged with cherry pipe tobacco, she found Cad sprawled back on the sofa, a full-bent pipe in one hand, playing cards in the other, a smug expression on his face. Spunky sat apart from him, chin in palm, brows furrowed, contemplating the cards in her own hand and those lying face up on the sofa between them.

"Pardon me, Mr. Blackburn. Harrison would like to see you."

Cad grinned self-assuredly. "Too bad, Spunky. You'll be deprived of the pleasure of having me beat you for the—what is it—fiftieth time since I came to North Manitou?"

"Don't flatter yourself, Mr. Chicago. I just let you win, that's all."

"On my dear grandmother's grave!" he retorted.

"It's a wonder to me a man like you ever had a grandmother!" Spunky quipped as Cad headed out of the room.

While Aurora was preparing a tray for herself, Cad walked through the kitchen to the rear entry and returned, carrying a bottle of some sort on his way upstairs.

Spunky, evidently having put away the cards, appeared in the kitchen. "I'm going to step across to Dixon's and fetch my weddin' present for you and Stoney. 'Tween Cad 'n me, we didn't have enough hands to bring it with us earlier. I'll be back in no time." Before Aurora had finished setting her tray, Spunky returned with a crate full of jars. "I put these up myself last summer. There's string beans, tomatoes, carrots, beets, and lots of applesauce, peaches, pears, and cherries, too. I'll put them away in the pantry."

"I'm really grateful for your generosity, and your help," Aurora said, genuinely pleased, but those thoughts were quickly forgotten as she sat down at the dining table alone. She just couldn't get off her mind how aloof Harrison had been since the wedding ceremony had ended. She was glad when Spunky joined her there with a cup of tea.

Pushing unhappy thoughts aside, Aurora glanced up at the other woman, and couldn't help noticing again her worn shirtwaist. Remembering the wedding present Harrison had given her, she said, "I've got a length of ivory broadcloth upstairs in my trunk. I'd be glad to make it into a new blouse waist for you, if you'll just give me your measurements. I've got the new sewing machine—"

"Crumb cakes!" Spunky's jaw set and her fist fell on the table. Then she winked so comically, Aurora couldn't help smiling. "The trouble with you seamstress ladies is, you think every woman oughta look just like a picture in a pattern catalogue."

"It was just a suggestion," Aurora said with a shrug.

"This shirtwaist I'm wearin' is an old friend, and plenty good enough for the chores around here," Spunky informed her, rambling on at length about the thrifty ways her mama had taught her before she had died.

When Aurora had finished eating, Spunky reached across the table and took her empty plate away. "I'll clean up. You go on upstairs and send Cad down with Stoney's dishes. It's time he took his leave and let the patient rest." As she stood, she added, "And you'd better check Stoney's wound tonight. When I changed the bandage this mornin', it seemed it might soak through by this evenin'. There's more bandages in the top drawer of his dresser when you need 'em. Strips of sheeting. I boiled 'em and rolled 'em so they'd be ready. And the carbolic acid is on the kitchen counter right near the sink. One ounce to a gallon of water if you need more than what's in the bottle I left on his closet shelf."

As Aurora climbed the stairs, she heard a sound she hadn't heard since Harrison had last visited her on South Manitou—his humming. He often hummed the song that had become popular last year, "Beautiful Isle of Somewhere," but a tuneless hum was coming from his room right now, and she hoped it was an indication he was beginning to feel better.

By the time she arrived at Harrison's door, the humming had ceased—with good reason. He was holding a wine bottle to his lips. He passed it to Cad the instant he saw her. The smell of fruity alcohol—the same as she had noticed this afternoon when she had first arrived—and the equally strong smell of a well-used chamber pot dominated the room. The smile with which Harrison greeted her proved an unconvincing effort to mask the more obvious look of guilt on his face. Never, in the five years Harrison had courted her, had she known him to consume alcohol.

"A little wine for medicinal purposes," he explained.

"From Spunky's cherry mash," Cad informed her. "It's just now right for drinking." He offered a toast. "In honor of your nuptials." He drew a swig, then wiped the top of the bottle, already half-empty, and offered it to Aurora. "Care for a taste, Mrs. Stone? Sorry I don't have a goblet so I can pour it out for you."

"Goblet or no, I wouldn't drink it," she said, barely civil. "I don't indulge in alcohol, and neither does Harrison, normally." Remembering her reason for coming upstairs, she noticed Harrison's dinner tray had been set aside on his dresser top. "Now, Mr. Blackburn, if you'll take the dirty dishes to Spunky, she'll wash up."

As Cad rose, he offered the wine bottle to Harrison, but Aurora's hand intervened, pushing it back to its owner. "You can take that downstairs with you, too," she told him.

"It's going to take more alcohol than he's got in him to get through the night, since he's sworn off the opium he was taking."

Aurora hadn't considered the idea of Harrison needing either opium or wine for pain. Very reluctantly, she accepted the bottle, setting it on the dresser, and handed Mr. Blackburn the tray. "Spunky is waiting for those dirty dishes, if you please, Mr. Blackburn."

"Of course." He took the tray in one hand, and with the other, reached beneath the bed and pulled out the pot beneath. "I'll empty this for you, pal," he told Harrison.

When he had left, Aurora turned to her husband. "I had better take a look at your bandage."

Though she expected some words of protest, he said

nothing. Slowly, she pulled back the sheet that covered his injured leg, but only as far as to reveal the wound. Modesty forbid her from imagining what lay beyond. In spite of herself, she blushed.

Just above the knee, the splints divided into two parts which were connected by pieces of arched iron. The curved metal allowed easy access to a separate padded dressing on the puncture wound. It showed a stain about three inches in diameter.

Fighting her delicate sensibilities and the uneasiness in her stomach, she told him, "I have to change your dressing," and was again surprised to hear no argument.

In the top dresser drawer, she found the supplies Spunky had told her about—cotton wadding, squares of muslin, strips of sheet, clean white towels, and a piece of rubber mattress pad. She also found a small pair of scissors, and in the closet, the bottle of carbolic acid.

Nursing did not come naturally. It had been her mother's domain as sewing was hers. Still, she had watched her mother often in treating her brothers' cuts and scrapes. Aurora was determined to prove herself no less competent a nurse than Spunky.

She set all the supplies on the seat of the chair. Harrison lifted his leg far enough for her to slip the rubber pad and a towel between his leg and the bed sheet so she could unwrap the muslin that was covering his wound. Then she removed the squares of cotton and the wadding underneath. From his quiet groans, she knew he was hurting. She dropped the old strip of muslin, soiled cotton squares and wadding on the floor.

The opening in the wound was not large, but the area around it had swollen considerably. When she poured carbolic acid over it, Harrison gasped, but still, he issued no complaint.

She covered the wound with clean cotton wadding and new squares of muslin, then began winding strips of sheeting over it, taking care to pull only tight enough to hold the bandage in place. Then she removed the rubber sheet and towel, and Harrison let his leg rest on the bed again while she tied the bandage in place.

She could feel his eyes on her every move as she picked up the scissors and clipped off the excess strip of sheet. Then he took the shears away, and enveloped her small hands inside his own large, warm ones. Her eyes met his, and for the first time since the wedding ceremony she saw a tenderness and warmth in their grayness.

Harrison wasn't sure what had come over him. Maybe it was the effect of the wine, but he was feeling incredibly blessed right now. Here was the woman he loved, caring for him as gently as if he were an infant—unlike Spunky's sometimes heavy-handedness with the medical supplies. He wanted more than anything to be a proper husband to her tonight—to hold her, and kiss her. He reached up and caressed her cheek, then slowly pulled her toward him.

Aurora wondered what had turned Harrison from angry to affectionate. Perhaps Spunky's brew had more medicinal value than she realized. Or had Harrison simply had time to consider how much he had hurt her feelings, and was now trying to make up for it? No matter. She wasn't about to resist the man she had grown to love more each day for the past five years.

Harrison covered her mouth with his. The pain of his leg had subsided and he was tempted to kiss her deeply, but he refrained, knowing if he did, he wouldn't want to let her go.

Aurora's breath came more quickly. Harrison had never kissed her like this before. Her pulse stirred. A fluttering like Monarch's wings set her heart tripping. She had to resist the urge to snuggle down beside her husband, reminding herself not to press against his broken leg. At this moment, the prospect of his recovery seemed a lifetime away, rather than weeks or months. How could she stand the wait?

Then she heard footsteps on the stairs—Cad's, bringing up the chamber pot. She sensed Harrison's reluctance to end the kiss, but when he did, she could tell from the intense look in his eyes, he had been deeply stirred by the exchange of affections.

Cad entered the room. "I'll come by again tomorrow," he said, setting the pot beneath the bed. "Good night."

"Good night, Mr. Blackburn." Aurora waited until he had gone, then leaned down and kissed Harrison's cheek. "Good night, Harrison. Call me if you need anything." Quickly, she put away the scissors, carbolic acid, and other supplies she had left on the chair, then she picked up the dirty bandages from the floor and took them out with her.

Harrison lay awake, sipping wine and listening while Aurora prepared for bed, angry for a moment that he could not lie beside his wife. He stared into the darkness until he fell into a stupor akin to sleep. Like a nightmare came dark thoughts carrying him back to troubled boyhood days—days he thought he had left forever in the past.

# CHAPTER

## 5

Harrison was thirteen, and back on his parents' farm near the northern end of the island. The fall breeze rattled painted autumn leaves, but the sun shone brightly on this warm Sunday in October.

The Anders family had come for dinner. Mrs. Anders had died the month before, and Harrison's mother considered it a neighborly gesture to invite the family over.

Harrison could smell the aroma of cinnamon applesauce through the open kitchen window. His mother promised that as soon as his grandpa came home from visiting his friend, they would all sit down to eat.

Meanwhile, Harrison, along with Peter and John Anders, took turns on the race course they had set up around the house and barn, timing themselves with the watch Harrison's Grandpa Harry had loaned him—with the standard admonition to be very careful with the timepiece.

While John was making his run, Spunky—the only girl in the Anders family--came out of the house to watch.

Until now, Harrison hadn't really noticed her. She was a little taller than he, with unruly thick dark blond hair that wouldn't stay braided, a square jaw line, and a dress she had obviously outgrown a season ago.

When John had finished his run, she boldly stepped up to the starting line. "Let me run next time."

"It ain't your place," Peter replied bluntly, turning to Harrison. "Give me the watch 'n get ready to run, Stoney."

"There ain't no reason why a girl can't run this race," Spunky insisted.

"There is so," John argued. "Girls ain't built to run fast. 'Sides, their dresses slow 'em down."

Spunky hiked up her skirt, unembarrassed to show her stockings from the knees down. "If you fellas won't time me, I'll just start out when Stoney does." She took a place at the starting line.

"Let her run," Harrison said. "I'll be so far ahead of her, she can't possibly get in my way!" He handed Peter the watch and crouched beside her, eager to win the foot-race and prove the girl wrong.

"Ready, set, go!" Peter shouted.

Harrison shot off the line faster than ever before, but Spunky stayed close behind. He moved to the inside to round the corner of the house, cutting her off. As he continued on the straightaway across the back yard, Spunky pulled up near him, running at his elbow. Behind the barn, she passed him. How could Harrison face his friends if their sister came around the far corner of the barn before he did?

The dread of humiliation spurred him on. He lengthened his stride, emerging ahead of Spunky, then dashed for the finish line. His chest burning from exertion, he crossed a nose ahead of Spunky.

When she finished, she dropped her skirt to its normal length, a few inches above her ankles, and walked toward Harrison, catching her breath. "My brothers were right," she admitted, her back to Peter and John. "I ain't no match for you, Stoney." Then she winked, and he was certain she could have won if she'd wanted to.

"Look! Your grandpa's comin'," John said, pointing down the drive.

"Maybe now we can eat. I'm hungry!" Peter stated emphatically, returning the watch to Harrison, who tucked it in his pants pocket.

As the wagon approached, he could hear his grandfather singing loudly and off key. "Bringing in the sheaves, bringing in the sheaves. We will come rejoicing, bringing in the sheaves." He pulled the wagon to a halt and smiled sloppily at Harrison, making him wish he were anywhere but here with his friends. He could feel his face coloring with embarrassment. Grandpa Harry had been having difficulty with alcohol since he had broken his leg and it didn't mend right. Harrison remembered keenly the old man's fall off a ladder, a sight forever etched in his mind.

He held his breath as his grandfather unsteadily climbed down from the wagon and pulled out his two canes. Leaning on them, he looked glassy-eyed from Harrison to Spunky. "You younguns go on, now. Get washed up for dinner. I'll be fine."

Harrison watched as the old man hobbled toward the front porch. Near the shrubbery, his body listed and his knees buckled. Twigs crackled beneath the weight of his fall.

Burning with shame, Harrison hurried to his side.

Peter and John snickered.

"You boys go in the house and wash up for dinner," Spunky ordered.

Reluctantly, they obeyed.

Kneeling by the old man, Harrison quietly asked, "Are you all right, Grandpa?"

He pushed prickly branches away from his scratched face. "I'll be fine if you younguns 'll just pull me up." He held out his hands.

Harrison took one while Spunky took the other, and together, they managed to pull him to his feet.

Spunky retrieved his canes while Harrison helped him to regain his equilibrium.

Looking ashamed, Grandpa Harry admitted, "I don't feel much like eatin'. If you'll get me to my room, I think I'll lie down a spell."

With Spunky, Harrison helped him up the steps and into the front door, grateful everyone was in the kitchen and not watching their painful progress. He wanted to shrink through the cracks in the wooden floor. How could he bear to face his friends again? How could he eat dinner across the table from them?

After what seemed like an eternity, they arrived at Grandpa Harry's small bedroom at the back of the house. The old man sat on the edge of his mattress and started to swing his legs up, then paused. "I'd best take off my boots, or your ma will have a fit," he told Harrison.

Immediately, Spunky began to unlace one of the boots. Harrison worked on the other, thankful for her helpfulness. She set the boots aside and pulled back the top blanket. "You just make y'rself comfy and rest, sir," she told him as she tucked him in.

Harrison remembered the timepiece and took it out of his pocket. "I'm setting your watch right here on your chest, Grandpa."

"Thanks, son. You know . . . " Harrison knew what was coming next. "That timepiece will be yours some day."

"I know. Rest easy now, Grandpa." When Harrison had closed the door, he turned to Spunky. "Thanks," he said awkwardly, unable to say more.

Spunky shrugged. "It was nothin'."

Despite her casual response, Harrison caught a look of understanding in her brown eyes that chased away some of his shame.

On his bed of pain, the grown Harrison unconsciously shifted, trying for a more comfortable position, and with his restless movements came a shift in memory as well.

Spunky was no longer with him, and the brilliant leaves of North Manitou's autumn hardwoods had faded and drifted from their branches. Snow crunched underfoot, and within him rose a sense of urgency.

He was the first one out that morning. He headed toward the barn, struggling through drifts that sometimes measured three feet high. The Manitou wind lashed against him, stinging his face with icy snowflakes. Despite his heavy woolen jacket, long muffler, and fur-lined mittens, the blizzard-like conditions were brutal.

He was worried about his grandfather. The old man had taken the wagon out yesterday afternoon before the storm hit, promising to be back in time for supper. When daylight broke, he still hadn't come home. Harrison's mother and father were sure the old man had stayed overnight with his friend. Harrison wasn't so certain.

Plodding along, he caught a glimpse of something in the snowdrift beside the barn door. He hurried forward, then stopped cold. His heart froze. Partially hidden by blowing snow, he recognized the unmistakable red and black plaid of the woolen blanket Grandpa Harry always carried with him in the wagon during bad weather.

A step at a time, against the bitter wind, Harrison approached the blanket, lifting one corner of it from the snow. Beneath it lay a sight so devastating, he bolted, following his own footprints back to the house.

The burial was delayed until spring, allowing Harrison ample opportunity to ponder his grandfather's fate, and his own uncertain future. After the graveside service, his mother told him to find himself a keepsake from his grandfather's room and put everything else into the trunk the old man had brought with him to the island.

The only thing Harrison wanted was the pocket watch he'd been promised. He searched and searched, but couldn't find it. Without the memento of better times, all that remained was the bitter memory of how his grandfather's drinking had destroyed him in the end, some worn clothing, and a few empty bottles. Putting the last of them into his grandfather's trunk, Harrison made a vow to God that alcohol would never pass his own lips, and a final decision about the direction his life should take.

Feeling the need to tell Spunky of his plans, he walked to the Anders's farm, finding her alone at work in the small garden behind the house. She had grown during the winter, taller than he, but her dress wasn't up above her ankles, as it had been last fall. Rather, she wore one that was too long, and he supposed she had started wearing her mother's clothes.

For a moment, they simply looked at one another. Despite the cramp in his throat, he was determined to speak of the important things on his mind.

"I'm leaving North Manitou soon, going to work on a schooner." With his older brothers already in a business partnership with his father on the fishing boat and farm, Harrison's best alternative as a fourteen-year-old seemed to be moving away from the island that would be a reminder of sadness and heartache for some time to come.

Spunky appeared on the verge of smiling and crying at the same time, but she managed to keep from doing either, and simply shrugged. "I'll think of you when y'r gone, friend."

Her guileless sentiment gave Harrison a small measure of comfort. As he slowly backed away and waved good bye, he knew he could count on Spunky's friendship to remain steadfast. In his dream-like memory, he turned toward home, but as he walked across the open field, his leg began to hurt.

The pain brought Harrison fully awake to a leg that hurt too much to sleep, a head that had begun to ache, and a desperate need to make use of the chamber pot he could not reach.

He was about to holler for Spunky when he remembered his most confounding problem of all. His longtime friend was no longer caring for him. Rather, he must now depend upon Aurora, whom he had never wanted to burden with his injury and his most private personal needs—a woman he considered too delicate, sensitive, and modest to face such intimate situations, despite her desire and willingness to take them on.

Frustrated and angry over his predicament, he shouted, "Aurora!" Moments later, she hurried to his bedside with a lantern.

"Harrison, are you all right?"

Angry with himself for worrying her, and embarrassed over his situation, he spoke too abruptly. "Set the pot on a chair and light the lamp on my bedside table."

She quickly carried out his requests and headed for the door.

"Aurora!" Again, he had spoken too harshly, and the fear in her eyes when she turned to him sent a dagger to his heart. He took a deep breath, determined to soften his tone. "Aurora, thank you for . . . " Renewed awareness of his complete dependence on her momentarily choked off his words. In a shaky voice, he said again, "Thank you."

"You're welcome, Harrison," she replied sweetly as she closed the door.

With great effort, Harrison made use of the pot. When he had finished, he lay in bed with a throbbing leg and a pounding head, his thoughts dominated by his loss of control over his temper, and the black memory of his Grandpa Harry's downfall.

Aurora barely slept, for fear Harrison might call again for help. When daylight finally broke, she pulled on slippers and robe, and went downstairs to heat water for her wash pitcher and start coffee.

The familiar smell of wood smoke and coffee comforted her as she looked out upon the thick blanket of snow left by last night's storm. Across the four miles of icy water that separated North from South Manitou, she could hardly pick out the neighboring island in the hazy distance.

Except for the soft crackling of burning wood and gentle perking of the coffeepot, the house was quiet—too quiet. With an unexpected pang of homesickness, she realized how much she missed the familiar voices that would be present at the breakfast table of the keeper's quarters on South Manitou. More than that, she missed the feeling of peace and happiness she had known there.

Shoving such notions aside, she filled her pitcher and carried it upstairs for her morning ablutions. When she had washed, dressed, and arranged her hair, she hunted in her trunk for her porcelain dishes, and carried them downstairs.

As she cooked breakfast, she took great care to brown the pancakes to perfection, fry the eggs without breaking the yolks, and leave the bacon on the griddle long enough to become crisp—all just the way Harrison preferred. Setting her portion in the warming oven, she carried his tray upstairs, balancing it across one arm while opening his door.

She stepped into his room with a smile on her face and a promise to herself to remain cheerful no matter what, but her spirits began to fade when she saw the pallor of his cheeks.

"Good morning, Harrison. I've brought your breakfast."

He pointed to the chamber pot. "I can't eat with that thing in the room."

Without a word, she set his breakfast on the bedside table and carried the chamber pot to the outhouse, wondering what had become of the kind, appreciative Harrison she had known before the accident. When she returned several minutes later, he had made little progress with his breakfast.

"Can I keep you company awhile?" she asked with forced cheerfulness.

"I don't like being stared at while I eat," he grumbled.

She headed for the door. "I'll come back in half an hour then."

Downstairs, she set herself a place at the table and tried to eat her breakfast, but her stomach was so tied in knots, she swallowed only a few bites and threw the rest in the scrap bucket, setting aside her dirty dishes to wash later with Harrison's.

Up in her room, she put away the clothes in her trunk, discovering one last package at the bottom. She had forgotten entirely about her wedding gift for Harrison!

She picked it up and read again the card she had penned last week when wrapping the gift over which she had labored for a month.

> *To Harrison,*
> *I love you with all my heart!*
> *Aurora*

She was reminded of the sheet-draped gift from Harrison standing in the corner. She went to it now, lifted off the white muslin, folded it, and put it on the shelf in her closet. Then she reread the beautiful poetic lines on his card which she had so unexpectedly discovered the previous evening.

She must thank Harrison for both the gift and the sentiments. With the card Harrison had given her in one hand, and her gift and card to him in the other, she crossed the hall, hoping he would have cleaned his plate and improved in disposition by now. She was disappointed to discover he had barely touched his breakfast.

"Take this away. I'm done," he said brusquely.

Unwilling to be so quickly dismissed, she held up the card he had penned to her. "I should have thanked you for your card and the sewing machine earlier."

He grabbed the card and studied it for several moments, his features darkening. Suddenly, he ripped it to shreds and stuffed them into his dirty coffee cup.

"Forget you ever saw that!"

# CHAPTER

## 6

Aurora was stunned, then anger boiled up inside her. Raising her gift above her head, she threw it down, landing it with a plop near his feet. Her card flew out from beneath its ribbon, hitting the wall, then coming to rest on the floor beneath his bed.

"There's your wedding gift. I hope you like it!"

Not trusting herself to get his dirty dishes from the bedroom to the kitchen intact, she left his tray on his bed stand and stalked out, aching to slam the door behind her. She only refrained for fear of cracking the new plaster walls.

In the kitchen, she heated water to wash her own breakfast dishes, not caring whether Harrison's ever got washed, or whether he ever ate another meal. No matter how much his leg hurt, he had no right to destroy the only romantic sentiments he had ever written to her! Maybe he didn't love her after all!

The thought that he might not love her upset her so, her hands began to tremble, and she had to be extra careful while washing her porcelain plate, cup and saucer, and putting them in the china cabinet, which looked horribly empty with only her place setting in it—as empty as she felt inside without Harrison's loving companionship.

When she had stoked the fire, she wandered into the pantry to look at the stores Spunky had brought to her last night. She had counted a dozen jars of canned fruit when she heard a pounding on the front door and opened it to find Keeper Dixon well-wrapped in muffler, stocking cap, and a woolen jacket so thick, it made his medium build appear muscular.

"Good morning," she greeted, sounding more cheerful than she felt. "Can I get you a cup of hot coffee?"

He pulled off his cap and ran a hand through his mop of gray hair, then brushed snow from his thick mustache. "Coffee would be much appreciated. Cream and sugar, if you please, Aurora." He took a thick book from beneath his coat and set it on the stair step while removing his outerwear.

Aurora read the title, *The Cottage Physician*, as she returned to the kitchen to prepare a tray with coffee. A few minutes later, she joined the head keep' at the dining table where he sat studying his book. His soft, hazel eyes showed dark circles, and she could well imagine the strain he had been under with Harrison unable to perform his usual duties.

When Keeper Dixon had liberally doctored his coffee with cream and sugar, he slid his book toward her. "I've been reading about fractures of the thigh. The divided splint Harrison has on right now will be all right until the swelling goes down. Then he'll need a new splint. You'd better read this." He pointed to the paragraph on compound fractures.

Aurora silently read.

**Compound Fractures.**—*Treatment.*—

. . . During the stage of formation of matter (supperation), the patient will require tonic medicines, as bark, porter, etc., and small doses of opium at night, and nourishing diet, if the stomach will bear it; but this treatment should not be carried too far. Strong purgatives are injurious. The case will continue to progress very slowly for some weeks; abscesses may form; and, should matter collect under the skin so as to be felt on examination, or the skin become red and thin, the part should be punctured, and great relief will be afforded by its escape.

The splints should be removed as often as the matter renders the pads foul, or the wound appears to suffer from their presence; perhaps this may be required every other day, or even oftener. When the supperative stage has passed, which may occupy from one month to two, the wound will look florid and healthy; and as soon as it begins to heal, the bone will begin to unite, but not until then. A month or five weeks will still be required before the union is complete, and two or three weeks yet longer before the patient is enabled to use the limb.

Aurora's heart sank. Harrison's bone wouldn't begin to mend for a whole month, maybe two. Even then, he would require another two months before he could make use of his leg. One night of caring for him had seemed a trial. How would she manage until spring, when he would be healed?

She supposed she couldn't begrudge Harrison the cherry wine, since the book *had* recommended tonic medicines and opium for pain, and according to Mr. Blackburn, Harrison had already decided to stop taking opium.

She studied the figure showing the splint Keeper Dixon had spoken of, and turned to the beginning of that passage on the previous page.

... When inflammation has subsided, and the pressure can be borne, the case had better be treated in this way: let the patient lie on a hard mattress, with the leg extended and uncovered; then commence operations by bandaging the leg evenly from the toes to the knee; then place the splint, previously well padded, in its place, and make it fast with rollers to the foot, ankle and leg, taking care that the former is in the position which it is to occupy—that is, pointing straight upward; next, take a silk handkerchief, in the middle of which some wool has been rolled up, to make it of considerable thickness, and pass it between the legs, bringing one end up behind, and one before; these ends pass through the holes at the top of the long splint, and tie them as tightly as possible, without displacing the fracture. Then after confining the splint to the waist, with a bandage, insert a short stick between the loop of the handkerchief, and give two or three turns; this will have the effect of shortening the handkerchief, and pulling down the splint, which will carry with it the part of the limb attached to it below, producing the necessary extension. Keep on at this until you find that the injured leg is as long as the sound one; and when this is the case, lay a short splint along the inside of the thigh, and bandage tightly and smoothly, from the knee up to the hip. When it is completed, the patient will appear as in Fig. 125. The extension must be kept up for about six weeks, at the end of which time the fracture may be sufficiently united to bear the strain of the muscles upon it.

FIG. 125

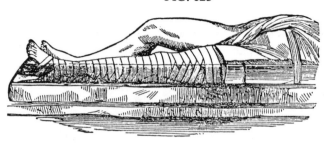

"From the figure and description, I'm not certain exactly how the new splint would go on," Aurora admitted, still
studying the drawing.

Keeper Dixon pulled a folded paper from his flannel
shirt pocket, opened it, and laid it beside the figure in the
book. It showed a short splint, and a long one with holes at
the top per the description in the reference manual. "Here's
what I think we need, but I don't know the dimensions. I
thought maybe you'd help me measure Harrison. Then you
can go with Spunky and Cad this morning and take the
diagram to the Freilings."

Aurora had visited the Freilings with Harrison a couple
of times the previous summer when he had brought her to
North Manitou for the day. She remembered the charming
home, and Mr. Freiling's carpenter shop, up the road a
piece from the light station.

Keeper Dixon continued. "Mr. Freiling made the splint
Harrison has on right now, but of course, that one with the
metal arches is only good until the swelling has gone down.

"Freiling has been working on crutches. He promised to

have them ready today. The sooner we can get Harrison up and around for a little while each day, the better. It would be good to take his splints off for a spell now and then, too. But like I said, I need measurements."

"I can help you take them," she said, though she dreaded going into Harrison's room again. Maybe soon, with crutches and an increase in mobility, Harrison's disposition would improve.

A few minutes later, they went upstairs. Aurora immediately noticed Harrison was wearing a thick gray sweater over his nightshirt, the extra heavy one she had knitted of wool for his wedding present. The tissue wrapping paper lay neatly folded on the chair beside his bed. But the plate on his tray looked the same as the last time she had seen it, and his expression was still glum.

Keeper Dixon was evidently not deterred by Harrison's brooding, for he offered a broad smile. "Good morning! How are you feeling today?"

"Poorly."

"You look improved from yesterday. I knew having Aurora here would pick up your spirits!"

Aurora nearly choked, fighting the urge to say Harrison was even more cantankerous today than before, but she would keep their differences private.

"I want to take some new measurements for a different splint, the one I showed you in this book a couple of days ago. You were feeling so pained then, maybe you don't remember." Keeper Dixon opened to the illustration. "If you don't mind my sitting with you for a couple of hours, I thought I'd send your wife over to Freilings with Cad and Spunky to leave off the measurements and pick up your crutches. Mrs. Freiling is eager to see Aurora. Says she's

71

got a wedding gift she wants to give you. A right neighborly woman, Mrs. Freiling is."

"That would be fine," Harrison said, though his scowl
told otherwise. "Send Cad up when he comes. I want to
see him."

Keeper Dixon nodded, and turned to Aurora. "Have
you a measuring tape we can use?" He moved aside the
chair by the bed. As he did so, the tissue wrapping fell to
the floor, slipping partway beneath Harrison's bed.

Aurora moved to retrieve it, but Keeper Dixon stopped
her. "I'll get that. It's a good thing I'm not this clumsy
when I clean the glass in the light tower!" he quipped,
stooping down. He picked up the paper, then reached
farther beneath the bed, rising with a blank white card in
hand. "What's this?"

Aurora immediately recognized it as the backside of the
gift card that had fallen when she had thrown the sweater at
Harrison's feet, but before she could move, Harrison leaned
over and took it.

"Thanks. I lost that a little while ago." He turned it
over immediately.

Aurora let him read her one-line sentiment, then she
swiped the card from him. "I believe you're mistaken. It
was *I* who lost it." She ripped it in two, stuffed the pieces
into his coffee cup, and with a swish of her skirt, headed
out the door to get her measuring tape.

Half an hour later, measurements had been taken and
duly noted on Keeper Dixon's diagram. "I'll go on home
and tend a few chores," he said, folding the paper and
handing it to Aurora. "Cad should be coming up from the
barn with the carriage for you and Spunky in a few
minutes. Then I'll come back and sit with Harrison."

72

Aurora saw the keeper out, then sat down to put on her boots. Moments later, Cad knocked on the door.

"Good morning, Mrs. Stone!" His greeting sounded almost like a baritone solo.

"Come in, Mr. Blackburn. I'll be ready in a minute. Harrison wants to see you. Why don't you go on up while I put on my coat and hat."

Cad stomped the snow off his boots, then headed up the stairs.

Harrison could hear him coming. Before he even reached the room, Harrison spoke plainly. "Get in here, Blackburn, and close the door."

Cad came to stand at the foot of Harrison's bed, his cocky smile in place. "Good morning to you, too, Stoney."

Harrison glared at him. "You had no right to interfere!"

Cad offered an innocent, puzzled look. "I don't know what you're talking about, Stoney. Can you give me a hint?"

"The card to Aurora."

Cad broke into a grin. "Oh, that."

"How *could* you?" Harrison demanded. As his anger intensified, so did his headache.

Cad shrugged. "I studied your entries in Keeper Dixon's log book. That's more than enough for any forger worth his salt."

Such arrogance only worsened the uneasiness in Harrison's stomach. "That's not what I mean and you know it."

"Stoney, you've said yourself, you're not much with words. I was only trying to help. I wrote notes like that to the coeds all the time when I was at the University of Chicago. Women like to know how you feel about them."

Harrison sat erect. How he wished he could stand on

73

both feet and face Cad eye to eye! "This isn't some college literature class. I won't have you toying with Aurora's emotions, you silver-tongued rogue!"

Cad put his hands palm out, his impudent smile still intact. "Wait a minute. I tried very hard to express accurately the way you feel about your wife. What harm was there in putting your emotions into words? Women adore romantic poetry. If you'd ever bothered to think about it, you'd already know that. The way you act, sometimes I think you've spent your whole life working in fog signal buildings and light towers, without the slightest acquaintance with the intricacies of the female mind, or heart."

Harrison sighed. He just didn't have the strength to argue with the likes of Cad. "I will let Aurora know how I feel about her in my own way, in my own time."

Cad rolled his eyes, obviously unconvinced. "Your intentions are good, but will your words come too late?"

Harrison leaned back, exhausted. "Talk is cheap, Cad." He closed his eyes, listening while Cad's boot heels retraced their path out his door and down the stairs.

Dressed in her warmest cloak, Aurora waited for Cad in the rear entry.

"I see you're ready for the cold out-of-doors," Cad commented pleasantly as he held the door open for her. His hand came to rest at her back as she stepped past him. "I'll help you in the buggy, then I'll tell Spunky and Keeper Dixon we're ready to go." He opened the carriage door and lifted her by the waist, though she could have easily made the step up on her own.

Had Aurora imagined it, or had Cad's hands lingered a bit too long? The incident made her uncomfortable, and she was thankful he would be sitting on the driver's seat out front while she and Spunky snuggled beneath deer hide robes inside for the cold ride.

Harrison watched with envy from his window as the carriage pulled away from the keeper's quarters and headed toward the road to the Freilings. Normally, he wouldn't mind missing an outing to the neighbors. This time was different. This time, the woman he loved was leaving in the company of Cadwallader Blackburn, and Harrison knew he couldn't trust Cad any more than he could trust a red fox in a chicken coop.

Why Keeper Dixon couldn't see that, he didn't know, except for the fact that Keeper Dixon had been working extra hard since Harrison broke his leg, taking all-night watches each of the last four nights. He probably hadn't had much chance to observe Cad in operation.

In a day and a half, the dadblamed shifty Chicagoan had already gotten Harrison into more trouble with Aurora than he would be able to explain in a lifetime. Without Cad, Harrison would never have begun drinking wine to relieve pain. Every night, Cad had brought another bottle, and every night the pain had been so bad Harrison had indulged despite promises to himself he wouldn't. If he hadn't been in such a foul mood from drinking alcohol for which he had little tolerance, he probably would have been able to temper his reaction to the forged wedding card.

*A soft answer turneth away wrath.*

He remembered the biblical proverb his mother had taught him, one he had lived by until his accident had changed everything. He wished he hadn't ripped up Cad's wedding card, nor spoken as he had about it. After all, it had been a true expression of his feelings for Aurora. He just wouldn't have come right out with them the way Cad did.

He sighed. None of it mattered. What he wished most of all was that he had never gotten himself into this tangled mess. His leg would never be right again. He was certain of it.

# CHAPTER

## 7

Cad stopped the carriage by the front porch of a modest two-story home with the white clapboard siding and black shutters. Just beyond lay a red, vertical-sided building of moderate size, the workshop Keeper Dixon had told him about. Off to one side was a leanto housing a one-lunger hit and miss stationary engine. It was silent now, but Mr. Freiling obviously used it to power his woodworking equipment by means of the jack-shaft through the side of the building. It all looked rather sophisticated for a woodworker on an island the size of North Manitou.

He hopped down from the driver's seat and opened the carriage door. "I'll see you ladies into the house, then I'll look for Mr. Freiling in his shop," he said, offering Spunky an arm to lean on as she stepped down. When Aurora emerged, he lifted her to the ground, his large hands nearly circling her waist. She really was quite attractive—petite and fair, with pretty curves, unlike Spunky who, like his preconceived notion of a backwoods girl, was tall, ruddy-cheeked, and built like a six-by-ten. "Do you have the measurements for the new splints?" he asked Aurora as they stepped onto the small front porch.

She found the folded paper in her pocket. "Keeper Dixon says Harrison will need them by Christmas," she reminded Cad as he tucked them away.

When the front door opened, the aroma of fresh baked cinnamon rolls wafted out. A woman as wide as a cookstove greeted them with a jolly smile. "Do come in, all of you! What an unexpected pleasure!"

Spunky entered ahead of the others. "Good mornin', Mrs. Freiling. We've come to pick up the crutches for Stoney. You've met Aurora, haven't you? She and Stoney was married yesterday afternoon."

"My best wishes to ya, Mrs. Stone! I remember when you and Harrison came calling last summer. It's good to see ya again." She enfolded Aurora's hand in her plump ones.

"And this gent," Spunky continued, "is Mr. Cadwallader Blackburn, from Chicago. I believe I mentioned last time I came to call that he's stayin' at Pa's place for the winter."

"My, my! I've been lookin' forward to meetin' ya! The Anders's farm must be some change from your Chicago home, I'll reckon, Mr. Blackburn." She shook his hand.

"Right you are, Mrs. Freiling."

"Well, Matthew has the crutches ready. He's out in his shop."

"Then I'll leave you ladies and tend to business," Cad said.

"I expect the both of ya at my kitchen table for coffee in half an hour," Mrs. Freiling informed Cad.

"We'll be in, ma'am."

Cad followed the path through the snow to the side door of the workshop and let himself in. The potbellied stove in the center of the room had brought the temperature to a tolerable degree, adding wood smoke to the fragrance of freshly worked lumber. The rhythm of Mr. Freiling's hand planer greeted him, uninterrupted by the sound of the door closing.

Cad took a few moments before announcing himself to quietly marvel at the treasure trove of woodworking equipment—leather belts descending from the jack shaft to drive a wood lathe, table saw, jigsaw, and drill press. Hanging on the walls in neat order were a plethora of hand tools—coping saws, crosscut saws, hand planes, chisels, and off in the corner, a bench with a treadle and grinding wheel that spun in a tub of water for sharpening the chisels. It fueled Cad's dream of turning out wooden parts for an automobile frame of his own design one day. He was convinced the time would come when this innovative mode of transportation would replace the horse and carriage, and he was determined to be in on it from its infancy.

"Good morning, Mr. Freiling." Cad spoke a little louder than usual to make himself heard above the plane's song.

The slender, silver-haired man set down his planer and turned about, a questioning look in his soft blue-gray eyes. "Mornin'. Don't believe we've met, have we?"

"I'm Cad Blackburn. Keeper Dixon sent me to fetch Harrison Stone's crutches."

"Now I know ya. I was expectin' Walt to come by, but I suppose he can't get away much with his wife gone to the mainland for the winter and my friend, Stoney, laid up. Here are the crutches." He took them down from a bracket

79

on the wall and handed them to Cad. "Made out of oak to fit Stoney's height, sanded smooth as can be, and well varnished. Stoney oughta be pleased with 'em, don't ya think?"

Cad looked them over carefully, pretending to know a good crutch when he saw it. He *did* know a good wood finish, and the crutches were smooth and shiny, held together neatly by pegs. He tucked one crutch beneath each arm and took hold of the handgrips which had been padded and covered with calico.

"My wife done that padding. She thought it'd make 'em easier to use. Stoney can take it off if he don't like it."

Cad's height was similar enough to Harrison's to fit the crutches nearly perfectly, and he tried them out for a few steps. "These are fine. The finest crutches I've ever seen, Mr. Freiling." Since he'd never tested any others, he wasn't stretching the truth, a rarity for him. He leaned them up against the wall and took the dollar Keeper Dixon had given him out of his pocket. "Here's your payment. I have another job for you, too. A second set of splints for when Stoney's wound heals. Keeper Dixon sent along the plans." He unfolded the paper. When he handed it to the old gent, he noticed Mr. Freiling's left thumbnail had been damaged, likely from an encounter with a saw blade.

Freiling brushed sawdust and shavings aside and smoothed the page out atop his workbench. "Yah. I see what he's after. Shouldn't be no problem. I've got some wood that'll do just right."

"I was supposed to ask if you can have them ready by Christmas. Do you suppose that's possible?"

"I'll have 'em for ya tomorrow night, if ya want. I didn't get much notice on that first set of splints I made for

Stoney. Started work on 'em early in the mornin' and finished 'em the same day. 'Course, I knew he'd be in mighty bad pain till he got 'em."

"You can take your time on these, Mr. Freiling."

The old man took a hammer and small nail and tacked the plans on the wall beside his workbench, then checked his pocket watch. "We got a few minutes 'fore the misses expects to serve coffee. I wanna show you what I been workin' on. Got my Christmas presents all made already!" He bent down, lifting a piece of canvas shroud from the shelf below his bench top to reveal half a dozen beautifully finished gifts.

Cad was deeply impressed. His own need surfaced for gifts to give at Christmas time. An idea came to him, and he pointed to four of the items.

"Mr. Freiling, how much would you want for these?" Though Cad had no money to call his own, he knew where he could borrow some.

"Oh, these ain't for sale," said the man, rubbing his hand over the finish on a small cabinet-like piece. "No, these ain't for sale. They're for beneath our tree on Christmas mornin'."

"But if they *were* for sale, how much would you ask?"

Mr. Freiling studied them and scratched the stubble on his chin. "Never gave it any thought. I just don't know. Doesn't make no difference, since I ain't sellin' 'em."

"Could you make another copy of each of them for me? I know folks who would like them as Christmas gifts. I'll pay you a fair amount. Name your price."

The old man scratched his chin some more, and shifted his weight. "I'd have to give it some thought."

"You figure up what you'd need in payment. You'd be

81

helping me out a lot. I've got no other way of getting presents to give this Christmas, unless I buy them from you. I can't make them. Even if I had a nice shop like you do, I wouldn't know how."

"Well, now, maybe you should learn. I could show ya how to make them."

"I'm afraid I'd be all thumbs, Mr. Freiling." The thought occurred to him some acquaintance with woodworking might come in handy making wooden car parts one day.

"Just maybe we could strike a deal here, son. Ya know, I was all thumbs when I got started forty-some odd years ago, workin' with wood in my pappy's shop. How 'bout if I show ya how to make these things. Two dollars will cover the cost of the wood, the finish, and the power to run the tools. Every man should know *this* much about woodworkin'. Since you've got no experience, it's time ya learn."

Cad instantly decided he would prefer passing his time in Mr. Freiling's cozy workshop over doing chores and making repairs in the freezing out-of-doors at the Anders farm.

"I could give it a go."

"Good." Freiling went to a sliding door left of his workbench. "Come. We'll pick out some pretty wood for your presents." He pushed the door aside.

Daylight streamed in windows on each of three sides of the room. Against two walls were neat stacks of lumber, but the object which commanded Cad's attention stood in the center—the wooden chassis, frame, axles and wheels of what would eventually be a phaeton.

"Are you building this all by yourself?" he asked,

running his hand over the finger joints.

"Yah. Started back in September. It's for the Benson family over t'other side o' the island.

"Nice work. Your joinery is smooth and well-fit. I've seen frames in Chicago that can't match this for quality."

"I take my time. When ya work for someone on an island, ya gotta do the job right. If y'r customer's disappointed, it don't take long 'fore the whole island knows about it. Then y'r out o' business."

Cad studied the members of the oak frame. "This seems to be built heavy for a small runabout. And what is the purpose of these?" He ran his hand over two runners extending off the back.

"The frame is thicker than usual. Mrs. Benson wants it plenty strong for the trunk she asked me to mount off the back. She don't care much for goin' to town in a wagon. This way she'll be able to cart home big sacks of flour, cornmeal and beans, and any other sundries she's in need of, right here in the back end of her phaeton."

The concept of a heavier frame seemed perfect for the automobile Cad dreamed of owning, and eventually producing in number. It would hold up better than a regular frame under the stress of an internal combustion engine. He knew men in Chicago who could add the springs, and finish the body. With the engine mounted beneath, he would have his own design of the automobile. It would be remarkably similar to the electric vehicle he had worked on with Mr. Roberts in Chicago, but better!

"I'll give you eighteen dollars for this," he offered, knowing he could soon put his hands on that sum.

"Beg pardon?"

"I'll give you eighteen dollars for this, as is."

83

"As is? Why, in heaven's name . . . ?

"I'd ship it to Chicago and make it into an automobile." Cad described his plans for finishing the vehicle, and how it would be an improvement over those he had seen. "If my idea works, I could bring you quite a lot of business. Will you sell it to me?"

Freiling shrugged. "Eighteen dollars sounds fair enough for my labor and materials, but I can't sell this one. If y'r interested, we could build another one together, after Christmas, that is. By then, you'll have some experience under y'r belt, making those presents, and you'll be handy enough 'round here to help me out, as my assistant, like."

Cad offered his hand. "It's a deal. When do we get started?"

"Tomorrow?"

"I'll be here. You've got to promise to keep our presents a secret, though. No one is to know. Otherwise, my Christmas surprises will be spoiled."

"I won't breathe a word." The old man pulled out his watch. "It's nearly time for coffee. We'd best pick out that wood for your presents and get inside 'fore my misses comes out here lookin' for us and discovers the Christmas surprises I left uncovered beneath my bench."


"Soon as I start a fire in the parlor stove to take the chill off, Mrs. Stone, I want to give ya the wedding gifts I've been saving for you and Harrison. Then I'll show ya the ornaments I've been making for Christmas," said Mrs. Freiling, leading her guests to the sitting room.

"Let me help you with the stove, Mrs. Freiling," Spunky offered. "Aurora, why don't you take to the sofa. It's my favorite place in Mrs. Freiling's house."

While Spunky and Mrs. Freiling tended the stove, Aurora sat on the green velvet divan. She recalled sitting there beside Harrison last summer, but their time with Mrs. Freiling had been so brief, she hadn't noticed the softness of the cushion, nor the pleasant feel of the room. Mrs. Freiling's parlor, with rose-striped wallpaper above varnished wainscoting, and Nottingham lace curtains and lambrequins at the windows, had a warm, inviting feel to it, regardless of the cool winter temperature. Interesting whim-whams and what-nots filled every available surface, yet the room didn't appear cluttered. Each item seemed carefully chosen and thoughtfully placed to give just the right effect—a small wooden heart, a cornhusk doll wearing a white kerchief and blue gingham skirt, a sweet grass box, a shelf dripping with lace and lined with a collection of gilt and embossed greeting cards.

The oak center table immediately caught Aurora's eye, with gargoyle heads on brass feet holding wooden balls, and creatures halfway up the rope-turned legs that supported a medial shelf. The table top was adorned with a crocheted doily and handsome parlor vase lamp. On its dome shade was hand-painted the image of a sailboat on a small lake, with a grapevine arching above the scene. Beside the lamp lay a small gift-wrapped box.

When the fire had begun crackling, Spunky sat beside Aurora, and Mrs. Freiling pulled her rocker up near the sofa.

"Mrs. Stone, the package on the table there is for you to open. It's our wedding gifts to you and Harrison."

Aurora picked up the small box and slid off the delicate white satin ribbon, then pulled the shiny white paper off. Beneath the lid, a man's pocket watch and a ladies' gold pin lay side by side, nestled in fluffy white cotton batting.

She lifted the pin from the box to admire it. "Thank you, Mrs. Freiling, for your thoughtfulness. These are truly lovely."

"There's a little story I must tell ya about those pieces," said Mrs. Freiling. "Years ago, before Mr. Freiling and I came to the island to live, we were great friends with Harrison's Grandpa Harry and his Grandma Lacy. We lived just down the road a piece from the farm they had near Leland. Lacy and I, we were always helpin' one another. Two or three times a week, if we could, we'd get together, her kitchen or mine, and brew ourselves a pot of strong coffee and chat while we set to work on our mending, or putting up preserves, or what have ya.

"As the years went by, hard times hit Lacy and Harry. He took a fall off a ladder one day. Broke his leg real bad. That left Lacy with a load more of work. Well, she was kind of a delicate woman, like her name. After awhile, she got real tired, and her heart just stopped.

"But before she died, she gave me the gold pin she always wore. I don't think I hardly ever saw her but what she had it on. Even if she was just wearin' her everyday calico dress, she'd pin a piece of lace at the neckline and make herself look just a little nicer. I always admired that pin of hers. Solid gold. Now, it's time to pass it on to the next generation. I hope you'll wear it in good health."

Aurora ran her finger over the star-shaped pin. "Thank you very much, Mrs. Freiling. I'll treasure it, always."

"Why don't you put it on?" Spunky suggested.

Aurora pinned it near her collar then lifted the pocket watch from the box. "Was this—?"

"Harrison's Grandpa Harry's watch. Poor Harry. He

had a rough time of it before he died. We'd all moved over to the island by then, and Harry swapped that watch for somethin' he wanted more. When I found out Harrison was plannin' to marry, I went to the man who'd taken the watch in trade and made a deal with him so's I could give it to Harrison."

The thought occurred to Aurora that in these few minutes, she had learned more about Harrison's family than he had shared with her over the past five years. Until now, she had known little more than the fact that Harrison's parents and older brothers had moved from North Manitou many years ago, following his Grandpa Harry's death, to take up ranching in Montana. Now she suspected from Mrs. Freiling's tone, that Harrison had some painful memories concerning his grandfather. She hoped one day he would be willing to share them with her.

"Thank you your kindness, Mrs. Freiling. Harrison will be pleased with such a special gift, I'm sure."

"You're welcome, my dear. Now, I'm just itchin' to show ya the ornaments I've been workin' on. I'll fetch them."

Mrs. Freiling soon returned with a large cloth bag. From it, she took a fabric strawberry. "This here's my favorite, made from a semicircle of cloth. You can make 'em real quick on a sewing machine. It ought to be real easy on that new one Harrison gave ya. I knew about it before you did. Spunky told me when it was delivered." Mrs. Freiling handed Aurora a red velvet berry dotted with tiny clear beads to resemble seeds. To the top had been stitched green velvet leaves, and a loop of green thread had been added for hanging on the tree.

"You keep that one," Mrs. Freiling told her. "I'm sure

ya could use some tree decorations, this being your first Christmas on your own. Did you bring any ornaments from home?"

Aurora shook her head. In her mind, she envisioned a whole tree decorated with red fabric strawberries, but the vision vanished when she thought of the sewing machine. She had no intention of touching it anytime soon. "I probably should have at least brought some colored paper for a chain, but the thought never occurred to me."

Mrs. Freiling took a dozen sheets of colored paper, and as many paper doilies from her bag, and handed them to Aurora. "Here. These 'll do for more than a few paper ornaments." As she closed her bag, she caught sight of something out the parlor window. "I see the men are comin' in from the workshop. I'd better get the coffee poured and the plates set out."

Aurora helped Spunky and Mrs. Freiling set places, and everyone sat around her large kitchen table to sample fluffy glazed cinnamon buns and rich, steaming coffee.

Too soon, the fellowship ended, for when it came time to return to the keeper's quarters, Aurora found herself wishing she could extend her pleasant visit.

As Cad drove the carriage beneath bare hardwood branches, Aurora reflected on Mrs. Freiling's warm and welcoming hospitality. What a change from the emotional seesaw Aurora had been on since her arrival at North Manitou!

Suddenly, she turned to Spunky. "Why don't you and Mr. Blackburn stay for dinner? We can have boiled potatoes, and fry up some of the ham you left for us in the icebox. I'll ask Keeper Dixon, too. It's only right, since you cooked for me and Harrison last evening." Besides,

Aurora couldn't face being with Harrison alone again.

"I'm sure the men 'd like somethin' other than turkey 'n gravy," Spunky acknowledged. "I'll be the first to admit I ain't got much imagination when it comes to Thanksgivin' leftovers. Before we sit down to a meal, though, I wanna see Stoney on them crutches!"

When the carriage stopped in front of the keeper's quarters, Cad helped Aurora down. She was again troubled by his straying hand that smoothly shifted from her elbow to her lower back as she touched the ground.

"I'll be in as soon as I've unhitched the rig," he promised, standing very close.

Aurora stepped out of his reach. "No rush. It will be awhile before I have dinner ready."

"Besides, we ain't eatin' till we've seen Stoney on crutches," Spunky put in. "Dependin' on his mood, it could take awhile!"

Aurora hung up her coat, put the things Mrs. Freiling had given her in a kitchen drawer, and busied herself peeling potatoes while Spunky carried the crutches upstairs. Moments later, she came down with Harrison's tray of dirty breakfast dishes in one hand, and the pitcher from his washstand in the other.

"Keeper Dixon and I are gonna get Stoney up off the bed so I can change it. By then, you'll have dinner simmerin', and Cad will be in, and the two of you can come up and help us convince our patient to try out those new crutches he's already claimin' he's got no use for." She took the kettle from the stove, filled it at the pump, and set it on a front burner. "And bring a pitcher full of warm water when you come. Stoney could do with some washin' up."

A quarter hour later, when Aurora heard Cad coming in

from the barn, she thought it wise not to be caught alone with him. Quickly, she poured warm water into Harrison's wash pitcher and headed upstairs before Cad had removed his coat and boots.

When she entered Harrison's room, he was sitting on a chair while Spunky changed his bed, lecturing him as she dropped a dirty sheet in a laundry basket, then fitted the clean one to his mattress. "Now that y're up, make use of that warm water Aurora's heated and wash yourself. Then you can try out them new crutches Keeper Dixon is inspectin'."

When Aurora stepped past Harrison to set the pitcher on his washstand, his eyes rested on the pin at her collar, and she thought he was about to say something, but instead, Keeper Dixon spoke up.

"This is a mighty fine pair of crutches. They'll certainly outlast that broken leg of yours, Stoney."

Harrison didn't give two hoots about the crutches. He *did*, however, wonder about the pin Aurora was wearing. He'd seen one like it before, but where? Too tired to ask, he longed for privacy again, and the comfort of his bed.

No sooner had the thought crossed his mind, than Cad entered. When Harrison saw the bottle of red liquid the Chicago man set on the dresser, he realized this was one visitor he welcomed.

Cad offered his usual cocky smile. "Stoney, my friend, seems to me you've got it mighty easy with two nurses on hand to tend you." He slumped onto a chair.

Spunky went to the washstand, poured warm water into the basin, and worked up a suds on Harrison's washcloth before handing it to him. She laid the towel across his lap.

Harrison felt keenly the indignity of having to wash and

dry himself with a roomful of company. When he had finished, he watched Spunky avidly, impatient for her to finish making up his bed. The moment she turned back the covers, he reached for the bedpost, but try as he might, he couldn't get up.

"Help me back to bed, Aurora," he requested grumpily.

"Don't you dare!" Spunky quickly countered. "If all you want is to waste away in bed the rest of the day, Stoney, you'll have to get there by y'rself."

"My, but you are a cruel taskmaster," Cad teased.

Keeper Dixon handed Harrison the crutches. "Here. Try these."

"Yeah. This is a good time to start usin' 'em," Spunky put in. "In fact, y'r gonna have to use 'em all the way down the stairs to the dinin' room. Aurora will have dinner on soon, and it's time you took a meal with the rest of us."

Harrison's temper flared. "The dining room? That's impossible!"

"Nothin's impossible. Least not if y'r hungry."

"I'm not hungry," Harrison grumbled. In truth, he was starved, but he wasn't about to admit it. Surely someone would bring him a tray.

"Not hungry?" Spunky questioned. "But you barely ate any breakfast!"

Harrison glared at her, then concentrated on pressing himself up. The chair started to slip out from under him, but Aurora held it steady behind him. After a struggle, he gained his balance on the two crutches and his right foot. He didn't care what Spunky said about the dining room, his destination remained his bed. He took one hesitant step toward it before Spunky stepped squarely in front of him.

"Sorry, friend. I meant what I said. Hungry or no, y're

gonna have to learn to get around on those things. Y're a strong man, Stoney. You can do it if you want to."

Harrison's cheeks began to burn.

"The sooner you get up and around, the sooner you'll be back to your duties here," Keeper Dixon reasoned, "and the sooner I'll get caught up on my sleep!"

His boss's logic only amplified Harrison's frustration, and his guilt at being unable to work.

"You'd better do as Spunky asks if you ever hope to get between those sheets again." Cad's casual advice fueled Harrison's anger. His fingers tightened about the handgrips on his crutches.

Simmering inside, he turned to Aurora, expecting her to add another voice to those already stacked against him. Instead, her silence, and the pity in her eyes spoke louder than words, making him boil over.

"Get out of my room!" he shouted. "Get out, all of you! And don't come back!"

# CHAPTER

## 8

Aurora trembled. She could feel the color draining from her face. Despite the weakness in her knees, she was the first to walk out Harrison's door. The others followed her down the stairs.

"These last couple of days, Harrison has been worse than a grizzly," she heard Keeper Dixon murmur to Spunky. "It was no joy sitting with him this morning while you folks were off to Freilings."

"I've known him for twelve years, and I've never seen him so angry and unreasonable," Spunky admitted. "Kinda takes y'r appetite away. Maybe by the time Aurora and I get dinner on, we'll feel more like eatin'."

Aurora arrived in the kitchen feeling sad and sick inside. All she could think of was that she had married a man she no longer recognized.

The thought so frightened her, she scarcely noticed Cad following her to the stove, or the fact that Spunky had headed off to the dining room with place settings for the table. Keeper Dixon was in the sitting room, leaving her alone with the Chicagoan. She reached for the two-pronged fork and checked the boiled potatoes to see if they were tender.

Cad came up close beside her and rested his hand on her shoulder. "Don't feel bad. Harrison is just having a rough time of it. I'm sure his temper will improve once his leg starts to heal."

Badly in need of some kindness, she allowed his hand to remain. When she turned to leave the stove, his nearness and the sympathetic look in his brown eyes comforted her. For one brief moment, she thought he might put his arms around her.

An instant later, she recognized the trappings of a compromising position and backed away. "I'm sure you're right, Mr. Blackburn. Harrison will be back to normal in time." She didn't believe her own words right now, but as she headed into the pantry to find a jar of fruit to serve for dessert, she wondered if God might soon work a miracle in Harrison. Too late, she realized Cad was following her through the door. He had started to close it when Spunky's voice floated in from the dining room.

"Cad?"

He swiftly retraced his steps. "Were you calling me, Spunky?" His mellow baritone voice bespoke innocence.

Hurriedly, Aurora picked a can of peaches off the shelf and returned to the kitchen where Spunky was setting out the bread board and a sharp knife.

"Cad, do me a good turn and fetch a loaf of the bread I baked this morning from Keeper Dixon's kitchen," Spunky said.

A quarter hour later, the bead had been sliced, the ham fried, the potatoes poured into a serving dish, and all had been carried to the dining table. Keeper Dixon asked the blessing.

"Dear Heavenly Father, we thank you for this our food, for the shelter you have provided, and we ask that you put your comforting hand on Harrison, to heal his heart and his leg. In Jesus' name, Amen."

Keeper Dixon had offered exactly the prayer Aurora carried in her heart, but she still could find no appetite for the food she had just prepared. Instead, she gazed out the dining room window, looking for South Manitou, remembering the joy she had known there. But a haze obscured the island from view, fogging her memories just like the cloud over her heart shrouded her dream of a happy future.

Harrison had *thought* Spunky was his friend, but he was beginning to tire of her bossy ways. At least she had drawn Cad to the keeper's quarters, and with him, more pain medicine.

He spied the bottle of wine on the dresser, reached for it, and downed several swallows, then he leaned back against a pile of feather pillows propped against the headboard. How sick he was of being confined to this room. He had studied its every detail for endless, painful hours. No matter what the future held, he would always associate the worst pain he had ever felt in his life with the white plaster and oak woodwork of this room.

As the alcohol took effect, he began to relax, and gradually, his hunger increased. He could no longer ignore it, nor the fact that downstairs, four people sat at the dining table enjoying dinner. The sound of serving spoons against dishes floated up to him, as well as the enticing aroma of fried ham.

He glanced at his crutches. Spunky was right. He was capable of using them if he wanted. But did he want to?

"I'm not accustomed to silence at the dinner table," Cad commented. "If no one else has anything to say, I suppose I'll just have to tell Mrs. Stone about the automobile I helped build in Chicago before I came to visit the island. Has your husband mentioned it to you, Mrs. Stone?"

Aurora wasn't much interested in anything Cad had to say, but at least it would take her mind off her problems. "I'm afraid Harrison hasn't spoken a word about it, Mr. Blackburn. Probably because, with the exception of sewing machines, I don't understand the first thing about mechanical devices."

"Ah, then I'll take this opportunity to enlighten you. My father's friend, Mr. Roberts of the Steel Screw Company, undertook to build an automobile last year. At first, he thought he might power it with one of those—"

"—infernal combustion engines," Spunky put in. "I've heard this story so many times since Cad first set foot on the island, I can tell it by heart, but you go ahead, Cad."

"Thank you. As I was saying, he thought to power it with an *internal* combustion engine, but then he had a better idea. Why not use electricity?"

"I'll tell you why not," Aurora replied, "because you would only be able to drive as far as the cord could reach."

Keeper Dixon chortled. "That's the best reason I've heard yet. Better than the one I gave him, which is that too many people have no place to plug it in. Can you imagine one of those here? Automobiles! Pooh! You'd be better off spending your time making a really fine horse harness. Those auto contraptions won't ever replace the horse and buggy."

Having shared his opinion, Keeper Dixon cocked his

head, as if listening for something, then put his napkin beside his plate. "Excuse me a moment, if you will."

Cad continued. "Folks can make fun of automobiles, if they wish, but the day of the motorcar is coming!" he prophesied.

To his captive audience he recited chapter and verse of the development of the automobile, including experiments in Europe, such as Nicolas Cugnot's steam-driven wagon, the first powered vehicle which ran across a field in France and straight into a wall.

Cad described the first internal combustion engine built in 1860 by Ettienne Lenoir which ran on illuminating gas, and Nikolous Otto's four-stroke gasoline engine which was patented in 1876 in Germany. Begrudgingly, Aurora admitted to herself that Cad had captured her interest on a topic she had previously thought boring.

He went on to say Daimler, another German, had worked on a four-wheel, gasoline-powered automobile which, if Cad was to be believed, had been discussed in 1888 with William Steinway, the piano maker, with the intention of manufacturing it in the United States.

"And three years ago this very month, the Chicago *Times-Herald* sponsored the first automobile race ever held in this country," Cad continued, "from Chicago—"

"To Evanston and back," Spunky put in, evidently tired of listening to a story she had heard before. "That was a total of fifty-two miles. An automobile called the Duryea won the race. That contraption was named for the pair of brothers who built it—Frank and Charles." She turned to Aurora. "And how fast do you think they was goin', on average?"

Before Aurora could offer a guess, the answer came

from the direction of the doorway. "Five and five one-hundredths miles per hour."

Harrison stood at the entrance to the room, propped on his crutches, a look of satisfaction on his face. Keeper Dixon was at his side.

Still in nightshirt and sweater and bare-footed, Harrison made his way toward the table, the tips of his crutches clunking against the maple floor with each step. Keeper Dixon pulled up a chair beside Aurora while Spunky and Cad slid theirs over to make room for him.

"You make a good case for sticking with a horse, Cad." Harrison commented as if nothing unusual had taken place upstairs. He set his eyes on the platter of meat, still half-full. "That ham looks mighty good."

"I'll fetch you a plate," Aurora quickly offered, wanting to pinch herself to make sure she wasn't imagining Harrison next to her. Of one thing she was certain—he carried the smell of wine on his breath.

She set Harrison's napkin, plate, silver, and a cup of coffee in front of him and passed him the meat, potatoes, bread, and peaches. He helped himself to small portions of each. His presence seemed to take the tension out of the air, and the others all took second helpings while conversation flowed, mostly between Keeper Dixon and Cad, comparing the horse and buggy to the automobile.

Aurora  heard little of it, so preoccupied was she with wondering how Harrison's moods could fluctuate so widely. She couldn't help thinking he owed her and the others an apology, but if they were willing to overlook that point, she supposed she should do the same.

When he had finished eating, he pushed back from the table, making ready to get up on his crutches.

Keeper Dixon rose. "Very good dinner, Aurora. I'll sleep well on it." He pushed his chair in. "Before I go, I'll make certain Harrison gets safely upstairs."

With Spunky's help, Aurora cleared away the dishes. She couldn't help peeking into the front hall, where the stairway led up to the bedrooms. Spunky came up behind her. Though Keeper Dixon and Harrison had left the table several minutes earlier, they had only made it up three steps to the first small landing.

"I think we should move your bed down to the sitting room," Keeper Dixon was saying. "It would be easier for you at mealtimes, and Aurora wouldn't have to run up the stairs to care for you during the day."

"I can manage," Harrison said determinedly. He set the tips of his crutches on the next tread and attempted to hoist himself up, but his broken leg, extended by the splints, bumped the riser. He inhaled sharply, and Aurora could almost feel the pain that must be shooting through his thigh as he retreated to the landing.

She stepped forward. "I couldn't help overhearing, Keeper Dixon. I like your idea, moving Harrison downstairs."

"I'll get Cad to help," Spunky offered. "The four of us could do the job in no time."

Harrison turned toward them and for a moment Aurora feared angry words were about to be hurled at them again. Then, a look of relief overspread his features and he started down the stairs with Keeper Dixon at his side.

He sat quietly in the corner of the sitting room while Aurora and Spunky moved the chairs and tables to make a place for his bed by the window. Soon, Cad and Keeper Dixon had carried the frame, springs, and mattress downstairs and set them up.

Aurora and Spunky began putting the sheets and blankets on, but before they had finished, Cad and Keeper Dixon had come down with another piece of furniture.

"Where do you want this, Aurora?" Keeper Dixon asked, his voice strained from holding up his half of her new sewing machine.

How she wished Keeper Dixon had left the machine upstairs, but it was too late now. Quickly, she glanced around. "In the dining room." She hurried through the connecting door to find a location. With Spunky's help, she moved the dining table and chairs closer to the window at the far end, allowing Cad and Keeper Dixon to set the sewing machine by the door to the sitting room, though she was in no hurry to make use of the wedding gift.

Keeper Dixon looked over the arrangement with satisfaction. "Now that we've got things nearly back to working order, I think I'll go home and get some sleep. With the days growing short, it will soon be time to light the lamp."

"You go home an' rest easy. I'll come wake you half an hour before sunset," Spunky assured him. "And I'll come with you when you put the light in the tower, like I been doin'. For now, I'm gonna help Aurora." She turned to Cad. "It's time you got back to the farm, don't you think? Pa and my brothers could do with another set o' muscles to help with chores, even if yours are a titch soft from city life."

"Again I say, you're a stern taskmaster, Spunky." To Aurora, he added, "I'll be by in a day or two to check on the patient."

As soon as the men had gone out the door, Aurora and

Spunky returned to their task of making up Harrison's bed. Though he said little, he seemed relieved to settle beneath the covers when they finished.

Then Aurora went upstairs with Spunky to fetch the bandages, medicines, the bottle of wine—now half empty—and other necessities stored there.

After they unloaded all the supplies onto a table in the sitting room, Spunky put on her coat. "It's near dusk. I'd best go and wake Keeper Dixon. I'll prob'ly see you tomorrow."

"Good night, Spunky, and thanks for all your help."

Spunky shrugged as if it were nothing. Aurora was ashamed of herself. Spunky was proving to be a true friend not only to Harrison, but to herself as well.

After Spunky left, Aurora poured herself a cup of coffee. She dreaded returning to the sitting room now that she and Harrison were alone again. She lingered by the warm stove while she sipped the strong brew, then set her half-empty cup on the counter and went to check on her husband.

He had fallen asleep. From the window beside his bed, she could see Spunky and Keeper Dixon making their way along the boardwalk to the tower. Keeper Dixon was carrying the service lamp. The weather was too cold now to leave it in the tower where the oil would be too chilled to light. Aurora wished she could trade places with Spunky, spending her evening on duty watching the light from an upstairs bedroom window like her mother had on South Manitou, instead of taking care of a man who didn't seem to want her around.

Rather than wallowing in self-pity, she had better start planning gifts and making decorations for Christmas,

Aurora chided herself. In her trunk upstairs, she found scraps of red silk to make a Christmas strawberry like the one Mrs. Freiling had given her.

She took the red silk down to the kitchen, brought the most comfortable chair and the small wooden footstool in by the stove, then took out the strawberry Mrs. Freiling had made.

As Aurora began to cut a circle of red silk using a dessert plate as a template, she was reminded of the happy times she had spent on South Manitou preparing for Christmas celebrations in the past. How she longed for those times when Harrison had been attentive and adoring!

*I will be happy again. I will!* she thought, folding the circle in half and cutting it on the fold line. Onto the half-circle of fabric, she stitched several pearls to look like the seeds on a strawberry, then she folded the semi-circle in half. How quickly she could stitch the seam by machine. Through the doorway to the dining room, she glanced at Harrison's wedding gift.

*I will not use that sewing machine!* Into her mind flashed the image of Harrison ripping up his poetic card to her. It tore at her heart!

She threaded her needle, and began to take painstakingly tiny stitches by hand. She had been working for several minutes when, from the darkness of the sitting room, Harrison's soft humming came to her as in times past.

Heartened by the sweet sound, she couldn't resist joining her words with his melody in a duet like they had sung so often on South Manitou.

> Somewhere the sun is shining,
> Somewhere the songbirds dwell;

102

Hush then, thy sad repining;
God lives, and all is well.

At the chorus, she put aside her sewing and carried a lamp to his bedside, forgetting for now his past anger.

Somewhere, somewhere,
Beautiful Isle of Somewhere!
Land of the true, where we live anew
Beautiful Isle of Somewhere!

By the flickering light she could see that he had a peaceful look on his face. In fact, he was almost smiling! A feeling of relief washed over her.

"Are you hungry? Would you like a ham sandwich?"
He nodded. "With mustard."

"With mustard," she repeated, and couldn't help grinning. Many times in their five-year courtship, they had debated the best way to make a ham sandwich. He held forth for mustard; she, for cheese. "I'll bring it on a tray so you won't have to get up," she offered, thinking his move downstairs on crutches had caused enough strain for one day.

He shook his head. "I'd rather eat with you at the table."

Overcome by surprise, she could not answer for a moment. Then, "Of course. I'll only need a few minutes to make the sandwiches and set the places."

Before she turned to go, Harrison caught her by the hand. "No rush. We've got . . . all evening." He gave a squeeze before letting go. A thrill went through her. At long last, he was acting like his old self again!

# CHAPTER

## 9

While Aurora was preparing the ham sandwiches, she could hear Harrison making his way to the table. The dining room was so dark, she worried that he would collide with the rearranged furniture. Chewing the inside of her lower lip, she prayed silently until she heard his chair scrape across the floor, then set her tray with milk and sandwiches and carried it to the dining table.

Harrison took her hand in his and bowed his head in prayer. "Thank you, Lord, for Aurora, and this food. In Jesus' name, Amen."

As Harrison ate, he stole glances at the woman beside him. The soft light of the single candle became her, dancing upon her pert nose, enhancing the oval face he had found beguiling from the very first time he had seen her over five years ago. Had he really been angry enough to raise his voice to her earlier today? The incident seemed unreal. He kept wishing he would wake up and discover his broken leg had been only a nightmare, a trick of his imagination.

But the splints, the crutches, and the pain were very real. Thank goodness, his leg wasn't hurting much tonight. Maybe each day from now on would be a little better than the last. Maybe he wouldn't feel the need for wine ever again. Maybe, just maybe, he would be able to endure the frustration of waiting to take his wife into his arms. He prayed it would be so.

Harrison had always been quiet, but Aurora couldn't help wondering what he was thinking tonight. Her thoughts raced ahead, filling the silence with the unvoiced hope that he would continue to behave like his old self from now on.

Harrison finished his sandwich and milk, and laid his napkin beside his plate.

"I'll help you back to bed," Aurora offered, staying beside him while he made his way to the sitting room. Then she left him alone and went about cleaning up the dishes.

A few minutes later, she took Mrs. Freiling's gift to Harrison. The moment he saw the watch, his pale face turned even whiter. He took it in his hand and turned it over, reading the initials engraved on the back side.

"H.S. I never thought . . . " His voice caught with emotion, and his eyes grew misty. A minute elapsed before he could continue. "Where did Mrs. Freiling find this?"

Aurora had never seen Harrison so moved. "She said your grandfather traded it for something else he wanted, and she bought it from the owner when she learned you were getting married."

Harrison's focus shifted to the pin at Aurora's collar. "Then that *is* Grandmother's pin."

Aurora nodded.

Harrison admired the watch again, then set it beside the wine bottle. The two together would serve as a strong reminder not to fall victim to his grandfather's ways.

He lay back. Fatigue was beginning to set in and his leg pain returned.

Aurora brushed a lock of hair off Harrison's forehead,

checking at the same time for any sign of fever, but he felt cool. "I'd better change your bandage again before you go to sleep. I'll go wash up."

When she removed the dressing, she saw that his wound was not seeping as much as before, but seemed more swollen.

Harrison could barely stand Aurora's touch, even though it was more gentle than a butterfly. He clamped his teeth together to keep from crying out, but couldn't suppress a grimace.

Aurora worked carefully and quickly to apply the disinfectant and wrap a new bandage around Harrison's thigh. Gathering up the soiled bandages, she told him, "I'll set these to soaking."

Harrison could hear Aurora pumping water in the kitchen and knew she would be busy there for a time. He reached for the bottle of wine. At first, he simply stared at it, wishing he could do without alcohol, but the throbbing was too great to ignore.

He glanced at the watch and thought of his grandfather, then set the wine back on the table and began softly humming the first tune he could think of to take his mind off his aching leg.

Aurora finished in the kitchen. Carrying her lamp with her, she went to say good night to Harrison. In the pale light she could see a haggard look on his face, and softly stroked his cheek. "I'm going up to bed now. Call me if you need anything."

Harrison caught her hand in his and kissed the palm. How he wished he could rid himself of his leg trouble and go upstairs with her! Weariness returned full measure, prevailing over his discomfort. "Good night, Aurora. I . . ."

In his gray eyes she saw his lassitude. She waited expectantly for him to finish his sentence, but his eyes drifted shut. His breathing fell into a rhythm, and eventually his hand went limp in slumber. She drew away.

What had he left unsaid? I'm sorry? I love you? The incomplete thought and her need to hear him say he was sorry for his angry outbursts haunted her as she climbed the stairs to her bedroom.

The next morning, when Aurora checked on Harrison, he seemed neither better nor worse, despite the fact that the wine bottle on his table was now empty. He remained in bed, napping much of the time while she went about her morning tasks, cleaning the chimneys of the lamps and refilling them.

At ten o'clock, she set a stew to simmering, and while it sent a delightful aroma of thyme and parsley throughout the house, she started knitting a blue and white wool cap for Keeper Dixon's Christmas present. By the time the cap was half finished, the stew was ready. Much to her surprise, Harrison hobbled to the kitchen on crutches as she was ladling the stew into a serving bowl.

"I hope you're planning to set a place for me at the table." He smiled at her for the first time since she had arrived on North Manitou, making her forget for now that she had been waiting for an apology.

In return, she grinned broadly. "Of course. Dinner will be on the table soon. Go and have a seat."

Though Harrison said little throughout the meal, he ate the portion she gave him and more. When he had finished, she fluffed his pillows and helped him back to bed. He took her hand in his as she arranged the blanket over him, and she was sure he was about to apologize for yesterday's anger.

"When you're done washing up, would you take my splints off for a while?"

Aurora put aside her disappointment, remembering that Keeper Dixon's book had recommended the splints be taken off every two days. "I'll tend your leg in a few minutes, when I'm done in the kitchen."

While she worked, she heard Harrison humming "The Man Who Broke the Bank at Monte Carlo." She would serve him stew more often, if it would make him hum such a lighthearted tune. As she dried and put away the dishes, she sang the chorus with him.

> As I walk along the *Bois Boolong*,
> with an independent air,
> You can hear the girls declare
> He must be a millionaire;
> You can hear them sigh,
> and wish to die,
> You can see them wink the other eye
> At the man who broke the Bank at Monte Carlo.

Harrison continued his humming while she tended him, unwinding the bandage that held the splints in place. Then he quieted down, napping much of the early afternoon while she finished knitting the cap.

By late afternoon, Harrison was wide awake and commenced singing quite boisterously in his own rendition of "Asleep in the Deep," substituting "la, la, la" for the words. Within minutes, Spunky showed up at the door, going straight to Harrison after Aurora let her in.

"I thought I heard music. I just had to come and find out for myself if you was caterwaulin', or if my ears was playin' tricks on me."

"You were hearing things," Harrison said, a grin teasing at the corner of his mouth.

"You're feelin' better, Stoney. I can tell."

Actually, his leg pained quite a bit, but the more it hurt, the louder he rendered his tunes in an effort to keep his mind off it. He just didn't want to admit he wasn't improving. "It must be Aurora's cooking," he said with a half smile.

"Don't believe a word of it," Aurora put in, joining them at Harrison's bedside.

Spunky turned to her. "The place does smell good."

"I made stew for dinner. There's plenty left. Let me send some along for you and Keeper Dixon. I'll put it in a bowl while you and Harrison visit."

While she was busy in the kitchen, a knock came at the rear door. She opened it to a strapping fellow who looked vaguely familiar. He was about the same age as Harrison.

"Sorry to bother ya, ma'am. I'm Peter Anders. Is my sister here?"

Aurora remembered him now. She had seen him play baseball on the North Manitou team when they had visited South Manitou. "Come right in, Mr. Anders. You'll find your sister in the sitting room with Harrison."

"Thank you, ma'am." He took off boots soiled by farm work and left them in the entryway before walking through the kitchen to the sitting room.

Harrison had heard the knock on the door, but he hadn't expected Spunky's brother to show up. Their friendship had dissolved years ago, when Peter had ridiculed him for his grandfather's drunkenness. Harrison would never forget the taunts that had made him decide to leave the island the spring following his grandfather's death. Since Harrison had returned to North Manitou in the prestigious position as assistant lightkeeper, his relationship with Peter had been civil, but cool.

In the kitchen, Aurora could barely hear the conversation in the sitting room, but she was desperately curious to know what had brought Peter to her door. She put a plate over the bowl of stew and quietly moved into the dining room.

"I came lookin' for Blackburn," Peter told his sister. "He was supposed to do the milking this morning. When I heard Bessie bawlin' her head off, I knew that Chicago freeloader had taken off before he'd done his chores."

Aurora thought it was just like Cad to let the cow suffer while he indulged his own whims. She pulled a chair up behind her sewing machine. Though she had no intention of sewing, it provided the perfect vantage point from which to watch and listen. Despite her resistance to using Harrison's gift, she opened the lid, raised the machine, wrapped the leather belt around the wheel, then sat at the treadle. It felt so natural, so comfortable.

"I haven't seen Cad since last night when I sent him home," Spunky told her brother. "Where do you suppose he could be?"

"I don't know, but I'm 'bout ready to put a tether on him." Peter turned to Harrison, looking at his broken leg, still free of its splint. "Sorry to hear what happened to ya out on the lake the other night."

Harrison made no response. He didn't believe Peter's

sympathy was sincere.

Peter's eyes shifted from the leg wound, to the bedside table. He picked up the empty wine bottle and stared at it.

"So *this* is where my sister's wine is disappearin' to." He looked Harrison in the eye, then set the bottle down. "And all the time, I thought that city rat, Blackburn, was usin' it for his *own* pleasure."

"Now, Peter," Spunky warned.

"It cuts the pain," Harrison stated bluntly.

"I remember your grandpa was mighty fond of my ma's cherry wine. When his friend on the north end o' the island run outta hard cider one winter, your grandpa would come near five miles down to our farm, poundin' on our door. He'd stand there beggin' my pa for a bottle of wine. Pa would tell him to go home, and your grandpa'd say, 'Just one more bottle and I promise I'll never bother you again.'"

"Peter, stop," Spunky begged.

Aurora could hardly believe what she was hearing. No wonder Harrison had said so little about his grandfather.

Peter ignored his sister. "I remember one night, the weather was bad, but it didn't keep your grandpa away. Pa told him to git on home. He said we had but one bottle left, and the whole winter ahead of us. Pa said he needed that bottle in case we kids took sick with a cough, but your grandpa just kept on a-beggin'. Finally, Pa shoved the bottle in his hands and pushed him out the door."

Peter paused, then he went on. "Next day I heard . . . " His voice grew quiet—"I heard your grandpa was dead."

Harrison could hardly believe what Peter was telling him, but at the same time, with a sinking heart he knew it was true. When he looked up at Spunky, her eyes were full of regret, but the sorrow he saw there couldn't quell the anger building inside him. How could she have let her father turn his grandfather out in the cold with a bottle of wine?

Harrison looked away, catching sight of Aurora at her sewing machine. She glanced down the moment their eyes met, and he knew she'd been listening to every word. His stomach knotted. Peter had shamed him again. This time, in front of his wife!

"Your pa killed my grandpa!" He told Peter. His words were laced with quiet rage.

"That ain't so!"

"Both of you, stop it!" Spunky scolded.

"Be quiet, Sis. This is between me an' Stoney." Peter turned again to Harrison. "Your grandpa's drinkin' killed him. As for you . . . " He scanned the room. When his eyes met Harrison's again, there was no mistaking the spark of resentment in their blue depths. "I don't expect you'll be around here too much longer. That leg o' yours, it won't never be right again. Come spring, there ain't no way you're gonna get up and down them stairs to the tower." He buttoned his jacket, making ready to go. "Besides, they don't let no drunks stay on in the light service." Peter pulled on his cap and let himself out.

Harrison wanted to go after the fellow and give him the whipping of his life! But it was impossible. Frustrated, he turned to Spunky. She simply looked at him, her eyes filled with tears.

Bitterness rose within him. She had betrayed him, keeping this secret from him all these years. She had called herself his friend, while her father was to blame for his grandpa's death!

"Get out!" Harrison said angrily.

"Stoney, no. Don't—"

"You heard me! Get out!"

She set her hands on her hips. "No! I won't go just 'cause you tell me to. Not till I've had my say. Your grandpa had a problem, Stoney. It's like Peter said. His drinkin' killed him, not our pa!" She turned and stormed from the room.

# CHAPTER

## 10

Spunky was so furious, she barely took time to pull on her boots. Without even a good bye to Aurora, she yanked on her coat and flew out the Stones' back door, running headlong into Cad.

His arms clamped around her. "Spunky! What an unexpected pleasure!"

"Let go of me!" She twisted violently.

He relaxed his embrace, surprised to see tears running down her cheeks. He'd never expected to see her cry.

"What's been going on in there? I just saw Peter come stomping out. Now here you are, looking as though you lost your best friend."

She felt trapped in Cad's arms, but too troubled to fight him. In a moment of weakness, she took advantage of his broad shoulder, brushing her damp cheek against it.

"I *did* lose my best friend," she murmured.

He stroked her hair and pressed his cheek against hers, then held her face gently in his hands and looked straight into her sad eyes.

"But that's impossible," he quietly reasoned. "I'm right here!"

Spunky's forlorn look promptly turned indignant. "You conceited . . . *donkey!*"

"What?"

The mock surprise and disbelief in Cad's smooth voice and on his handsome face was enough to make Spunky want to spit, and laugh at the same time. She finally opted for the latter.

Cad smiled innocently, putting his arm about her shoulder. "Suppose we go inside, pour ourselves some nice hot coffee, and you tell me what this is all about?"

"I'll tell you, *after* you tell me where you've been today. You were supposed to be helpin' at the farm. Peter says you took off first thing this mornin'."

Cad opened the door to the Dixon side of the house and ushered her in. "Coffee first, explanations after." He helped her off with her coat, then removed his own.

Spunky ran up the half-dozen steps to the kitchen, filled mugs with coffee from the pot she kept for Keeper Dixon on the back burner, set a tray, and carried it to the table by the sofa where Cad had already made himself at home behind his favorite book, the one about horseless carriages.

"I hope you've got that memorized. The lighthouse tender 'll be comin' by soon with our supplies for the winter, and they'll bring us a different set of books. Then you'll have to say good bye to that old friend."

Cad set the volume on the table, took a sip from his mug, and laid his hand on Spunky's shoulder. "Speaking of old friends, what happened with Stoney to get you so upset?"

Spunky stared down at the cup in her hands until Cad took her by the chin and gently turned her toward him. She studied the pleasing angles of his clean-shaven jaw and cheeks, the way his light brown hair fell into a center part and two perfectly matched waves, and the tenderness in his uncommonly blue eyes.

For the first time, he looked concerned for someone other than himself. For the first time, the words he had spoken showed compassion for others. For the first time, the subject he had raised was too personal to warrant an answer.

Cad considered the woman beside him. As usual, her dark blond hair stuck out in all directions from the loose knot she had pinned slightly off center atop her head; as usual, her chin looked too square to be pretty; as usual, her cuffs were threadbare and her skirt faded from too many washings. Nevertheless, there was something *un*usual, indefinable, even vulnerable about her right now.

Her brown eyes, often sparkling with laughter or mischief or some headstrong notion, were darkly troubled in a way he'd never seen before. Yet, even as he watched her, a trace of the old fire began to warm their depths, and a smug smile started to form on her generous mouth.

"Nice try, Mr. Cadwallader Blackburn, but it's your turn to speak first. You've got some explainin' to do concernin' y'r whereabouts today. Now, start talkin'!"

Cad raised his brow, the corner of his mouth tipping into a cunning grin. "I've got nothing to be ashamed of. In fact, when I tell you what I've been doing, you'll be so pleased, you'll hardly know what to do with yourself. I spent my day with Mr. Freiling in his workshop. He's teaching me how to use his woodworking tools and helping me to make Christmas presents, and one of them is for you!"

Her mouth dropped open in surprise. "Well slap the

dog and spit in the fire! I can't figure what put you in such a charitable frame of mind, but I ain't gonna complain, even if Pa and Peter *are* a bit provoked by y'r absence." Spunky wondered whether Cad was being honest, and if so, what really lay behind his actions. She was pondering these points when Keeper Dixon came to the sitting room, evidently finished with his nap.

"Spunky, I'm going out to put a light in the tower."

She jumped up. "I'm comin', too. Cad was just leavin'. He's got a load o' work ahead of him at the farm. Ain't that right, Cad?" Spunky gave him an arched look as she took the mug from his hand and picked up the tray.

"I can take a hint."

"Hint, nothin'! I'm tellin' you to get y'r things and get goin'. We both got jobs to do." She carried the tray to the kitchen, then wrapped herself warmly in her winter things.

While Spunky and Keeper Dixon made their way to the light tower, Cad stepped up to the Stones's door. He felt the large inside pocket of his heavy jacket, reassuring himself it still held the bottle he had placed there early that morning before going to the Freilings, then he knocked loudly on the door.

When Aurora answered, she looked as though she'd had a long day. He offered a wide smile, stepping inside before she invited him. "Good afternoon, Mrs. Stone. I've come to say hello to your husband."

"Mr. Blackburn, perhaps you could come back at a different time. Harrison isn't feeling much like company right now."

He stepped past her and started up the stairs. "He'll want to see me. I'll only be a minute."

Aurora followed Cad up the stairs and through the

kitchen, determined that a minute was all he would get. Despite the upsetting time with the Anders, Harrison had calmly helped Aurora put his splints back on and was now resting peacefully, and she didn't want him disturbed.

When Cad entered the sitting room, Harrison appeared to be sleeping. Cad reached inside his jacket, pulled out the bottle of wine, and set it on the table beside the empty one.

At the gentle sound of glass connecting with wood, Harrison's eyes opened, taking in the new bottle of wine, then Aurora, then Cad. "Blackburn. It's you."

"Of course, Stoney. I'm here with your new supply of medicine. You didn't think I'd let you down, did you?"

Harrison propped himself up, his sober gray eyes remaining on Cad's impish blue ones. "I've got something to say to you, Blackburn. Now hear me, and hear me well." His tone was daunting. "That's the last bottle of wine you'll bring into my home. Understood?"

Cad nodded.

"Good. Now take your leave."

Harrison caught Aurora by the hand, holding it in both of his while he listened to Cad's departure through the kitchen, down the stairs and out the rear door. Then his eyes met Aurora's. He saw a trace of fear, and he hated knowing he had put it there. He must remain in control of his emotions from now on. It wouldn't be easy with the injury and pain, but for Aurora's sake, and his own, he *must!*

Aurora was certain by the look in Harrison's warm gray eyes that he was about to apologize for all the times he'd been unpleasant and unkind. At last, they would talk things out and put anger and resentment behind.

Harrison prayed for wisdom and strength, and told the

118

woman beside him, "I don't like drinking wine, but I'm going to need relief from pain for a few more nights. Then, when the spirits in that bottle are gone, and my leg has improved some, I'll rely on your spirit to see me through." He gave her hand another squeeze, pulled the blanket up beneath his chin, and let his eyes drift shut.

Aurora tiptoed from the room, filled with a curious blend of relief and disappointment. *Oh, Lord,* she silently prayed, *grant me strength!*

Hours later, the increasing soreness in Harrison's leg woke him, or was it the sound of the fog whistle starting up that had disturbed his sleep? He counted the seconds between blasts. The timing was close, but not as perfect as he knew he could make it.

He looked out at the light tower, still lit, though its brilliance had been diminished by the vaporous shroud, and he counted the seconds between the red and white flashes. Keeper Dixon may be an expert with the clock mechanism that kept the light changing at ten-second intervals, but fog signal equipment like that on North Manitou was definitely not his specialty.

Harrison had spent years running similar equipment on South Manitou, learning all the cunning tricks to keep it functioning properly. That, and Keeper Trevelyn's recommendation had earned him his position here on North Manitou, and now, he couldn't even uphold his duty!

Feeling guilty, frustrated, and too pained to sleep, he reached for the bottle Cad had set on the table, uncorked it, and took several swallows. He lay back, thinking of Spunky. The old nightmare about his grandfather falling off a ladder came in flashes, mixed with troubled thoughts of his drunkenness and Peter's tormenting revelations.

*Your grandpa had a problem . . . His problem was what killed him, not our pa!*

As Harrison contemplated her words, the Lord began to reveal to him their truth. His grandpa had let alcohol control him, and he had paid the ultimate price.

As the dose of wine began to take effect, his leg didn't hurt as much, the fog signal seemed to fade into the distance, and the tower light dimmed. His last thought before he drifted off to sleep was a prayer to God to help him find the right words to apologize to his old friend.

"Spunky, do you know what day this is?" Keeper Dixon asked the following morning as they walked from the tower toward the keeper's quarters after dousing the light.

It had been a long night, with fog moving in and out, requiring both the whistle and light to be kept in full operation. At the moment, she was so tired, she felt as if a fog had settled over her brain. She yawned. "If I'm not mistaken, today is Wednesday, the thirtieth of November."

Keeper Dixon held the door open for her. "That's right. And you and I have some business to take care of this morning. Go sit at the dining room table. I'll be there in a minute to square up with you for your first month's wages."

Spunky had been looking forward to this day for the entire month. She wasted no time removing her boots and hanging up her coat.

She waited at the dining table while Keeper Dixon put away the service lamp, went upstairs, then came down to join her. He fanned several bills on the table in front of him. "I like the way you've been willing to take on the extra duty of watching the light in the tower this past week, waking me up when the lamp needed filling, and when fog came in. When I hired you, I had no idea I'd need your help outside the keeper's quarters, but with Harrison off his feet, I don't know what I'd have done without you. Between fog, darkness, and snow, one fella could pretty well stay awake twenty-four hours a day this time of year on North Manitou. I'm glad today marks the official end of the navigation season on the lakes. Pretty soon, we won't worry about the light or fog signal—unless the passage freezes hard enough for folks to start walking to the mainland." He slid the bills across the table to her.

Spunky picked up the money, jogged it into a neat pile, and set it in front of her. "I know I ain't the most educated person on this island to help out at a light station. I'd be hard put to write an entry in your log book that would make sense to anybody else, least of all that inspector who's gonna be stoppin' by any day now. But I know fog when I see it, and I know a flickerin' lamp, too. Watchin' for those two things ain't hard for a farm girl like me, even if I can't seem to remember the fancy name for that light."

"Fresnel."

"That's it. I know you told me that a dozen times. I know you said the lamp and lens was made in France, and they're called Fourth Order, but I'm too tuckered out at the moment to remember what it means."

"Fourth Order refers to the size, but that's not important right now. I think you'd better get some sleep. I'll sit by the window in the parlor in case the fog comes back. You rest easy."

Spunky waited until he had moved to the other room, then took her tea tin down from the china cabinet shelf. She counted the bills he had given her—ten one-dollar bills.

If the truth be known, it was the easiest ten dollars she had ever earned. She opened up her tin and counted the money inside—a little over eight dollars. The sum puzzled her. She was certain she'd had over ten dollars last time she'd counted, but a second counting bore out the lower figure. Her memory must have slipped. At least the eighteen dollars would be more than enough for her passage to Chicago and back in a cabin aboard the *Missouri*. Now, she needed money for a room, meals, and for spending. By spring, she would have plenty to cover all her expenses, and to do some shopping in Marshall Fields, Montgomery Wards, and Sears & Roebuck.

She made one thick stack of the folding money, which was in one-dollar bills, curved it to fit atop the coins in the bottom of the tin, and pressed on the lid. Returning it to its place on the shelf beside the sugar bowl, she yawned once again, then dragged herself upstairs and quickly changed into her nightgown. As she hung her worn blouse waist in the closet, she thought she just might change her mind and take up Aurora on her offer to make her a new one. Maybe her neighbor would make her a new skirt, too, and she could wear them to Chicago.

As Spunky snuggled into her feather bed, she saw herself standing on the deck of the *Missouri* in the new clothes, waving good bye to Cad. He'd be staying on North Manitou until he'd earned enough for passage home, and would be mighty put out that she'd go and leave him.

She chuckled to herself. She'd miss him. Especially if he ever acted again the way he had when he'd seen her so upset yesterday.

But as she drifted off to sleep, her final thoughts were not of the trip she would take come spring, nor of the tenderness she had noticed in Cad the last time they were together. Rather, her mind was on Stoney, who was obviously troubled by the truth about his grandfather's death, and his own denial over its cause.

The following morning, Aurora made pancakes and fried bacon for breakfast, but despite the delicious aroma that flowed through the house, she could interest Harrison in nothing more than black coffee. She wondered if his lack of appetite was due in part to the half bottle of wine he had consumed during the night.

When she had finished her morning chores, she sat by the kitchen stove and resumed work on her strawberry ornament. As she pushed the needle through the fabric, she thought of the sewing machine in the other room. How she missed the seamstress work she used to do by machine!

On South Manitou, she had spent every summer since she turned sixteen, sewing for the visitors. During winter, she had sewn occasionally for islanders, and made up all the garments necessary for her mother, sisters, and brothers, as well. Sewing had been her life, and how she loved it!

When her needle ran out of thread, she reached for the spool of scarlet mercerized cotton. Why not take it to the dining room, wind a bobbin on her new machine, and quickly finish the ornament?

Instantly, the memory of Harrison ripping apart his card flashed before her eyes. A sharp pang shot through her, reminding her of the hurt he had caused.

*I will not use that machine!*

Determinedly, she unwound a strand of cotton from the spool, threaded her needle, and took up her work again.

As the day wore on and the effect of the alcohol diminished, Harrison's leg ached more and more. Somehow, he endured the changing of his bandage without wincing. Certainly Aurora treated him as gently as humanly possible. Nevertheless, he'd had to invoke an unusual measure of self-control to suppress the groans that remained locked in his throat.

Late in the afternoon, when he heard Spunky stirring in the other half of the house, he called Aurora to his bedside.

"Aurora," he spoke quietly, taking her hand. His gray eyes gazed at her. She was sure he was about to deliver the apology she had been waiting for.

"Yes, Harrison? What is it?" she asked tenderly.

"Aurora, would you *please* go next door and get Spunky?"

She chewed the inside of her lip, biting back disappointment and angry words. What could Spunky do for him that *she* couldn't? But the earnest tone of his voice, coupled with the look of discomfort on his face told her this was no time to argue. A few minutes later, she brought their neighbor in through the back door.

While Spunky went to the sitting room, Aurora set a pan of stew on the stove to reheat—the leftover portion Spunky had forgotten to take home the day before in her hasty exit. Then Aurora lingered near the kitchen door, listening.

Harrison heard Spunky pause at the open hallway door behind him. With a wave of his hand, he beckoned her in. She came to stand at his bedside, her expression solemn, but without a hint of condemnation.

He studied her brown eyes, as clear and confident as

ever, but lacking any trace of the mirth and sparkle he so often found there. Taking a deep breath, he made his simple speech.

"I was wrong yesterday. I'm sorry. Can you forgive me?"

In the kitchen, Aurora's hands knotted into fists at her husband's words. If he could apologize to a friend, why couldn't he apologize to *her?* Instead, she pressed her hand over her mouth and continued to listen.

In the sitting room, Harrison was relieved to see Spunky's mouth turn up in a quirky little smile. "Stoney, you know I ain't any better at Bible learnin' than I am at cipherin', but there's one verse in the Good Book Preacher Mulder was readin' to me awhile back, and I ain't forgotten it yet. Seems a man asked if he should forgive his brother seven times, and Jesus told him he oughta forgive seventy times seven. I ain't sure how many times I still owe *you* forgiveness. I suspect y're past y'r allotment by now, the way you been actin' since that leg o' y'rs went bad.

"But one thing I *do* know. We've been friends for a lot o' years, almost like brother and sister. What you said to me yesterday, you said 'cause you was hurtin', both in y'r leg, and in y'r heart. That don't make it right, but it leaves a lot more room for understandin'. As for forgiveness, I got room in my heart to forgive you one more time. Maybe even a hundred more times!"

Hearing Spunky's words made Aurora yearn to talk things out with Harrison, and to forgive, but she felt too hurt and resentful to do either!

Harrison looked up into Spunky's eyes and mouthed a silent, "Thank you."

Spunky squeezed his shoulder, then took a moment to

press the covers snugly around him. "You rest easy now. Let that leg heal. Don't mind what Peter said yesterday. This spring y're gonna be climbin' the tower, and back to y'r old good-natured self!"

As she left the room, he silently prayed, *I hope she's right, Lord. I sure hope she's right.*

Aurora heard Spunky's footsteps and hurried back to the stove to stir the stew. Spunky paused by the kitchen counter where Aurora had left her strawberry ornament sitting out beside Mrs. Freiling's.

"That's mighty pretty, Aurora. Maybe even a touch nicer than Mrs. Freiling's," she concluded, hanging it on her finger to dangle in the air. Then she laid it in the palm of her hand for a closer inspection. "Hmm. I ain't much on sewin', but it sure looks to me like you put this seam in by hand. Don't y'r new machine work?"

Aurora shrugged, offering no explanation.

"Haven't you tried it?"

Aurora felt her face coloring as she continued stirring the stew. "I guess I haven't felt much like sewing by machine lately," she said lamely.

Aurora's fragile excuse cautioned Spunky to go easy. She came up beside Aurora, taking the spoon from her hand and laying it on the spoon rest, giving Aurora no choice but to face her. "What's botherin' you?" she asked sympathetically. "Whatever it is, there ain't no use sufferin' in silence. Just tell me, and I'll fix it."

Aurora hated the way Spunky always seemed to be in the middle, between herself and Harrison. She knew she should be more appreciative, but she couldn't help wishing Spunky would just go back to her farm. "You can't fix *this* problem," Aurora said bluntly.

"Sure I can," Spunky insisted. "Y're my friend. I wanna help you."

Aurora wanted only to drop the subject, but suddenly her heart was in her throat, and words came pouring out. "You can't get back the card Harrison gave me with the sewing machine—the love poem he wrote, and then—" Her throat suddenly constricted with emotion, but she forced the words out. "Ripped to shreds!"

"I didn't know nothin' about a card."

Aurora forced back tears. "It was the only poem he ever gave me." She could see him ripping the card to pieces and shoving it into his dirty coffee cup. Resentment overtook her. "I don't care if I never sew a single stitch on that machine!"

"I can understand you bein' miffed, but not usin' the machine—that's silly! There must be a reason why Stoney did what he did. Let's just go and ask him." Spunky headed toward the sitting room.

Aurora held back. "He won't talk about it."

"We'll see about that. Come on."

Reluctantly, Aurora followed Spunky to the sitting room. Harrison appeared to be napping. Spunky lit a lamp on his bedside table to chase away the dusky shadows and jostled his shoulder. "Stoney, wake up. We gotta talk to you. It's important."

Harrison blinked awake. "What is it?"

"Stoney, Aurora and I was wonderin' why you ripped up the card you gave her with her sewin' machine?"

Half asleep, Harrison answered without thinking. "Cad forged it."

Spunky turned to Aurora. "See? I told you there was an explanation for it. Now you know. It wasn't Stoney's card

127

after all. It was another o' Cad's tricks."

The revelation was even more disturbing. Maybe Harrison didn't love her after all! But she had only a second to think about it before Spunky went on.

"I'm glad there ain't no good reason why you can't use the machine, 'cause I've decided to take you up on the offer you made the other day to make me a new blouse waist. And after that, I'll need a skirt. Can you do that for me?"

"She can do it," Harrison answered for Aurora. Coming wider awake, he added, "I've been telling you for five years, there's no finer seamstress in the Manitou Passage. Maybe not in all of Michigan."

"How can you say that?" Aurora demanded, unable to contain herself. "How can you spout compliments when you've never even told me you're sorry for the times you yelled at me? You apologized to Spunky. What about me? You're like a different person where I'm concerned!"

"I'm sorry!" Harrison shouted, then he lowered his voice. "I'm sorry. Now please let me rest, both of you." He closed his eyes.

To Aurora, Harrison's apology seemed forced, and of little consolation considering the possibility he didn't even love her. She had no choice but to take it at face value, but she was so distraught by the thought of being trapped in a loveless marriage, she hardly heard Spunky's words as she saw her to the back door.

"I'd better be on my way. It's pretty near time to help Keeper Dixon with the light. I'll come back tomorrow."

After seeing Spunky out, Aurora dished up one plate of stew and ate alone, still vexed by the realization that Harrison hadn't written the romantic poem. Thinking back, she realized in all the five years she had known him, he hadn't actually ever told her he loved her. She had only assumed it because when they had been together on South Manitou, he had paid her much attention, shown her much respect, and had asked her to become his wife.

How could she have been so mistaken?

Aurora shoveled ash from the stove into a bucket, lit a fire to start the morning's coffee, then pulled on her coat and carried the ash out to the barrel in the barn where Keeper Dixon had told her to dump it. She probably shouldn't have left the chore for Sunday morning, but she hadn't had time for it yesterday or the day before.

Harrison had worsened slightly each of the past two days, and whether he loved her or not, she loved him, and had sat with him and read to him to help pass the time. The days had slipped by before she could finish her work. Even the kitchen floor hadn't been mopped. Perhaps tomorrow, she could catch up.

Right now, she was too worried about the increase in the swelling on Harrison's leg, the worsening soreness, and the fever he had developed overnight. She had noticed the changes when she had removed his bandage first thing this morning. His leg was so tender, in fact, she had suggested leaving the bandage off for a few hours.

She pulled her collar up around her ears as she left the barn and headed to the house, veering at the vee in the path to knock on Keeper Dixon's door. Spunky answered.

"Harrison has a fever and his leg is badly swollen. I think you and Keeper Dixon should take a look."

Spunky's brow furrowed. "We'll be over soon as I can wake him."

Aurora put away the ash bucket, then emptied the

chamber pots. She was measuring oatmeal into a pan of water to cook for breakfast when Spunky and Keeper Dixon arrived.

Dark circles rimmed the gray-haired keeper's eyes, accenting his look of concern. He had brought his book, *The Cottage Physician*, and carried it with him to the sitting room.

"Aurora says you're feeling under the weather this morning," he said to Harrison, touching the back of his forehead.

Even though Harrison had opposed consulting Keeper Dixon, he was glad Aurora had disregarded his wishes. Nevertheless, his pride demanded a protest. "You should be in bed."

"The sooner I get you up out of *your* bed, the sooner I'll be able to spend more time in *mine*," Keeper Dixon teased. "Now let's take a look at that leg."

Harrison rolled back the bedclothes, exposing the swelling. The area was extremely inflamed.

Keeper Dixon reached for his book, opening it to a marker. "I'm no expert, but I believe we'll find the advice we need right here." He scanned the page, then began reading. "'Should matter collect under the skin so as to be felt on examination, or the skin become red and thin, the part should be punctured, and great relief will be afforded by its escape.'" He closed the book and turned to Aurora and Spunky. "Ladies, I'm sure with your natural nursing instincts, you won't need my help to drain the infection. I'm going back to bed. I'll be over later to lead worship service. Meanwhile, I leave the patient in your capable hands."

*Lord, have mercy,* Harrison silently prayed.

# CHAPTER

# 11

Spunky picked up Harrison's razor from his bedside table. "Gotta make sure there ain't no germs on this."

Aurora quickly reached for the bottle of carbolic acid solution, then held out her other hand. "If anyone is going to take a razor to my husband's leg, it's going to be me."

Spunky hesitated. She had seen her brothers and father through plenty of farm injuries that had resulted in infections. But what did Aurora know? Reluctantly, she set the razor in the woman's open palm. "I'll put some water on. We'll need it for cleansin' the wound once it's open."

Harrison waited in dread. He prayed Keeper Dixon's book was right, and the procedure would bring him relief. But suppose the infection only worsened after it was drained? He prayed for God to guide Aurora's hand and help Spunky show a little mercy!

Aurora went to the kitchen to wash her hands and disinfect the razor, then returned to Harrison and swabbed his wound with diluted carbolic acid.

He inhaled sharply when the cold, wet cotton touched

his leg. He hadn't wanted to show his discomfort, but he couldn't help it.

Spunky came with the pot of water and set it on the bedside table. "Better find somethin' nice to look at out that window for a spell, Stoney, 'cause this leg o' yours ain't gonna be a pretty sight for the next few minutes."

Harrison gazed through the four-pane window by his bed at the barren trees, snow-swept sand, the teal blue water beneath the gray sky, and began humming "Beautiful Isle of Somewhere."

Aurora held the razor above the wound. Her hand trembled. She steadied it with the other, held her breath, and pressed the blade against the red, swollen flesh.

Harrison's humming stopped with a grunt.

The wound burst open, spraying the front of Aurora's dress with pus and blood. Her stomach turned.

Spunky quickly pressed a warm, wet towel to his leg. "No wonder you was feelin' so poorly, Stoney. That old leg o' y'rs was just full o' bad blood. There won't be no more evil spirits left in you, once we've got it drained. Y're gonna heal just fine."

While she took her dirty towel to the kitchen, Aurora picked up a clean one, dampened it, and laid it against Harrison's leg as gently as possible. Now she understood better why Harrison had been difficult this past week.

With his pain subsiding, Harrison turned to look at his wife. A ray of sunshine peeked through the window beside his bed, surrounding Aurora with a halo of gold, making her more beautiful than the morning brightness for which she was named.

It was as if the shaft of light had pierced his heart as well, filling it with a love overflowing. *Thank you, God for putting Aurora by my side, for giving me a woman who is strong when I am weak!*

Then the heavenly light faded, and he saw the worry in her blue eyes.

He took her hand in his. "I'm feeling much better, thanks to you."

Aurora drew a deep breath and let it out slowly. In her mind, she knew Harrison would be able to heal now, but would her own hurt ever go away? *Thank You, Father for healing Harrison. Please, heal my wounded heart!*

"Here's the things you was askin' about," Spunky told Aurora, setting a crate on the kitchen counter.

Five days had passed since Harrison's infection had been drained. He was feeling so much better, she had altered a pair of his old pants, making the left leg baggy enough to fit over his splint so he could get dressed. She had even been able to sew the blouse waist for Spunky, and to stand watch one night for Keeper Dixon then sleep through the following day, confident Harrison could manage to serve himself the ham sandwich she made ahead of time and left in the ice box for his lunch.

To Aurora's way of thinking, the big indication of his improvement had been in his teasing her to start making Christmas treats. Being newly married, she lacked the variety of spices, flavorings, utensils, and other special ingredients required to create traditional holiday confections. Last night, Keeper Dixon and Spunky had offered to loan the items from Mrs. Dixon's kitchen, and Spunky had kept her promise to gather them together and bring them over this morning.

Now, she unpacked them, pausing to read the

labels—blanched almonds, confectioners sugar, popping corn, cinnamon disk candies. Beside these, she set a meat grinder, a collection of cookie cutters, and several small bottles of food coloring, extracts, spices, colored sugar crystals, tiny red cinnamon hearts, silver balls, and multi-colored candy decors.

"There you be. You and Stoney have yourselves a good time today. I'm goin' home to get some sleep, and when I get up, I'm comin' over here for some samples!"

Aurora began with sugar cookies, cutting out Santas, reindeer, Christmas trees, and stars, each with a hole in the top so it could be hung on the tree. Harrison sat at the dining table with a batch of icing, the colored sugar crystals, and other cookie decors, applying the finishing touches.

The morning passed quickly. By midday, the kitchen was cluttered with dirty baking dishes, the dining table was covered with frosted cookies waiting to dry, and the floor beneath was scattered with crumbs and sugar crystals in a rainbow of colors.

"I think I'll serve our sandwiches on trays in the sitting room, and clean up afterwards," Aurora told Harrison.

While she prepared trays with tin plates and cups, sliced the bread, and made the sandwiches, Harrison's humming of "Deck the Halls" floated to her from the sitting room. She was carrying his tray to him when suddenly his humming stopped and she heard the clunk, clunk, clunk of his crutches crossing the hardwood floor much faster than usual.

He was leaning against the sill of the east window when she entered the room. He turned to her, a profound look of dread in his gray eyes. "The light tender is docking. In-

134

spector Gordon will be here any minute, and this place is a mess!"

Aurora scanned the room. Medical supplies cluttered the table beside Harrison's bed, which had been left unmade when her morning work routine had been interrupted by Spunky's delivery.

"I'll make my bed and straighten up here," Harrison said, indicating the table top crowded with medicine and bandages. "See what you can do in the kitchen and dining room."

"I'll put our sandwiches in the icebox." Aurora hurried back to the kitchen to tidy up.

Harrison pulled off the covers of his bed, smoothed out the bottom sheet, and tucked in square corners. Getting around was awkward, but he managed to put the covers and chenille spread on so his bed looked nearly as good as if Aurora had made it.

Turning to the bedside table, he wondered how to hide rolls of bandages, bottles of carbolic acid, scissors, cotton pads, cotton wadding, and the empty cherry wine bottle?

His gaze settled on the lump of pillows on his bed. He slipped the pillowcase off one of them and tucked the pillow back under the spread.

A knock sounded at the front door, and he heard Aurora answering. "Inspector Gordon, how good to see you again! Come in!"

With a sweeping motion of his arm, Harrison shoved the bandages and scissors into the pillowcase and tossed it beneath his bed. Hurriedly, he draped the bedspread so it met the floor, then he sat on the edge of his bed and looked around the room once more. He had forgotten to hide the empty wine bottle!

Inspector Gordon's voice floated to him as he came up the front stairs. "Harrison is in here?"

"Straight through that door," Keeper Dixon answered.

Harrison grabbed the bottle, set it on the floor, pushed it beneath his bed, and sat down on the edge just as the inspector opened the door leading from the front hall.

"Inspector Gordon, good to see you!" As Harrison greeted the neatly uniformed, older man, he saw Aurora discreetly closing the door to the dining room, and prayed she would have an opportunity to tidy up there before the inspector moved on.

Cap tucked beneath his arm, Inspector Gordon offered a handshake. "Sorry to hear about your accident, Keeper Stone." He glanced down at the splint showing beneath Harrison's left pant leg. His forehead wrinkled curiously.

Harrison looked down. The neck of the wine bottle was peeking from beneath the bedspread! He shifted the drape of the fabric to hide it.

Inspector Gordon went on as if nothing were amiss. "Keeper Dixon tells me you've had an infection, but you're on the mend now."

Harrison could feel his face coloring as he pulled his thoughts together for a reply. "Yes, sir. I'll be good as new in a few more weeks."

"Glad to hear it." The inspector glanced about. "I'll see the rest of the house now, but I'll be back to talk with you before I leave."

"This way to the dining room, Inspector Gordon," said Keeper Dixon. Harrison's heart skipped a beat as the head keep' and the inspector walked toward the connecting room. When the door opened, he saw that Aurora had draped the dining table with a cloth, and had swept the

136

floor and put the chairs in perfect order. He let out a sigh.

Inspector Gordon and Keeper Dixon moved to the dining room. Aurora closed the door to the kitchen and scrambled furiously to straighten the clutter there and put dirty dishes out of sight.

Christmas cookies still covered a good share of the counter top and her center work table. Swiftly, she set as many as would fit, into her cookie jar, then hurried to the pantry. Every container was full except a few empty quart jars! She took out her cracker tin, dumped the crackers onto the shelf in the cupboard, and closed the door. She was at her work table, carefully filling the cracker tin with the last batch of cookies when Inspector Gordon came through the door.

"The smell in your kitchen is wonderful, Mrs. Stone! Reminds me of baking day when I was a boy." He came to stand beside her. "Ah. No wonder. Look at those Christmas cookies you've been making!"

"These are for you and your crew on the tender." She offered him the canister.

"The fellows will sure appreciate your generosity, and your holiday spirit! This time of year, we're always anxious to finish our last tour for the season and get back to Detroit for the winter." He set the tin on the counter by the exit to the front hall. "Don't let me forget these on my way out. Now, if you don't mind, I'd like to see the upstairs."

"I'll take you up," Aurora offered, leading him to the three bedrooms. All but hers remained nearly empty. She had left her own room in good order, a habit cultivated through a lifetime of living at light stations.

When they had reached the downstairs hall again, Inspector Gordon turned to Aurora and Keeper Dixon. "I'd like a few minutes with Keeper Stone alone, if you don't mind."

Harrison sat on his bed, his left leg propped on a cushion when Inspector Gordon came through the door from the front hall for the second time. Harrison set aside the old issue of *Timely Topics* left behind months ago by a visitor from Lansing. His thoughts hadn't been on the article about the Spanish-American War; rather, what the inspector might have to say to him. In his mind flashed images of his drunken grandfather, weaving his way from the wagon to the front door on a pair of canes.

In Harrison's memory echoed Peter Anders' words: *I don't expect you'll be around here too much longer. That leg o' yours, it won't never be right again. Come spring, there ain't no way you're gonna get up and down them stairs to the tower.*

Harrison glanced down at the fringed hem of his bedspread, then reached beneath and deliberately set the empty wine bottle on the table in full view.

Would Inspector Gordon believe Harrison had only drunk the wine to ease his pain, and that he would make a full recovery in time to climb the tower in the spring? Or would Harrison find himself out of work before the lighthouse tender left North Manitou?

# CHAPTER

## 12

Inspector Gordon closed the door behind him. Immediately, he noticed the empty bottle on the table. He picked it up and took a whiff, then set it down and pulled up a chair beside Harrison.

The seat of the inspector's pants had barely made contact with his chair when Harrison opened the conversation. "I drank that wine to ease my pain, Inspector Gordon."

The inspector nodded. "Keeper Dixon informed me you had taken small amounts of opium for the first few nights, then relied on wine to help you sleep."

Harrison gathered his courage and made his next bold statement. "Come spring, I'll be good as new."

Inspector Gordon's expression held many messages—hope in his kind eyes, skepticism in his wrinkled forehead, encouragement in the slight upturn to his mouth. "I trust you're right, but we could both be wrong. Have you given any thought to what will happen if you need more time?"

Harrison replied confidently, "Aurora will be my legs. She'll tend the light. I'll work the fog signal." He couldn't help thinking, *But it won't be necessary. I won't sink in defeat the way the* Merrimack *did in President McKinley's*

139

*"splendid little war" down in Santiago Harbor.*

Inspector Gordon offered a smile. "I can tell I needn't waste any time this winter worrying over the situation here on North Manitou. I'll take you at your word." He extended his hand. "Until next spring, Keeper Stone."

"Until spring."

Aurora tied spices in a bag, dropped it into the pan of cider, and set it on the stove to simmer. The aroma of cinnamon, allspice, and clove began to filter throughout the warm kitchen, overpowering the last remnants of the beef and pork roast she had served Harrison and Keeper Dixon for Christmas dinner.

In the sitting room, Harrison and the head keep' were talking, passing the time until Cad and Spunky arrived from the Anders's farm, where they were celebrating the holiday with her father and brothers. Already, the overcast sky was turning to the dusk of a late winter afternoon. From the window beside the stove, she looked across the expanse of snow-covered sand to the lake and beyond, but couldn't make out South Manitou Island through the falling snow. She couldn't help wondering what Dorin and Eli had thought of the flannel shirts she had made last fall and left for their Christmas gifts. She wondered, too, whether her mother and sisters were pleased with the blue serge skirts she had sewn in the latest style, fastening at the side.

She set the tray with the rope hot pad and coasters Harrison had so cleverly fashioned as his gift to her, placed a large glass bowl in the center, and around it, the small glass cups borrowed from Mrs. Dixon's kitchen. She was filling a plate with the sweetheart cookies she had baked the previous day of egg whites mounded into heart shapes and colored a delicate pink, when she heard Spunky and Cad coming in the rear entry. She hurried down the steps to welcome them.

"Merry Christmas, both of you!"

"Merry Christmas, Aurora!" Spunky offered a hug.

Cad set down the bulging burlap sack he carried. The top fell open, and Aurora could see it was brimful of gaily wrapped gifts. "Do I get a hug, too?"

Before Aurora could think to avoid it, his arms were around her. She allowed a brief hug, then pulled away. "Merry Christmas, Mr. Blackburn. I hope you're not too homesick for your family in Chicago." Despite Harrison's improvement these last two weeks, Aurora had occasionally felt longings to be with her family on South Manitou for the holiday.

"Me? Homesick? Not likely. I keep thinking of all the expensive gifts I didn't have to buy, staying here for the winter." He helped Spunky off with her coat and hung it on a peg, then began unbuttoning his own.

"Ain't it like him, always thinkin' of himself?" Spunky commented wryly as she pulled off her boots.

Aurora saw that Spunky was wearing her new ivory blouse waist with a beautiful red satin bow tied at the neck. "The shirtwaist looks good on you."

"Today is my first time wearin' it. I woulda put it on for the inspector's visit, but I was so sound asleep when he came, Keeper Dixon couldn't wake me up, and I slept right through his inspection!" She chuckled. "I hope you can make me a new skirt soon to go with it. This one's pretty shabby at the hem." She grabbed the sack of gifts. "I'll go set these under the tree."

Aurora took Cad's coat and hung it on a peg. When she

turned to face him again, his arms went quickly around her. She tried to back away, but he trapped her against the coat-lined wall, clamping her in an embrace, his lips meeting hers in a disgustingly familiar kiss. "That's the gift I've been wanting all day," he said in a smooth, seductive voice.

"Let me go!" she demanded. With all the force she could muster, she pushed against him, but he kept his hold on her.

"I'd have thought you'd have welcomed a little affection, with that husband of yours laid up like he is." A sardonic smile appeared.

She twisted hard, and he finally set her free. "It's his leg that's broken, not his lips or his arms!" she reminded him angrily. "Besides, his hugs and kisses are a thousand times more pleasing than yours!" As she made the claim, she was painfully aware that since Harrison's accident, his affection had seldom amounted to more than hand-holding and cheek-pecking, but the attention Cad forced on her turned her stomach.

"Then I'll just have to get in some more practice!"

He reached for her, but she escaped, dashing up the stairs, Cad close behind. She grabbed a large meat fork from the counter and turned to face him as he was about to embrace her a second time. "Don't you ever touch me again, Cadwallader Blackburn! Do you understand?" Her words were like steel.

He held his hands up in surrender, a cherubic smile giving him an innocent look, then he sidestepped his way past her and headed toward the door at the other end of the kitchen, meeting up with Spunky as she came through from the dining room.

"You oughta see the tree Aurora and Stoney put up. It's really somethin', all decked out in strawberries and fans and lanterns!"

"I'll have to take a look," Cad responded casually, as if nothing were amiss.

Aurora set down the fork, picked up her wooden spoon and went to test the mulled cider. Her mind was in a scramble over the kiss Cad had forced on her. How could she stand to be in the same room with him and pretend nothing had happened?

She mustn't let him ruin her Christmas. She mustn't! She burned at the humiliation he had caused.

Spunky came beside her. "You feelin' all right? Your face is mighty flushed."

She thought for a moment of telling Spunky what had happened, then decided against it, since this was Christmas Day.

"It must be the heat from the stove," she said, lifting a spoonful of mulled cider from the pan. "Try this and see if it's ready."

Spunky rolled it around on her tongue before swallowing. "Tastes mighty fine to me. Let me help you pour it out." She carefully emptied it into the glass bowl on Aurora's tray, and together they carried the cider and cookies into the sitting room and passed them around. For a few minutes, conversation raged about the roast Spunky had cooked for Christmas dinner at the Anders's household, and the resulting complaints about its toughness.

"Enough talk about food," Keeper Dixon said, patting his stomach. "I've already eaten enough for the next three days. I say it's time we open gifts. Harrison, if you don't mind, I'll be Santa for a minute and hand around the presents Cad and Spunky brought in. Here's one for Aurora from Cad," he said, setting a box-shaped present on her lap. Aurora held it gingerly, wishing she didn't have to lay a finger on it, despite its beautiful gold foil wrapping and huge red bow.

Keeper Dixon continued his rounds. "And here's one for Spunky, and one for Stoney, and one for me." He then distributed four small identical packages from Spunky. The maple candies she had made were opened and sampled and pronounced delicious. Spunky accepted the compliments graciously, then turned her attention to the flat square-like object from Cad, peeling off the paper.

She couldn't miss the smug look on his face when she revealed a breadboard. As she inspected the piece of maple carefully, she realized it was no ordinary breadboard. Running her hand over its smooth cutting surface, she flipped it over to find a fancy medallion pattern chiseled into the backside. The back of the board and handle had been stained, varnished, and polished to a lovely, warm satin finish. Deeply impressed, she ran her finger along the grooves, then turned to the man beside her. "You made this in Mr. Freiling's workshop?" She couldn't help sounding skeptical, but it looked more like Mr. Freiling's work than that of a man who had once told her his only experience with woodworking had been to whittle a point on a new pencil.

"Of course I made it! Especially for you!" he said, obviously injured. "I'll have you know I now possess great talent where woodworking is concerned."

She admired the board again. "This is real pretty, Cad. Too pretty to use!" She looked up into the blue eyes that always seemed to twinkle with mischief, and thought again that they were the handsomest she'd ever seen. "Thank you!" She leaned over and kissed him on the cheek.

He put his arm about her shoulders and gave a gentle squeeze. "You're welcome. Now I expect you to make firewood out of that old, carved-up board in your father's kitchen, and hang this one in its place."

"I'll take it down soon as we get home," she promised.

"Now it's my turn to see what Cad has been learning from Mr. Freiling," said Keeper Dixon. Tearing foil from a bulky object, he revealed a wooden toolbox with two open, oblong compartments. They ran either side of a center divider and a large handle. "With all the tinkering I do to keep things running around here, I'm sure to make good use of this. Thanks, Cad."

Harrison slipped the red bow from around the flat, square object Cad had handed him, pulling back the gold wrapping paper to discover a highly varnished piece of wood painted in a checkerboard design.

"Stoney, catch!" said Cad, tossing him a small pouch.

Harrison untied the string on the muslin bag and dumped out the contents—wooden disks for checkers, some of light wood, others stained dark.

"That's to help you pass the time while your leg heals," Cad explained. He turned to Aurora. "Don't you want to see what I've made you, Mrs. Stone?"

Aurora was still wishing he hadn't brought her any gift at all. Carefully, she untied the bow, then pushed back the paper to find a small, beautifully crafted pine cabinet.

Inside were narrow shelves inset with pegs that would hold at least four dozen spools of thread.

"This is quite something," Aurora said, unable to thank the man she now feared and despised.

"I'll hang it over your sewing machine for you, with Stoney's and Keeper Dixon's permission."

Harrison simply shrugged.

"I have no objection," Keeper Dixon said.

"Then perhaps you could loan me a nail, hammer, and two screws, and I'll put it up straightaway."

"I'll fetch them from the barn, along with my tape measure," Keeper Dixon said, rising. "In fact, I'll take this new toolbox along to collect what we need."

"If you fellas are goin' out to the barn, I think I'll take a jaunt out there myself. I could do with some fresh air," Spunky said.

While they pulled on coats and boots, Aurora began picking up wrappings, stuffing them into the kitchen stove to burn. When the rear door had closed, she joined Harrison in the sitting room. His expression was glum as he stared at the cabinet Cad had given her.

"Quite a present, Cad's," he said ruefully.

"That isn't all he gave me for Christmas." The words were out of Aurora's mouth before she could stop them.

Harrison's brows knitted. "Meaning?"

Her stomach knotted. She wished she could have kept her awful secret until the day had passed, but she felt so wretched inside, she simply had to share it. "He cornered me in the back entryway when he came in today. I tried to get away from him, but he . . . "

"What? He what?" Harrison's face flushed deeply. "Thunderation! Tell me what he did!"

She pressed her lips together, but she couldn't stop the words from escaping. "He kissed me! Most improperly!"

Harrison's jaw tightened, and his whole body went rigid. "Why that miserable, low-down . . . " He grabbed

146

his crutches and began pushing to his feet. "I'll see to it he never sets foot in this house again!" Recklessly, he clunked his way out of the sitting room heading for the back door, moving faster than he had at any time since his accident.

"Where are you going?" Aurora demanded.

"To the barn to give that scoundrel a piece of my mind!"

"You can't go on crutches. Not with all the snow and ice. You'll surely fall and break your leg all over again!"

# CHAPTER

## 13

Harrison's pace scarcely slowed at all as he negotiated the few steps leading down to the back door. He leaned his crutches against the wall long enough to pull on his woolen jacket, scarf and cap. From the back window, he looked out on the hundred feet or so which separated him from the barn—a hundred feet of snow-covered walkway. But three sets of footprints had tamped down the snow ahead of him. He should be able to get there without any mishaps. He swung open the back door.

"Harrison, *please* don't go out there!"

The fear in Aurora's voice was obvious, and when he glanced back over his shoulder at her, it was equally evident in her blue eyes as she stood watching from the kitchen door.

He turned away, crossing the threshold. Two steps separated him from ground level, and they were glazed with a thin coating of ice. The leather sole on his shoe would be more slippery than the rubber tread on his boot, but he couldn't take time for boots now. Cautiously, he lowered himself down, one level at a time, standing safely on the walk. Like a cripple escaping from a house afire, he headed toward the barn, his crutches poking holes in the snow on either side of the path.

Hesitating in disbelief a moment longer, Aurora grabbed up her own coat and threw it over her shoulders, following as quickly as conditions underfoot allowed.

The barn door stood ajar. Harrison swung it wide open. It banged against the siding. A broad shaft of light from the bright snowy outdoors streamed across the three figures within.

His gaze locked on Cad, standing to the left of Spunky and Keeper Dixon. In a fleeting moment, a look of dread crossed the other man's face, and Harrison was sure Cad knew why he had come.

Cad put on a solicitous smile. "Stoney, you shouldn't be out here." His mock concern, delivered in his smooth-as-silk baritone voice, only fueled Harrison's anger.

He hobbled forward, stopping two feet away from his nemesis. He'd take that smile from the city slicker's face and teach him a lesson he'd never forget!

Leaning on his right crutch, he swung his other one toward the side of Cad's head.

A moment before impact, Harrison's balance faltered. He took a hop, losing some of the leverage aimed against his opponent.

Nevertheless, his blow sent Cad tripping backward to land on a mound of hay. Harrison stood over the downed man as he lay moaning, his right hand clamped to the side of his face. Through clenched teeth, Harrison delivered a warning.

"You kissed her once. Try it again, and your kissing

days are over!"

Without a moment's hesitation, he pivoted away. Aurora stood in the doorway, her hands over her mouth. Pushing past her as he hobbled out of the barn, he heard Spunky's voice.

"Cad, are you all right?"

He didn't have to look back to know she was kneeling beside her fallen hero, inspecting the damage to his Greek god-like cheekbone. It burned Harrison up inside that Spunky paid so much mind to that good-for-nothing. Couldn't she see past his polished manners to the manipulative, unprincipled soul beneath?

All the way back to the house, with his wife trailing at a slower pace, Harrison seethed with anger so intense, he was surprised the tips of his crutches didn't melt the snow to leave patches of bare sand in his wake!

Harrison set his crutches on the first step and tried to hoist himself up, but his splint-bound left leg, sticking straight out, prevented him. He was reminded of his own limitations and the reason his bedroom had been moved to the first floor. Using his crutches more for balance than for lift, he hopped backward up to the top step and somehow managed to get inside.

As he took off his things and hung them up, Aurora came in and quietly hung hers up, also. Her face wore a pensive, unreadable expression. She appeared to be thinking long and hard about his actions. Her continued silence troubled him as he hoisted himself up the six steps to the kitchen.

Making his way to the sitting room, he collapsed on his favorite chair, lifted his left leg and set it on the stool in front of him. Then he leaned back, suddenly exhausted.

His gaze fell on the thread cabinet sitting on the floor a few feet away where Aurora had left it. His anger began to rise again when he thought of the gift's giver.

"Aurora!" he bellowed.

She hovered in the doorway, her mouth open slightly as though she herself had been about to speak. At last she asked, "What is it?"

Harrison pointed to the thread cabinet. "Please get that thing out of my sight."

She carried it out of the room, wondering where to go with it, then decided to take it to the back entryway. How insignificant the gift now seemed compared with the enormity of Harrison's reaction to it. Perhaps he did love her, after all, for surely he would not have defended her so vehemently otherwise. Looking away from the small cabinet, she saw through the window that Spunky, Cad, and Keeper Dixon were heading toward the house. Cad was holding a handkerchief to his right cheek, and she couldn't help thinking the rogue had gotten what he deserved, and feeling a little pleased that Harrison, despite his limitations, had laid a blow against him because of what he had done to her.

Now she was fairly certain he loved her. Then came the niggling thought—maybe his pursuit of Cad was just to satisfy his own need to prove his manly strength, despite his injury. *Men!* Aurora despaired. Would she ever really know how Harrison felt about her?

As puzzled and troubled as ever, she returned to her kitchen chores. A knock at the rear door immediately summoned her away. She opened it to Keeper Dixon.

"Mr. Freiling finished these new splints for Harrison's leg. I'll take them in and show him."

When Harrison heard Keeper Dixon's voice, he wondered what his boss would have to say to him about the incident in the barn. His concerns were allayed when he saw the splints.

Keeper Dixon, ignoring the incident altogether, said, "Mr. Freiling finished these several days ago." He crossed the room to show Harrison the molded, polished wood. "Now that your swelling has finally disappeared, it's time to straighten out that thigh bone so it will knit properly. Not today, of course. The change will be uncomfortable for you at first. No sense ruining the holiday with pain."

"My holiday can't get any worse. Let's put it on right now," Harrison said, eager to push thoughts of Cad out of his mind.

Cad lay down on the sofa, his head against the mound of towels Spunky put behind him. She brought a basin of water and two washcloths, knelt beside him and carefully removed the handkerchief he had been holding to his injured face. A deep gash two inches long, bleeding profusely, marred his cheek. She wrung out a washcloth and pressed against the open wound to stem the flow of blood that threatened to run into his ear.

"Lucky for you, Stoney ain't quite up to full strength, or you'd be out cold on the barn floor," Spunky concluded, exchanging washcloths.

Cad groaned. "This hurts worse than a visit to the dentist." He spoke slowly from the left side of his mouth. "Blast Stoney! If he left a scar—"

Spunky shook her finger at him. "Cadwallader Blackburn, you oughta count y'rself lucky this is the only wound you got!" She placed his hand against the cloth and started to get up.

Cad moaned, and propped himself on one elbow. "I thought Mrs. Stone would appreciate my attention, considering her husband's condition."

Spunky picked up the washbasin. "With an opinion like that, it's no wonder you been havin' trouble since you came to this island." She started toward the door.

Cad lay down again. "When you come back, bring a mirror, will you?"

Spunky made no reply, but returned to the kitchen for fresh water and bandages. Working the pump handle, she filled the basin with clear water, took a bottle of lamp oil down from the shelf and poured some into a small dish. Then she chipped several pieces of ice off the block in the icebox, wrapped them in a dry towel, set all her supplies on a tray and carried them to the sitting room.

"Hold this ice to y'r cheek a few minutes," she said, then she fetched her sewing basket and pulled up a chair to sit beside him.

"Where's the mirror?" he asked, pressing up on his elbow again.

"You don't need a mirror just yet," she said, pushing him back down, then lifting the ice pack from his face. The bleeding had nearly stopped. She threaded her needle with silk thread.

"You're not going to take stitches in me, are you?" Cad asked, his eyes wide with concern. "Remember what I told you. I don't want any scars."

"You shoulda thought o' that when you kissed Aurora. Now lie down and stay still a minute." As she dipped the thread in the oil, she wished someone else--*anyone* else—were holding the needle. She thought of Aurora's skills as a seamstress. How much better suited she was for sewing up this cut! But the thought of asking her to repair the damage to Cad's face was just too absurd. Besides, the way Stoney was feeling, he wouldn't let Aurora within sight of Cad.

Spunky inhaled slowly, then held her breath. Her hand shook as she poked the needle through Cad's skin. He grunted, but didn't flinch. She made the stitch about an eighth of an inch deep, then crossed to the opposite side of the wound and took a second stitch. Afterward, she cut the thread and tied a knot. The process was repeated two more times. When she had finished, she was pleased with the neat manner in which she had closed the wound.

"Now let me see," Cad said, sitting up.

"If you promise me to lie still for a half hour longer, I'll fetch you the mirror."

He sighed. "I promise."

She hurried upstairs, dreading his reaction when she handed him the silver-backed mirror.

He stared into the glass, turning his head this way and that, studying the slightly swollen cheekbone and each stitch of her sewing job, then handed the mirror back. "I didn't think you knew how to use a needle. Guess I was wrong." He couldn't let her know how upset he really was at the way he looked.

Spunky was pleased with his reaction. "Now put the ice back on it. It'll help keep down the swelling."

She returned to the kitchen, to put away the washbasin and oil, then came back to sit with Cad. As she gazed upon the man who had been causing havoc since his arrival on the island six months ago, she realized how fond of him she had grown, despite the difficulties he had caused. She realized, too, that her feelings would never be returned, and in time, he would depart for good from North Manitou.

Nevertheless, he had some things to learn about life from his sojourn here, lessons he seemed thus far willing to ignore. "Cad, when you go takin' somethin' that don't belong to you, like stealin' that kiss from Aurora, you gotta expect to pay a pretty heavy price."

Cad shrugged. "I didn't think one kiss would matter. I stole them all the time from the coeds at school. Besides, you didn't mind that time I kissed you in the barn last summer, at least not at the first. In fact, for quite some time, I got the impression you rather liked it!"

Spunky could feel her face growing hot with humiliation. What Cad said about her was true. She had enjoyed the kiss they had shared at the end of the summer when he had first learned he was stranded on the island for the winter and she had offered to take him in. They were alone in the barn when he had thanked her with a kiss that had started gentle, and grown long and strong and deep.

At age twenty-four, it had been a very startling experience for a plain-faced, simply dressed young woman whose best years for finding a husband had already passed her by. How often her brothers had told her she would wind up a spinster!

But when Cad was kissing her, she was overwhelmed by the thrill of his touch, the taste of his lips, the feel of his strong body pressed tightly against hers. Her head was so carried away by her heart, she clung to him and returned the ardor of his kiss—until he started to pull her down in the straw.

Then, she came to her senses, realizing there would soon be no stopping the flow of passion. She pushed away, kicked him in the shin, and ran to the house. He had limped around the farm for two days.

"I did like your kiss," she frankly admitted, "but I'm not married. I'm not even spoken for! Aurora is a married lady. There's a whole world of difference."

Cad thought of how he had always helped himself to whatever he wanted, then if trouble rose, he talked his way out of it. He hadn't counted on Stoney being so short on words and long on action, especially while his leg was broken. Cad knew this time, he would just have to live with the consequences of his miscalculation.

Another person he had miscalculated at the start was Spunky. When he had first met her, he had quickly dismissed her as just another backwoods farm girl, neither pretty nor smart. She had proven herself full of good sense, grit, and pluck, and had come to serve a very important purpose in his life, in more ways than even she herself yet understood. He wanted to stay on her good side, at least for the time being. He knew what words she wanted to hear, and they rolled easily off his tongue.

"I'll behave myself from now on. I promise."

"Good. Now you just lie still for a while longer. I'll go brew some tea." She went to the kitchen and set the kettle on to boil. No sooner had she poured hot water into Mrs. Dixon's pretty Bavarian china teapot, than Keeper Dixon came in.

He glanced at the teapot, with the steam rising from its spout, and the cups and saucers she was setting on the tray with it. "I trust you've fixed up Cad's face by now."

"That I have."

"Good, because I came to ask your help with Harrison. We've taken the old splint off and padded the new one.

The tough part will be in putting it on and getting his leg straightened out. You know what kind of patient Harrison can be. I need more than Mrs. Stone to help. If you've got any more of that wine, bring it along. Harrison will probably need it, even though *he* doesn't think so."

# CHAPTER

## 14

Spunky grabbed a bottle of wine Cad had brought from the farm and followed Keeper Dixon next door. She could hear Stoney groaning even before she reached the sitting room. He greeted her with a grimace.

His leg had been bandaged from his toes to his knee, and now Aurora was starting to bind on the new splint, beginning at the roller she had placed beneath his foot.

Spunky set the wine by his bed and held the roller and splint in place while Aurora bound them with the long narrow strip of white cotton.

"Thanks, Spunky. I didn't seem to have enough hands," Aurora said, wrapping the bandage about Harrison's foot and ankle.

"Take care that his foot is pointing straight up," Keeper Dixon advised as he rolled a silk handkerchief around soft wool padding.

Spunky adjusted Harrison's toes from their outward position.

The pain traveled from his foot all the way to his teeth. "Thunderation, Spunky!"

"Oh, hush, Stoney! You gotta expect to hurt some if y're gonna get this new splint on the way it's supposed to be. You don't want that leg o' y'rs lookin' like y'r grandpa's did, do you?"

When Aurora tightened the binding to hold Harrison's foot in proper alignment, he groaned, making her ache in sympathy. She continued wrapping his leg, working her way up the shin, around the knee, to his thigh.

When she had finished, Keeper Dixon stepped beside her, the silk and wool padding in his hands. "I'll have to slip this between your legs and pass the ends through the holes in the top of the splint," he told Harrison. When he had finished, a considerable gap kept the uppermost end of the splint from lying flat against Harrison's side.

Aurora handed Keeper Dixon the long strip of white cotton. "Here's a bandage to hold the splint to the waist." The head keep' tied it around Harrison like a belt, then picked up a short stick and inserted it in the loop of the handkerchief.

"This could trouble you some, Stoney," Dixon warned. "I've got to tighten down the upper end of the splint in order to bring that thigh bone of yours into alignment. It will extend the lower part of your leg, but it won't feel pretty. Maybe you'd better grab onto something so you can bear down when the pain hits."

"Hold my hand," Aurora said, slipping her small fingers into his palm. The look of dread on his face gave him the appearance of a condemned man.

Spunky reached across the bed and took his other hand, then Keeper Dixon began to turn the stick.

Harrison groaned and clutched Aurora tightly.

Keeper Dixon paused after one rotation. "I'll have to

159

go a couple more times around, Harrison."

With the second turn of the stick, Aurora thought her fingers would break. Harrison's eyes clamped shut.

"Once more," Keeper Dixon warned, and began to turn the stick again.

The grooves set in Harrison's face deepened with pain. Aurora's fingers went numb.

"*Ugh!*" The guttural sound came from deep within Harrison. His face screwed up tight in an agonizing grimace.

Keeper Dixon quickly gave the stick one more turn.

Harrison turned pale white, then went limp.

"He's fainted!" Aurora cried. A wave of panic tied a knot in her stomach.

"I'll get the smelling salts," said Spunky in her usual, efficient manner.

"Not yet," said Keeper Dixon, moving to the foot of the bed. He drew Harrison's good leg straight alongside the broken one, comparing lengths. "Good. They're the same. The extension worked," he concluded. "Now I'll bind the short splint against the inside of his thigh before he comes to. You ladies better look away."

Though Aurora's gaze was set on the snowdrift outside the window, she could almost see Keeper Dixon wrapping the second splint snugly from knee to hip.

"Okay, Spunky, now it's time for the smelling salts."

She held them beneath his nose, and within seconds, Harrison shook his head and opened his eyes, looking a bit dazed.

"Can I get you anything?" Aurora asked, tenderly stroking his forehead.

Harrison gazed up at her. "A sip of water, please."

His voice was so weak, she hardly recognized it.

"I'll fetch a fresh, cold glass from the kitchen," Spunky offered.

As Harrison slowly reoriented himself, his gaze traveled across the sitting room, pausing at the Christmas tree. Of the twenty-five Christmas Days he had experienced, this was the most unforgettable, and the one he least wanted to remember. How he wished his first Christmas as Aurora's husband could have been happier, for her sake and his own!

He looked up into his wife's eyes, blue to their depths with concern, and reached for her hand. *Thank you, Lord, for giving me a wife as gentle as the morning sun, and as strong as a Manitou storm. How I love her!* He would have told her so that very moment, if not for Keeper Dixon standing near, his nose in the medical manual he was studying by the light of the bedside lamp.

As Harrison held Aurora's hand in his, she thanked God the ordeal of applying the new splints was behind them, and asked for the strength to see Harrison through until spring. *And Lord, if Harrison loves me,* she silently prayed, *please give him the words to tell me so. I need to know! Amen.*

"As soon as you're finished with your kitchen chores, I'd like to have a talk with you," Keeper Dixon told Spunky on the morning of the last day of the year.

The smile beneath his thick gray mustache, and the friendly wink of his eye told her this was a meeting she looked forward to.

"Won't take me but another five minutes to finish tidyin' up," Spunky promised. Though the house still smelled like fried bacon, she had already washed, dried and

161

put away the cast iron skillet and the other dishes.

Sun streamed in the east window, a rare delight this time of year for the Manitou Passage. As she wet her dishrag and wiped up the kitchen counter, she smiled to herself. Today was payday, and tonight, Cad would come for dinner and a New Year's Eve celebration! Before he came back, she would empty her tea tin and count up the money she had saved for her trip to Chicago next spring.

She dumped out her dishpan, rinsed her dishcloth in the clean flow of water from the kitchen pump, and hung up the rag to dry. Keeper Dixon was waiting at the dining table, reading a history book from the portable library. He put it aside when she sat down next to him.

Reaching into his pants pocket, he produced several dollar bills. "Seems like we just sat here the other day talking about the end of the shipping season. How could a whole month have slipped by?"

"Time sure goes quick when y'r busy. Don't quite seem possible we're at the end of 1898, starin' a new year in the face." *And 1899 will be different for me. I'll take the trip I've dreamed about for years,* she was tempted to add, but instead, kept the secret hers alone.

Keeper Dixon counted out ten one-dollar bills and set them in front of her. "That ought to make a good end to your year, or a good start for a new one." He rose, picking up his book. "I've got some chores that need doing out in the barn, then I thought I might call next door and see what plans the Stones have for the evening. It's been mighty quiet over there since we changed Stoney's splint last Sunday. Maybe we should offer to bring our New Year's dinner and celebration to their place. What do you think?"

"Cad's comin' for dinner, and knowin' Stoney like I do,

he won't have a thing to do with Mr. Chicago anytime soon."

Keeper Dixon stroked his mustache. "I suppose you're right, but I'll make the offer anyway."

A few minutes later, when the rear door had closed behind Keeper Dixon, Spunky took her tea tin from the shelf. Visions of boarding the *Missouri* on a fine April day passed before her at the sound of the coins rattling inside. In her fantasy, she was wearing the ivory blouse waist Aurora had made, and the new navy blue skirt that would soon be finished to go with it. Making her way to the purser's window, she would proudly put down her eight dollars for a cabin and a meal, knowing that a leisurely lake cruise awaited her, and that a day and a half later, she would arrive at Chicago.

Chills went through her as she contemplated the adventure. Her first trip to a big city! The prospect was a bit frightening for a girl who had spent her life on North Manitou, with only occasional visits to South Manitou, and a handful of ventures to the mainland.

But for the past six years she had become well acquainted with North Manitou's summer cottagers from Chicago. Mrs. Boardman, Mrs. Shepherd, her daughter, Miss Katie, and of course, Cad, had all shared many details of the big city, and Spunky could hardly wait to see the bustling harbor, tall buildings, jammed streets, and elevated railroad for herself. The ladies had warned her about the smoky stench that sometimes hung over the city for days, but bad smells couldn't put off a farm girl who well knew the stink of a slaughtered hog!

She placed the metal can in front of her, and eased off the lid. Her stay at the Palmer House wasn't far off!

But when she peered inside the tin, visions of Chicago abruptly went black. All of her folding money was gone!

The only bills in sight were those Keeper Dixon had just paid her. Her heart pounding, her mind in a whirl, she poured out the coins and stared at the pennies, nickels, and dimes that littered the table.

"How could this be?" she wondered, but as she pondered her circumstances, the answer came to her. She voiced it to the empty room. "Cad took it. And he must have helped himself to the two dollars I was missin' last month, too." Anger raged within. Her fist slammed against the table. "It's a good thing y're not here right now, Mr. Chicago. If you were, I'd be tempted to whop you so hard, y'r left cheek would match the right one Stoney took a swing at a few days ago!"

She scooped up the money and stuffed it into the tin. "Ain't nothin' to be done about it till tonight. Right now, I gotta cool off." Setting the can on the kitchen shelf, she went to the rear entryway, pulled on her boots and coat, and took a walk in the brisk December air.

As the hours passed, Spunky's anger turned to disappointment. All she could think about was how she had taken Cad into her home, offered him meals and shelter, and in return, he had stolen her dream!

How she wanted to talk with him! Never had she lived through such a long day as this one, waiting for him to arrive. She was fixing dinner when he came pounding on the rear door.

His face was full of color, especially the place where she had taken the stitches, and he offered his usual broad smile when he stepped inside, pulling off his cap and handing it to her. Only now, she no longer found his features handsome, or his smile engaging.

"I've been looking forward to a cup of your hot coffee since I left the Freilings," he told her in his smooth baritone voice. "It's a mighty cold walk, even if it is only a mile."

Without a word, Spunky took his coat and scarf and hung them on a peg with his cap while he removed his boots. From her silence, Cad sensed something might be amiss, but he wasn't certain until he followed her up the stairs to the kitchen.

Tea tin in hand, she turned to face him, her expression more doleful than when she'd come running out of Stones' back door awhile ago after some sort of disagreement with Stoney. Her eyes glistened with unshed tears.

"You took my money."

He considered denying it, but her sorrowful look tugged at his heart, and he knew he couldn't lie to her. "I only borrowed it for a while—to pay Mr. Freiling for the automobile frame we're building. I'll pay you back the eighteen dollars and the two dollars I needed last month to buy wood for Christmas presents, as soon as I get to Chicago. I can't imagine you having a need of it, with your job here at the light station, and your papa's farm to go home to when it's over. Except for the summer tourists, there's hardly any local trade on this island. You'll have the money by the end of the summer. Honest!"

"But . . . " Her lips trembled, and when she spoke again, the words were barely a whisper. "The end of the summer will be too late."

He reached for her, but she stepped away. A giant tear rolled down her cheek, and she brushed it off with the back of her hand. The excitement he had felt, working with Mr.

Freiling today on the frame for his automobile, suddenly meant nothing, faced with Spunky's disappointment in him and her misery over her loss.

Cad didn't know where these new feelings came from, but it was as if his heart were in the vise grip on Mr. Freiling's workbench, and the handle was being turned, squeezing ever tighter. Cad offered Spunky his handkerchief, and she blew her nose loudly into it.

Spunky hadn't wanted to cry in front of Cad, but the disappointment of this day had overcome her. She cleared her throat and looked up into his deep blue eyes. Until today, she had thought they were the most handsome she had ever seen. Now, she saw only larceny and greed.

"I had plans for that money, Cadwallader Blackburn." She swallowed past the swelling in her throat and forced out the words. "I was gonna take the *Missouri* to Chicago in April. I ain't never been on a ship like the *Missouri*. I ain't never been to a big city." Her voice now a whisper, she paused, struggling to control her tears. "Now, I ain't never gonna get to see either."

As another tear rolled slowly down her cheek, Cad wished he could take her in his arms and make everything right again with one big hug and a pocket full of money, but that was impossible. The money he had taken from Spunky was long gone.

Somehow, he had to find a way to get it back! Somehow, he must revive her dream!

An idea popped into his head. He took her gently by the arms. "You'll see Chicago. When the summer visitors come in June, I'll offer island carriage tours. Before July is out, you'll be in Chicago. I promise!"

Spunky's head moved slowly from side to side. "That's

166

still too late. Pa will need me on the farm. I can't leave then. If I don't go in April, I can't go at all."

"Then I'll find a way to get you on that boat in April!" Cad's words were out before he had any notion how to make them come true, but he kept on talking. "I'll make sure you have a ticket for a first class cabin the very first time the *Missouri* comes next spring!"

Spunky had heard empty promises from Cad before, and these sounded no different. "I'll never see Chicago," she lamented, "or shop in Montgomery Wards, or Sears, or Marshall Fields."

"You will so! I give you my pledge!" he persisted.

Spunky seemed unconvinced as she released herself from his grip and wandered off to the sitting room, blowing her nose.

Cad stared at the tea tin she had left sitting on the kitchen counter and wondered how he could ever replace the money he had paid Mr. Freiling. How he wished he had kept his hands off!

But it was too late now.

He never would have figured that by year's end, he'd really start to care how Spunky felt. And he certainly hadn't calculated the cost of breaking her heart.

He had made a big mistake. Now he must make amends. First thing tomorrow, he would go to Mr. Freiling. Once he understood the problem, it should be easy to get him to return Spunky's money.

# CHAPTER

# 15

The following morning, Cad walked through new fallen snow from the Anders's farm toward the Freiling place. Even though he had originally planned to stay the night at the light station, it had seemed pointless with Spunky so disconsolate. Instead, he had spent the evening with her father and brothers, whose idea of a New Year's celebration had consisted of one glass of cherry wine, and lights out at nine o'clock.

Despite Cad's early bedtime hour, he felt more tired than if he had stayed up for an all-night card party, probably because he hadn't gotten any sleep. The whole night long, thoughts of Spunky, upset by the missing money and disappointed in him for taking it, had kept him awake.

Cad wasn't sure why he was so distracted by the problem. He'd never been this concerned over other young ladies in his acquaintance who had found reason to be displeased with him. In fact, he was usually relieved when they became miffed and decided to part company. With Spunky, his feelings were very different, and he couldn't understand himself at all.

He tried to puzzle out the mystery as he made tracks

toward Mr. Freiling's workshop. Smoke was rising from the stove chimney as Cad approached the red building. Letting himself inside, he found Mr. Freiling busy at his workbench, planing a piece of oak.

Cad drew a deep breath, taking in the scent of freshly worked hardwood that pervaded the shop. Since he had begun to work with Mr. Freiling several weeks earlier, Cad had really come to appreciate the aroma of new lumber, the orderliness of Mr. Freiling's tools hanging neatly from nails and pegs, and the camaraderie he had found working alongside the old gentleman. He had grown to respect Mr. Freiling for his vast knowledge of woodworking, and to treasure the secrets he had shared, including the best method to obtain a waterproof finish, and the proper construction of a strong buggy frame.

Aside from these, Mr. Freiling had imparted tidbits of island-grown philosophy, such as, "The man who lives only for himself runs a mighty small business," and "Happiness is what you feel when you try to make someone else happy." Until now, Cad had only chuckled at the old man's sayings. If only he had taken the advice to heart!

He was beginning to realize how smart Mr. Freiling was, despite the fact he hadn't had much formal schooling. Surely Mr. Freiling would see the necessity of returning Spunky's money, wouldn't he?

Cad forced a note of cheerfulness into his voice as he greeted the old man. "Good morning, Mr. Freiling! You're hard at work, even on a holiday, I see."

The old man set down his planer and brushed the wood chips off the piece he was shaping. "Good mornin', Cad. Sure wasn't expectin' you to show up to work today."   His gray eyes lingered on Cad's. "What brings you my way?"

Cad shifted his weight. He hated to sound blunt, but he seemed to have no choice. "It's about that twenty dollars I paid you for the Christmas gifts, and the automobile frame we're building. I . . . "

Mr. Freiling leaned against his workbench, casually crossing his arms. "Go on, son. What about it?" The kindness in his eyes was reflected in his voice.

Telling the truth was harder than Cad had thought. Reluctantly, he continued. "I need it back. It wasn't really mine to begin with. I borrowed it from a friend—without telling her."

Mr. Freiling offered a quizzical look. "Spunky?"

Cad nodded. "I planned to pay her back next summer." His words came tumbling out. "Yesterday she discovered her money was gone. When I saw her last night, she was dreadfully upset."

Quickly, he explained how Spunky had planned a trip to Chicago when the *Missouri* arrives in April. "Spunky acted as if her whole world would come to an end if she didn't go to Chicago in April. Honestly, I've never seen her so distraught! That's why I've got to get back the twenty dollars I gave you!"

Mr. Freiling scratched his chin. "I suppose I could terminate the agreement to build the buggy frame and return the money. After all, it is Spunky we're talkin' about here, and she's mighty special to me and my wife." Mr. Freiling continued scratching his chin and thinking. "I could sell that frame to somebody else come spring, either here on the island, or over on the mainland. There's always folks in need of a well-made buggy frame, and yours is gonna be built stronger than most."

Cad's hopes soared. The answer was so simple!

Mr. Freiling continued. "Yah, I could hand back the money." He paused to look Cad straight in the eye. "But that wouldn't be right—not any more than y'r takin' it in the first place. There's a mighty important lesson to be learned here. If I just give ya back the money ya paid for those Christmas gifts and the frame we're buildin', y'r gonna learn the *wrong* lesson. Y'r gonna go through life believin' ya don't have to be responsible, ya don't have to live up to y'r commitments. There's another way to solve y'r problem. An honorable way."

"How's that?" Cad asked cautiously.

Mr. Freiling paced across the workshop floor, and back again to face him. "It's the way we're taught by the Good Book. The Bible says, 'Let him that stole steal no more; but rather let him labour, working with his hands the thing which is good.' I'll give ya a chance to earn that money back, fair and square, before the *Missouri* comes steamin' up here, but it'll take plenty of hard work."

"You just tell me what's got to be done. I'll do it," Cad heard himself say, despite his aversion to labor.

"Y'r sure about that? These jobs aren't for quitters. Y've got to stay with 'em to the finish in order to earn the twenty dollars."

"I'll finish what I start, Mr. Freiling. You can count on it."

Mr. Freiling offered his hand. "Shake on it?"

Cad wasted no time placing his hand in Mr. Freiling's firm grip.

"Son, here's what I've got in mind . . . "

The cold, crisp, Sunday morning of January 1, 1899, had broken over the island with uncharacteristic brightness, lifting Aurora's spirits, and she couldn't help being hopeful for the year ahead. Her outlook had been further improved by Keeper Dixon's visit to share Bible readings and prayer.

Despite Aurora's buoyant mood early in the day, by afternoon, she had begun to feel troubled once again by Harrison's quiet, contemplative state. He had become melancholy after the new splint had been put on. This afternoon, the pall of sadness in the air seemed nearly palpable, and she could no longer ignore it.

Harrison put down the history book he was reading as Aurora pulled up a chair and sat beside him. He looked into her pretty blue eyes. Despite the sweetness in the smile she offered, he seemed unable to force the corners of his mouth upward. Though he cherished the warmth of her small hands as they enfolded his large one, and the loving tenderness imparted in her squeeze, he found it impossible to return the affection.

"Harrison," Aurora began, "we have a whole new year ahead of us. It's like opening to the first page of a blank book, starting over. Great new experiences are waiting to happen. Have you thought about that?"

Her hopeful frame of mind only served to push him deeper into the gloominess that had plagued him for several days. He voiced the words that dominated his every thought. "I can't believe I have to stay in this splint four more weeks."

Aurora tried to ignore the glumness of his tone. "I know it's tedious being laid up, but time will pass. Before you know it, we'll be taking off that splint."

Harrison glanced at the beside table and his grandfather's watch. Each hour felt longer than a day, each day passed more slowly than a week. Obviously, Aurora had no concept of the seemingly interminable amount of time before he would be free of the confines of the splints, and the keeper's quarters.

"After the splint comes off, I'll still have three more weeks before I can use my leg, and another six weeks or so before it's completely healed." He focused on the empty wine bottle beside the watch. Though he'd had no real pain since the day after the new splint had been bound onto his leg and hadn't really needed the wine, he often considered asking for another bottle. Drinking seemed like a pleasant alternative to the doldrums that were holding him hostage.

Aurora was determined to keep up hope. "You may be confined to bed for now, but you can still enjoy the simple pleasures of life, like the beauty of a gentle snowfall, or the precious moments of sunshine when bright rays find a rare opening in the wintry gray sky. You've got a wonderful view of the passage out your window," she reminded him. Picking up the book he had laid face down across his chest, she added, "And more good reading in the portable library than one person could hope to accomplish in three months."

Though Harrison heard Aurora's every word, their meaning was deflected as easily as a cotton ball off a knight's iron body armor. "Maybe my leg will never be right again."

Sensing the futility of further conversation, Aurora laid Harrison's book beside his grandfather's watch—now reading a quarter past four—and rose. "The afternoon is gone already. I'd best get started on supper."

"Nothing much for me tonight. I'm not hungry," he said.

As she put her chair away, she realized that this was the seventh time in seven days she'd heard those same words.

She wondered when his appetite would be restored. And what about his outlook on life? Would he ever be the man she had known before the storm?

Cad dropped one boot beside his bed in the back room at the Freilings, and bent to pull off the other. Every muscle in his body ached, from the top of his shoulders to the bottom of his feet. He was so exhausted, he hoped he would manage to get out of his pants and shirt and into his nightshirt before he slumped onto the feather mattress and fell into a dead sleep.

For one week, he'd been living and working with Mr. Freiling. From "kin see to cain't see" as the old man put it, they stayed in the woods, cutting down trees. It was the roughest job Cad had ever undertaken. He'd never imagined how hard he would toil when he'd said he would do anything to earn back Spunky's money.

Spunky's brothers and father hadn't been sorry to see him move off the farm. Remembering the cynical smile on Peter's face when he'd heard the news, Cad was put in mind of a dog finally rid of a flea.

His departure was probably for the best. He never could work up any enthusiasm for the chore of milking Bessie. The bovine seemed to know exactly how to kick over the milk bucket when it was nearly full, just to spite him.

As for Spunky, he hadn't seen her once the whole week long. He'd been too busy to call on her, and even if he'd had a few hours to himself, he'd have been too tired to walk the mile to the light station and back again, then get up in the morning for another day's labor.

Tomorrow was Sunday, a day of rest according to Mr.

Freiling. Maybe by afternoon, Cad could find the energy to hike to the Dixons'.

He sure hoped Spunky would appreciate the trouble he was going to, earning back the money he'd borrowed. If only she could have waited until summer for her trip, he could have solved the problem so much easier!

Instead, he would walk his legs off tromping through the woods, and work his end of a crosscut saw until his arms dropped off. By the time all the trees Mr. Freiling had marked for harvesting had been taken down, stripped of branches, and hauled to the dock, he'd be lucky if he could stand upright!

"Turn around and walk down the hall again. I want to check the hem one more time." Aurora watched closely as Spunky strolled down the upstairs hall. She was trying on the new skirt Aurora had just finished sewing, the perfect way to pass the lazy afternoon hours on the second Sunday in the new year.

Spunky was sorry now that she'd asked Aurora to make the skirt, but by the time she had discovered that Cad had helped himself to the money in her tin, the pattern had already been cut out.

"Your new skirt hangs very evenly, and it looks just right with your ivory blouse waist," Aurora remarked. Actually, Spunky looked better this minute than at any time since Aurora had arrived on the island. For a woman who was taller than average and built straight up and down, the side-fastening skirt appeared quite flattering, but Aurora kept that observation to herself. She also didn't tell her friend she was planning to make her a another petticoat to replace her old, frayed one. A new one would add fullness

175

to the hemline, making Spunky even more attractive.

A pounding commenced on the rear door, interrupting the thought. "You didn't tell me Keeper Dixon was planning to come over," Aurora commented as she headed toward the stairs.

"Maybe he's brought another book from the portable library for Harrison," Spunky suggested, returning to Aurora's room to gather her old skirt from the bed. She was on her way downstairs when Aurora came dashing up, a look of panic on her face.

"It's Cad!" she whispered.

Spunky's hand went to her waist. "I won't talk to him!"

"But you've *got* to!" Aurora insisted, sotto voce. "He's waiting for you on the doorstep. You know I can't let him inside. Harrison would have a fit!"

Spunky set her jaw and marched down the stairs.

# CHAPTER

## 16

Spunky sensed something different about Cad the moment she saw him standing outside on the Stones' doorstep. She wasn't sure whether it was the hint of fatigue about his eyes, or the improvement in the scar on his cheek—still pink, but fading. To her, he was as handsome as ever—no, *more* handsome than before, and she was thoroughly disgusted with herself for thinking so.

She pulled on her coat and stepped outside. "Good afternoon, Mr. Blackburn," she said in as formal a tone as she could muster.

Cad cocked his head, as if puzzled by her stiff reception, then he straightened and offered an engaging smile. "Good afternoon, Miss Anders. I've come calling in the ardent hope you might grant me a few minutes in the pleasure of your company."

Spunky had never been treated with such dignity, and she was instantly tempted to invite Cad in. But the disappointment he had caused, taking her hard-earned money, was plenty fresh in her mind. She wouldn't soon forget he had robbed her of her dream. Unfortunately, she would also not soon forget his charming manner, intriguing blue eyes, and melodic baritone voice.

But for now, she must stay clear, and she stiffened her resolve to keep away. "Mr. Blackburn, seein' as how I can assure you my company will not be pleasurable, I must ask that you be on y'r way." She headed toward the Dixons' door.

As she did, Cad caught her by the elbow. "Then just let me say one thing before you go."

With an impatient sigh, she turned to face him again.

"I'm earning back the twenty dollars I owe you. Mr. Freiling hired me. He says if I work hard each day for the next three months, I'll be able to pay back every penny I owe you before the *Missouri* comes in April."

Spunky's heart skipped a beat. Maybe her dream hadn't died, after all! Then she remembered that Cad's word was about as solid as a snowball on a hot griddle.

She chose her words carefully. "That's good news, Mr. Blackburn." Her tone was pleasant, but unenthusiastic. "Until such time as y'r debt to me can be paid back, I must ask you to refrain from comin' to call. Good day, now."

With a polite smile, she turned on her heel and let herself into the Dixons' house. Once inside, she leaned against the door, took a deep breath, and slowly exhaled. Then she peeked out the small back window and watched Cad as he headed down the trail. Were his steps heavier than usual, and his shoulders slightly slumped? How hard it had been to send him away!

But it had been equally difficult to accept the bitter disappointment of her stolen money.

"Serves him right, not letting him in!" she reassured herself, but as she climbed the stairs to the Dixons' kitchen, she grudgingly admitted she would miss having him around.

Three weeks had passed since New Years, and Aurora thought she had never been through a lonelier, quieter, more disheartening twenty-one days in all her life.

She sat at her sewing machine this windy, bleak, Sunday afternoon, working on her latest project, a white cotton petticoat for Spunky, with yard upon yard of lace trim. A ham was cooking, its succulent aroma spreading throughout the house, and the dining room seemed especially cozy with the additional warmth coming from the kitchen stove. Aurora looked forward to Keeper Dixon and Spunky coming to share dinner with her and Harrison in a couple of hours. They had already visited this morning for prayer and Bible reading. If not for their frequent calls these past few weeks, Aurora didn't know what she would have done.

She often thought of Mrs. Freiling, and yearned to go visiting. Even though Keeper Dixon would willingly stay with Harrison, the trail from the light station to the main road had drifted over so badly, there was no way of getting through.

Halfheartedly, she gave the flywheel of her sewing machine a pull and began working the treadle to stitch the insertion lace above the flounce. Seamstress work no longer provided the satisfaction it had when she had lived on South Manitou, and in the last three weeks, she had come to understand why. It wasn't that she didn't like using her new sewing machine. The new one worked even better than her mother's. And it wasn't that she didn't enjoy making petticoats. Even though she had made half a dozen from this same pattern, she still found the work interesting.

Her satisfaction had disappeared, she realized, because unlike the carefree days on South Manitou when sewing had given her great pleasure, she now spent many hours at her machine trying to forget the isolation she felt, living with a husband who had nearly stopped talking.

More and more often of late, she wondered whether Harrison really loved her. He had been so withdrawn these last four weeks that he barely spoke a dozen sentences a day. Some days, she was sure it was half that amount, from the time he awoke in the morning until he went to sleep at night, and he forever kept his eye on the time, staring at his grandfather's watch.

He hadn't hummed any tunes for a good long while, not since Christmas morning. Aurora couldn't help feeling that, aside from bringing him his meals and attending the other necessities, she served no purpose in his life at all.

Any efforts she made to initiate conversation failed abysmally. The isolation she felt left her plenty of time to ponder the question of his love. Again and again, she searched their past for a clue to the answer. Despite the fact he had shown her much attention during their courtship, she couldn't help remembering his forceful statement on their wedding day that he didn't need her.

Back then, she thought he didn't mean it. After all, he took his wedding vow a short while later, promising to love and cherish her. But that was the closest he had ever actually come to saying he loved her!

She thought about her own expressions of love. She had told him on her wedding day she loved him despite his broken leg, and she had put her love in writing to him, on the wedding card she had given him. But then, she had made great ceremony of ripping it up. Perhaps she was nearly as guilty as he!

The thought proved startling! She stopped the treadle, lifted the presser foot, and stood up. Slowly, she made her way from the dining room into the sitting room. She found Harrison staring at his grandfather's watch, again.

She stepped up beside him, but he paid her no mind.

"Harrison?"

He blinked and turned toward her, but when his gray eyes met hers, they held an empty expression, giving her the uncomfortable feeling he looked right through her.

She swallowed and forced herself to speak.

"Harrison, I love you."

Her words were tender, barely above a whisper, but at least she had said them, and meant them.

Harrison's blank expression remained unchanged. He looked down at the watch he was holding, then at her again. "One more week, then I'll be free of this splint."

Aurora wondered if he'd heard her, but was afraid to ask, unwilling to discover maybe he didn't love her, after all. She struggled to put the crushing possibility aside.

"One more week," she confirmed, taking a step back. Eagerly, she withdrew, returning to her sewing.


Cad checked beneath the seat of the sleigh one last time to make certain he hadn't forgotten anything--lumber, toolbox, hardware. Everything appeared to be there for the special project he planned to build.

He helped Mrs. Freiling into the sleigh, then climbed in beside her husband and adjusted the lap robe about his legs on this frigid, partly sunny Sunday afternoon during the third week of February. The old man slapped the reins and the sleigh lurched forward, bells jingling as it skimmed over the deep snow, heading to the lakeshore, then south along the ice toward the light station.

The tower and keeper's quarters were visible in the distance on the sandy southeast point of the island. Despite the cold, Cad slipped off his glove and jammed his hand into his pants pocket, fingering the ten-dollar gold piece Mr. Freiling had paid him for the work he had done so far. The old man had been so pleased with Cad's work, he had decided to make payments in two installments. The money burned a hole in Cad's pocket, and he could hardly wait to see the expression on Spunky's face when he handed it to her.

Cad jumped down from the sleigh the moment Mr. Freiling reined his chestnut mare to a halt in front of the keeper's quarters. After helping the elderly couple alight, he stepped up to the Dixons' door and pounded urgently. It seemed like an eternity before it opened.

For a moment, Spunky simply stood there. She wore a white blouse waist with a high ruffled collar. The large pink bow beneath her chin softened the jut of her jawline and muted the naturally strong hue of her complexion. Her blue skirt, narrow down to the fullness at the hem, gave her a more slender appearance than he remembered, and he wondered whether she had lost weight. He'd never seen her looking finer, and her mild rosewater scent made him want to get close.

At Spunky's first glimpse of Cad, her heart raced. How she had missed him these last six weeks! To look at him now, she could hardly believe the change. Despite the thick wool jacket he wore, she could tell he had put muscle on his chest and arms, working in the woods with Mr. Freiling. His handsome face had filled out some, and taken on a healthy glow from working outdoors. The scar on his cheek had nearly faded completely, and his light brown hair, no longer perfectly trimmed, now grew attractively over his collar and ears. Though he still parted it in the center, the more casual style only enhanced his appeal, giving the impression of country-rugged rather than city slick. Regardless that he hadn't seen a barber, she felt certain he had recently shaved, for his cheeks and chin showed no sign of stubble. The clean essence of his pine soap proved enticing.

How badly she wanted to invite him in! But she could not forget the debt he still owed, nor what it had cost her in shattered dreams.

"Hello, Cad." She kept her tone pleasant, but cautious.

Cad wanted to take her in his arms, but sensed he must go slowly. "Hello, Spunky. I've come to pay you."

Her eyes widened with surprise.

Quickly, he added, "I don't mean the whole twenty dollars, but I've got half." He held up the coin.

Deliberately, Spunky took it from him and turned it over in her hand. It was the real thing, all right. Slipping the coin into her pocket, she debated whether to invite Cad in. The entryway grew colder, and temptation stronger with every moment she spent gazing at him.

Cad sensed Spunky's hesitation. "The Freilings are coming to visit you in a while, after they've seen the Stones," he explained.

She opened the door wide. "In that case, it'd be right unneighborly of me not to have you in, too. Take off your wraps and go up to the sitting room. I'll tell Keeper Dixon we've got company."

This time when she spoke, Cad was aware of something different in her way of talking, but he couldn't figure out what. Silently, he followed her into the house.

Spunky hurried up to the dining room where the head keep' still sat at the table, patiently waiting to resume her reading lesson. "Do you think we could take this up later? Cad's come to call, and the Freilings will be along, soon." His brow furrowed until she flashed the coin in front of him. "I just canceled half Cad's debt."

His bushy mustache twitched upward. "In that case, I'm sure the lesson can wait."

Hastily, she tossed the coin into the tea tin on the shelf behind the dining table. "Promise me," she said in a half whisper, "that you'll stay in the sitting room with us."

Keeper Dixon nodded.

"I'll go fix some spiced tea while you fellas talk."

Several minutes later, Spunky brought a silver tray carrying delicate china cups, silver spoons, and a silver teapot to the sitting room. Cad was seated on the far end of the sofa while Keeper Dixon occupied his overstuffed chair. She set the tray on a table at the near end of the sofa, poured out the tea, then sat erect on the couch a good distance from Cad.

Cad couldn't help noticing changes in Spunky, from the tempting aroma of her cinnamon tea to the dainty flowered cups she used, to her erect posture as she took her place at the opposite end of the sofa.

He sipped the beverage. "This is the most delicious cup of tea I've had since I left Chicago," he said quite honestly.

"Yes, excellent spiced tea, Serilda. My compliments,"

Keeper Dixon confirmed.

Spunky caught the rise in Cad's brow at the use of her proper name, and she hoped he wouldn't tease her like he always had in the past. She hadn't allowed anyone to call her Serilda until recently, when Keeper Dixon had helped her to appreciate her name's beauty and meaning—"armored warrior maid."

"I like the name Serilda," Cad remarked unpretentiously. "It's very unusual and pretty, just like you, Spunky."

His compliment put her at a loss for words. As she took another sip of tea, her thoughts spun, searching for something intelligent to say. She recalled a recent lesson with Keeper Dixon. "I read an interesting fact in a biography about Mr. Lincoln the other day, Cad." Though she hadn't intended such an abrupt change of subject, at least she remembered not to drop the g on the end of "interesting." "Did you know that Burns and Shakespeare were two of his favorite authors?"

"Burns and Shakespeare. I didn't know. I'm impressed," Cad said sincerely, more amazed that Spunky had read a book, than at the revelation of Lincoln's literary preferences.

"Keeper Dixon's been helpin'—*helping*—me this winter with the book learning I would have got if I'd gone to school. I didn't get much schooling when I was young. I couldn't get to the schoolhouse in bad weather, or when there was work on the farm that needed doing. Then Mama died when I was twelve, and I quit school for good."

"What else have you learned since you began your lessons?" Cad wanted to know.

In the conversation that followed, he was surprised to learn that Keeper Dixon had not neglected the areas of mathematics and science in teaching Spunky. Cad sensed the improvement the tutoring had made in her self-esteem.

"I've received a remarkable amount of education this winter, myself," Cad said, admitting without shame that until he had worked with Mr. Freiling, his schooling had taken place in the classroom. He told how he was learning about survival in a rural setting, about felling trees and hauling them to the dock in preparation to shipping them to the mill in Manistee next spring, and more. "I'll be learning how to build a house as soon as the ground thaws. We're to put up a summer place for the Thurgoods, from Chicago."

Though he didn't say so, through his association with Mr. Freiling, he had come to understand there was a more important measure of a man--or woman--than formal education. There were the lessons of life, and of moral values. These counted more than any college diploma.

The conversation continued, taking other directions. Cad asked about Stoney. When he learned of the improvement to his leg, he broached the subject that had been on his mind for several days. "Keeper Dixon, I was wondering if you'd let me construct a set of parallel bars in the barn. As Stoney starts to put weight on his leg, he could use them to help build back his strength."

"Sounds like a mighty fine idea to me."

"Good. I've brought everything I need in the sleigh. If you'll excuse me, I'll get started right now. When the Freilings are finished calling here, ask them to drive around and pick me up there."

"Sure thing."

Spunky saw Cad to the door. He pulled on his heavy jacket, cap, and gloves, turning to her. The essence of rosewater seemed even more enticing now than when he had first arrived. And did that look in her warm brown eyes mean she didn't want him to go? He fought the temptation to reach for her.

"Thank you for the tea, Serilda."

She never realized how musical Cad could make her name, using the golden baritone sound of his voice, rather than the taunting, teasing tone in which he had last said it months ago. She wished he would say it pretty like this again and again. Then she silently scolded herself for having such a foolish thought. This was the man who still owed her a goodly amount of money, the man who still held the key to her dreams.

"Thank you for coming, Cad. Come again, the next time you get paid, that is."

# CHAPTER

## 17

When Aurora first heard bells tinkling on the third Sunday in February, she was certain it must be her imagination. But as the sound grew louder, she got up from her sewing machine to look out the front entryway window. Much to her delight, a beautiful sleigh carrying Cad and the Freilings came to a stop in front of the keeper's quarters! Cad jumped down and helped the older couple out, then disappeared inside the Dixons' house.

Aurora threw open her door before the Freilings had a chance to knock. "Welcome, neighbors! Come right in!"

"At last, my mister and I have come to pay you a call," Mrs. Freiling said, stamping the snow off her boots. "I've been lookin' forward to this since ya came to visit me in November."

"Didn't want to come by till Harrison had a chance to recover some," Mr. Freiling explained. "Then, y'r driveway got too thick with snow, and we had to wait for the ice to get plenty strong by the shore so we could run down here in the sleigh."

"How *is* Harrison?" Mrs. Freiling wanted to know.

As Aurora hung their coats in the entryway closet, she

answered with a brightness she did not feel. "He's been out of his splint for three weeks and using his crutches to get around the first floor."

Despite Harrison's physical improvements, he had remained as withdrawn as when he was bedridden, or maybe more so. His silence made her equally quiet, and they had all but stopped speaking to one another. Aurora felt more certain than ever that he didn't love her. Worse yet, she had begun wondering whether she still loved him!

But these were private matters, and she forced herself to remain cheerful. "Just today, he's begun to put weight on his left leg—only a little, but at least it's a start. In six weeks, it should be back to normal. Come into the sitting room and say hello." She led them up the stairs and through the hallway.

Harrison came across the room to greet them when they entered. His glum expression of the past several weeks had been replaced by a smile. Aurora couldn't remember the last time she had seen Harrison looking so pleased. "Mr. and Mrs. Freiling, come in and make yourselves comfortable."

Aurora positioned two straightbacked chairs near Harrison's.

"Well, look at ya. Gettin' about real handy on those crutches I put together," said Mr. Freiling.

"You look better than I expected," Mrs. Freiling commented. "Marriage agrees with you!"

"That it does."

How Aurora wished Harrison's rapid confirmation were spoken honestly! From his mood since New Year's Day, she knew better. If the truth be known, she had become no more than a nurse to her husband.

189

Regardless, she was determined to be a good hostess, and promptly offered refreshments. "I'll go get some coffee and cookies while the three of you talk."

While Aurora worked in the kitchen, filling mugs with hot coffee and arranging a plate of cookies, she tried to follow the conversation taking place in the sitting room. Though she couldn't catch every word, she could tell that Harrison had suddenly become more talkative than at any time since their marriage, and she resented him for being so silent when she was alone with him.

She carried her tray into the sitting room. Following several minutes of polite conversation about the weather and the holidays, Mr. Freiling started to get up. "If ya don't mind, Mrs. Stone, I'll step next door and say hello to Walt."

Aurora rose with him. "I'll get your coat."

"I'll be along shortly to visit with Spunky," said Mrs. Freiling.

Thankful for a few moments alone with the old family friend, Harrison pulled his grandfather's watch out of his vest pocket. He had spent countless hours contemplating the timepiece, his grandfather, and his feelings about them since he came into possession of the keepsake, and he needed to speak with Mrs. Freiling about it.

"I never thought I'd see this again. Thank you." Before she could respond, he continued. "When I was a boy, Grandpa told me this watch would someday be mine. Now, as it turns out, his timepiece isn't the only legacy he left me." Harrison indicated his left leg, propped on a footstool. Ruefully, he admitted, "I live every minute in the fear I'll end up like he did."

"But you won't!" Mrs. Freiling quickly assured him. "Your leg is mending much better than Harry's did. It's straight, and just as long as t'other one. Harry's wasn't that way a'tall. You're gonna be good as new in a few more weeks!"

Harrison took but small comfort in Mrs. Freiling's pronouncement, but he put those reservations aside. Right now, he felt the need to share something that had been eating him up inside since he'd acquired his grandfather's watch. He'd found it impossible to discuss the problem with Aurora, or even Spunky, but he believed Mrs. Freiling would understand. She had known his grandparents as well as anyone.

"You know . . . " His courage waned the moment he began. He struggled against the guilt that kept him bitter and silent for weeks, forcing himself to continue. "I've never forgotten the way Grandpa shamed me with his drinking, and I've never forgiven him for it." Through a clenched jaw, he added, "It makes me angry, to this day!"

"Oh, Harrison!" The sympathy and understanding in Mrs. Freiling's tone spoke volumes, and so did the kindness in the brown eyes that caught and held his gaze. "You know, son, your leg is gonna heal whether or not ya forgive your grandpa." She paused, then gently added, "But your spirit will be crippled till ya do."

Mrs. Freiling's words, and the compassion in her voice were audible to Aurora as she approached from the hallway after seeing Mr. Freiling out. Though uncertain of the deeper significance of the exchange, she sensed its delicate nature. Unwilling to interrupt, she went instead to the kitchen to draw water for another pot of coffee.

The older woman's wisdom cut straight to Harrison's troubled heart. He knew she spoke the truth, but he wondered whether he could let go of his anger and forgive.

191

She went on. "All of us who knew y'r Grandpa Harry were hurt by his drinkin', but I hardly ever think of those days. When I remember Harry, I think of the good times, like when you turned eight and he let ya help him drive the wagon to Leland. Do ya remember that?"

Harrison could see himself sitting on the wagon seat beside his Grandpa. Each of them wore overalls, the matching plaid shirts his grandmother had sewn, and straw hats to keep off the hot sun. How proud Harrison had been, knowing he was old enough to handle his grandpa's team! He had thought the world of his grandpa then.

Mrs. Freiling continued. "I remember it 'cause it seemed like we waited forever for ya to come back with the lemons so's we could squeeze 'em for lemonade and have your birthday cake and presents." Mrs. Freiling chuckled. "That was a mighty good time, and Harry Stone was a mighty fine gent' back in them days."

Harrison glanced down at the watch in his hand. As he stared at its face, the keepsake took on new significance—a remembrance of pleasant times. A rush of warmth went through him, rekindling a fondness for his grandfather that swelled in his heart. Suddenly, the shackles binding his spirit in resentment broke, freeing him to forgive, allowing him to cherish the watch twice as much as before.

*Thank you, Lord, for sending Mrs. Freiling here to show me the path of forgiveness.*

Peace flooded through him. He felt more tranquil than he had since his accident. He looked up from the watch, into Mrs. Freiling's kind, round face. "Thank you. You've helped me more than you know."

As he studied the watch again, it brought to mind another question that had nagged at him for weeks. He stared into the eyes of the only person who could provide the answer. "There's something I've been wanting to ask you." He paused only a moment before continuing. "Who sold you Grandpa's watch?"

Mrs. Freiling's eyes widened, then she answered very solemnly, "Spunky's pa. I thought you knew he had it."

Harrison felt his color rising, bringing with it an ill temper. Why hadn't Spunky ever mentioned it? After a moment of indignation, the peace he had discovered only minutes ago flooded back even stronger. He must no longer let anger rule him. The time had come for leaving animosity behind. "I didn't know, but it doesn't matter."

In the kitchen, Aurora sensed a lull in the conversation between Harrison and Mrs. Freiling. Carrying a second plate of cookies, she returned to the sitting room.

"Would you care for more cookies, Mrs. Freiling?"

"Gracious, no. I was just thinking it's time I visited Spunky." She pressed her plump form up from the chair. Smoothing the wrinkles from her skirt, she slipped her hand into her pocket and pulled out a folded paper. "I near forgot, I was s'posed to deliver this note." She handed it to Harrison. "Now the two of ya have got to come for coffee just as soon as y'r up to it. Promise?"

"We'll come calling," Harrison assured her, the corners of his mouth tilting up.

Aurora detected sincerity in Harrison's quick, agreeable response, and in his smile. As she saw Mrs. Freiling out, she wondered how the woman had caused such a difference in her husband's attitude. Her visit seemed to be just the medicine he needed, and she wished the neighbor woman could call on him every day to administer additional doses. But in her heart of hearts, she couldn't help thinking the

193

remedy had come too late to cure the ills that plagued their marriage.

When she returned to the sitting room, Harrison was reading the note Mrs. Freiling had given him. With a scowl, he handed it to her. She hastened to read the floridly penned words.

> *My dearest Mr. and Mrs. Stone,*
>
> *I write to express my deep regret for my transgression on December 25 of last year. In the weeks since, I have come to understand how wrong and selfish I have been in my past dealings with others. I humbly beg your forgiveness and a chance to begin our friendship anew.*
>
> *In the words of Tennyson: 'He that wrongs his friend wrongs himself more, and ever bears about a silent court of justice in his breast, himself the judge and jury, and himself the prisoner at the bar, ever condemn'd.'*
>
> *Please free me from my prison by accepting my apology, for as Robert Burton put it, 'As the sun is in the firmament, so is friendship in the world . . .'*
>
> *Most sincerely, Cadwallader Blackburn.*

Aurora folded the note and handed it back to Harrison.

He immediately ripped it to pieces. "Just another of Cad's tricks. I don't believe for one second he's changed, that silver-penned devil."

She kept her silence, but in her heart, she truly believed Cad's note was sincere, and she wondered when Harrison would realize that it was just as important to forgive Cad as it had been to forgive his grandfather.

Leaning on his crutches, Harrison easily hobbled down

the back steps for his second trip to the barn. The temperature was near forty degrees beneath a partly sunny sky on this second Saturday of March, and he savored the fresh Manitou wind coming up the passage from the southwest, nipping at his ears as he took his daily exercise.

Each day since he started putting weight on his leg nearly three weeks ago, he had walked to and from the barn at least twice each morning. Now, the strength in his left leg had improved enough to enable him to put half his weight on it, and he was certain Mrs. Freiling's prediction of complete healing would prove true with a little more time.

He opened the barn door and stepped inside, catching a whiff of the horse's stall in need of cleaning. Daylight slanted across the floor, hitting the set of bars Cad had built. Spunky told him about Cad's project the day it had been built, but as Harrison stood there, he saw not a piece of exercise apparatus, but the brazen Chicago man who had kissed Aurora on Christmas Day!

The memory still rankled. Determined not to touch the bars, Harrison turned away, recognizing at the same time his own reluctance to start back toward the house. Aurora seemed so unhappy these last few weeks. He wished he knew what was troubling her, but each time he had planned to ask, his jaw clamped up. The silence and uneasiness between them gradually worsened until he found his moments outdoors a relief from the tension, an escape from the worry that had plagued him since before their marriage. It seemed his worst fear had come true—that only hardship and unhappiness could come to a woman married to a man with a leg as badly broken as his.

A cold wind whipped through the open door, biting him

on the nose, reminding him he had nowhere to go but back to the house. From Dixons' back door, Spunky emerged, heading toward the barn with a bucket. He was still contemplating his return to the house when she entered the barn.

"Good morning, Stoney. I'm glad we crossed paths. I've been meaning to talk to you about something."

Harrison couldn't help noticing the improvements in Spunky's diction and appearance these last several weeks. She no longer spoke like an unschooled farm girl, and even when doing chores, her hair was pinned into a neat twist, rather than flying out in all directions from a loosely gathered bun.

"What's on your mind, Spunky?"

She dumped her bucket of ashes into the barrel, then turned to face Harrison. "Twice every morning I watch you come out here. You don't stay but a minute before you head right back to the house. Why don't you spend some time using those bars Cad built?"

"The answer should be obvious," he said shortly. Eager to escape the subject, he started toward the door, but Spunky stepped in front of him.

"I know I ain't—I'm not—the smartest person in the world. I'm certainly not near as smart as you, but I guess you're gonna—going to—have to explain the obvious to me."

"You're smart enough to figure it out," he quickly replied, trying again to pass through the door.

Spunky didn't budge. "All I can figure is you haven't forgiven Cad for what happened Christmas Day."

At mention of the incident, the hair on the back of Harrison's neck stood up. "And why should I?"

"Because you oughta forget the past!" Spunky told him, her grammar slipping in her exasperation. "The Freilings told me 'bout the apology he wrote. They've seen big changes in him. He's tried to make amends by buildin' those bars. I suppose it didn't occur to him you'd be so hard-headed as not to use 'em, even though they'd do you a world of good." She left her stance by the door and stepped over to the bars, testing them with her weight. "I suppose Cad just put in a wasted effort out here in the freezin' cold three weeks ago." She left the bars and came back to face Harrison, gazing directly into his eyes.

Harrison kept his silence, his fingers tightening about the handgrips on his crutches.

"You can stay mad if you want, but it would seem to me you'd be a whole lot better off if you was—were—willing to get over y'r anger long enough each day to use those rails."

She marched off to clean the horse's stall, leaving Harrison to think about what she had said. Reluctantly, he came to acknowledge one more prediction Mrs. Freiling had made. A heart that cannot forgive remains crippled. In order to heal completely, he must be willing to forgive Cad.

He limped over to the bars, running his hand along a rail. It was smoothly sanded and well-varnished, offering no danger of splinters. He laid down his crutches and stepped between the bars, testing them with his weight the way Spunky had. The rails bent only slightly, leaving no doubt they were strong enough to support him. Gradually, he made his way to the opposite end, putting about half his weight on his left leg. He turned around and began to walk back, aware of Spunky watching him.

It seemed nice to be able to move without a pair of

crutches jammed under his armpits, even though he was limited to the straight line down the center of the apparatus. After several minutes of effort, his leg felt fatigued, and he picked up his crutches. Spunky, evidently finished cleaning the stall, claimed her empty ash bucket and headed out the door with him. He proceeded toward the house somewhat reluctantly, knowing the atmosphere within was often as chilly as the cold outdoors.

About a third of the way along the path, he stopped. "Spunky, can we talk a minute?"

She offered a wry smile. "You know you can always talk to me, Stoney."

Her casual remark suddenly took on a deeper meaning. "Why is that?"

"Pardon?"

"Why is it I can always talk to you, but I can't talk to Aurora?" His words spilled out quickly, the way they never did with Aurora. "She seems terribly unhappy. We've hardly spoken to one another for weeks. But when I try to approach her about it, I can't seem to get out even the first word."

Spunky shrugged. "You're in love with Aurora. You're not in love with me. Maybe that's got something to do with it."

Her statement made Harrison pause and reflect. "But what should I do?"

Spunky's brows arched. "Next time you want to talk with her, pretend it's me you're talking to."

Harrison chuckled. "I don't believe I've got that much imagination."

She let out a hoot. "I guess that is a real stretch. No matter. You've got to talk to her, Stoney. And remember to go easy where her feelings are concerned. She's strong on the outside, but delicate on the inside." Spunky shook her finger at him. "You can't keep quiet forever. When was the last time you told her how you feel about her, anyway?"

Harrison could feel his face color. "That's none of your business."

"Maybe not, but if Aurora's unhappy, maybe she needs to hear you tell her you care about her."

Harrison started toward the house again, eager to leave the subject behind. "Surely she knows that by now."

No sooner were the words out of his mouth than a memory flashed into his head of Cad, the day Harrison discovered the forgery of the wedding card to Aurora. Harrison remembered saying he would let Aurora know how he felt about her in his own way, in his own time. But he hadn't.

Cad's response was clear in Harrison's memory. *Your intentions are good, but will your words come too late?*

Harrison propped his feet on the stool, picked up the library book, and attempted to concentrate on the description of the War of 1812, but his thoughts were elsewhere. In the next room, he was keenly aware of the *ch ch ch* of the sewing machine, and the fact that Aurora had shown interest in little else for several weeks.

Eleven days had passed since his talk with Spunky. Afterward, he had attempted to engage Aurora in a game of checkers in the hope they could begin talking with one another again. Her refusal to participate had caused him to lose confidence. A number of times since, he had been on the brink of complimenting her appearance, or saying how thankful he was to be married to her. One time, he had even popped pocorn and shared it with her, but after several futile attempts at conversation, his tongue had locked up, and those moments had trickled into the gulf of silence growing between them.

Taking out pen and paper, he reached for a book of poetry from the lighthouse library. If his tongue wouldn't cooperate, perhaps the written words of others could help him express the depths of his feelings for his wife.

# CHAPTER

## 18

Cad helped Mr. Freiling ease the oak display cabinet into place along the back wall of the general store. Together, they had designed, built, and finished the piece, giving it a durable coat of wax before wrapping it in old blankets, loading it onto the wagon, and driving four miles north to the village, where they were making the delivery to Mr. Cherryman exactly on time—Friday, the thirty-first of March.

The stout, dark-haired storekeeper, clad in his white shirt, black bow tie, red sleeve garters, and white apron, ran his hand over the finish. "Mighty fine job, Matthew. Mighty fine. That cabinet will be just right to hold the fancy goods I've ordered for spring delivery. I expect them to arrive real soon, now the passage has opened up. If the mail boat can get through, I expect the bigger ones will be steaming up from Chicago soon enough.

"By jolly, that reminds me. I've got a letter here just came in this morning for Keeper Dixon from his missus. I was hoping you could take it over to his place, seeing as how you're right close by. He seldom gets up this way, things what they are at the light station, and I hate for it to sit here for days."

"I'll see it gets to Walt," Mr. Freiling promised.

"Much obliged. I'll get it for you, and your payment for the cabinet. Come over to the front counter. I'll be with you in a minute."

While Mr. Cherryman disappeared behind the postal counter to locate the letter, Cad stood at the front with Mr. Freiling, listening to the conversation a few feet away. Peter Anders was beating Max Carleton in a game of checkers they had set up on the barrel by the stove while two of their friends—Cad heard them called Slim and Jack—stood by, sipping hot coffee, waiting their turn to play. Wood smoke tinged the air, hinting of the heat to be found by the fire. Cad wandered over to warm his hands which had nearly gone numb after the cold ride from the Freilings.

The others paid him no mind, offering not a single word of greeting as he stood among them. Cad was certain Peter's gossip had given him a bad name amongst the islanders, who never spoke to him unless he spoke first. Their chilly regard made Cad eager to get back to his friends in Chicago.

"Mr. Blackburn?" Mr. Cherryman had reappeared at the front counter. "I believe there's a letter here for you, too." The storekeeper, who was also postmaster on the island, held a long envelope up to the light. "Yes, sir. Looks like it might just be your ticket home."

Cad wasted no time claiming it. The address on the envelope bore his father's handwriting. He tore it open. Inside was a ticket for passage from North Manitou Island to Chicago aboard the *Missouri*, and a brief note from his father which he read eagerly.

*I've missed you, son. Ticket enclosed. Hurry home.
Affectionately, your father.*

He shoved the ticket and note back into the envelope, folded it securely and tucked it in his inside jacket pocket.

"Looks like you'll be leavin' us soon," Mr. Freiling commented.

Cad's happiness was instantly tempered by the trace of regret in his mentor's casual remark, realizing he would truly miss the old man. "It appears so."

"Here's the letter for Keeper Dixon, and your payment, Walt." Mr. Cherryman deposited several pieces of silver in one of Mr. Freiling's hands, and the envelope in the other.

Mr. Freiling handed Cad the letter. "I'd be much obliged if you'd put this in y'r pocket alongside that ticket. Then I know it won't get lost. Now hold out y'r hand. It's payday. One . . . two . . . "

Cad couldn't help noticing the conversation by the stove had ceased while Mr. Freiling counted ten silver dollars into his hand with the clinking of cold, hard cash.

"I expect you'll be callin' on Spunky soon. Ya can deliver that letter to Walt at the same time, if ya would, and save me the trip."

"I'd be glad to," Cad agreed, shoving the coins into his pants pocket."

"Cup of coffee on the house?" Mr. Cherryman offered. He set two empty mugs on the counter and retrieved the percolator from atop the stove.

"Sounds good," Mr. Freiling answered.

"No, thanks," Cad replied. Taking out his pipe and tobacco pouch, he realized couldn't enjoy a smoke in company the likes of the fellows by the potbellied stove. "If you don't mind, Mr. Freiling, I'll wait for you outside."

"I'll be out soon as I've had my coffee."

Taking his place on the wagon seat, Cad lit his pipe. He had barely taken a draw off it when Peter Anders slipped out the back door. "Say, Mr. Chicago, the fellas wanna get up a friendly card game tonight, here in the back room behind the store. There's gonna be some money at stake. Just maybe ya can turn that ten dollars o' y'rs into fifteen, or even twenty. Interested?"

A moment elapsed before Cad shook his head. "Not me."

"I was sure you'd want in. What's the matter? Our money not good enough for ya?" Peter taunted.

Cad was tempted to accept. The opportunity to show these island boys a thing or two about cards would be enjoyable, but he had other plans for his evening. "Tell you what, Peter, I wouldn't want to take unfair advantage."

"Unfair advantage?" Peter chortled and slapped his leg. "The boys was afraid if I invited ya, *they'd* be the ones accused of takin' unfair advantage." He laughed some more, then headed for the door, commenting over his shoulder, "If ya change y'r mind, you'll know where to find us. Seven o'clock."

A moment later, Mr. Freiling emerged, a candy cane in hand, which he fed to Acorn, his mare, whom he was always indulging with sweets. The old man climbed aboard and drove toward home, and as the wagon bumped and creaked its way over the rutted dirt road, Cad couldn't help thinking about the card game and Peter's remarks. He never had gotten along with Spunky's brother. He'd relish parting him from his money. With all the card tricks Cad had learned at the Monte Carlo cottage last summer and those he'd practiced during his years at college, there was no possibility he could lose to these ignorant island boys.

But it just wouldn't be a fair game. Besides, Cad planned to see Spunky tonight. Oh, how he'd missed her! Nearly six weeks had passed since he'd seen her, but he could remember the soft essence of her rosewater, the attractive blouse waist and skirt she had worn, and the pretty way she'd fixed her hair. He remembered, too, how her world had begun to open up under Keeper Dixon's tutoring. Until then, he hadn't realized Spunky was just a smart as she was sensible. She simply hadn't had the opportunity for book learning.

Cad fingered the coins in his pocket and counted them again. Ten silver dollars. The ticket his father had sent had cost eight dollars. He could give it to Spunky along with two dollars cash. That would satisfy the debt he owed her, and he'd still have eight dollars left for the game. The prospect held appeal, especially when he thought of all those times he'd been hauling logs to the dock with Mr. Freiling, and had stopped by the general store afterward to warm up, and those same fellas--including Peter--had ignored him, offering not even a single word of recognition.

Mr. Freiling drove the wagon into the barn and Cad helped him unhitch Acorn.

"You sure was quiet all the way home," the old man commented. Without waiting for a response, he continued. "Gave me a chance to think. Since y'r goin' to the light station soon, I might as well finish up the last coat of polish on the cane we made for Stoney, then you can take it along, too." He pulled out his watch. "Nearly supper time. We'd better get into the house and wash up. You know my missus. She can't stand havin' us come late to the table."

Mrs. Freiling served a supper of maple cured bacon and flapjacks, and lots of maple syrup. Mr. Freiling told her about Cad's ticket home, and that he had been paid for his labor.

"I'll miss y'r face at my table, Mr. Blackburn," said Mrs. Freiling. "It's been nice havin' ya here, with my own boys grown and gone."

Cad swallowed his last bite of flapjack and set his napkin aside. "I'll miss you, too, Mrs. Freiling," he said in all honesty, "especially your flapjacks. Excellent, as usual, Now, if you'll excuse me, I'd like to go change. I'll be stepping out this evening."

She smiled, a twinkle lighting her eyes. "You're excused, Mr. Blackburn, on the condition you promise to give Spunky my regards when ya see her."

"I'll do that, ma'am."

He changed from his flannel work shirt and overalls to a white cotton shirt and black wool pants, leaving off the bow tie when he discovered his neck had increased too much to button the collar, then he stopped by the workshop.

Mr. Freiling heard him enter and turned to greet him, giving the cherry wood cane for Stoney one last buffing with the polishing cloth. "Finished at last, and a finer cane can't be found on all of North Manitou, I reckon." He wrapped the cloth about it before handing it to Cad. "Might as well keep the fingerprints off till ya give it to Stoney. Looks nicer that way."

Cad was careful to hold it by the cotton rag.

"'Fore ya leave, come in here a minute," Mr. Freiling said, sliding open the door that revealed the automobile frame they had built over the past few months, as time had allowed. It was complete, but Mr. Freiling couldn't seem to resist tinkering. "I know ya was plannin' to put a sheet metal body on, and black paint once y've got the thing down in Chicago, but I've got some nice bird's eye maple that'd be just the thing for y'r door panels." He picked up two pieces from a stack of hardwood and held them in the light for Cad to see.

"I'll finish 'em for ya at no extra cost, if ya like, and ya can mount 'em in the metal after ya ship the thing home."

As Cad looked over the pieces of wood, he thought how they typified the quality he had come to associate with Mr. Freiling. Over the past three months, he had learned that despite Mr. Freiling's age, he was no soft pine. He was a very hard worker, and had always drawn a good day's labor out of Cad, even at those times when he'd felt too weary to get out of bed in the morning.

Mr. Freiling had instilled in him a new sense of values. Diligence, honesty, kindness. Cad knew he would miss the old fellow once he boarded the *Missouri*. It would be nice to have the bird's eye maple as a remembrance when he was back in Chicago.

"This is really fine wood, Mr. Freiling. If you're sure you want to part with it, there's one thing you can count on. I'll have the best-looking automobile in Chicago!"

"I'll get to work on 'em, then." He slid the door shut and carried them to his workbench. "Now there's one thing more I was gonna say to ya before ya go."

"What's that, Mr. Freiling?"

"Why don't ya ride Acorn? It'll take a load off y'r feet, and y'll have more time to spend with Spunky. The saddle is hangin' up beside Acorn's stall, and be sure to take along the lantern on the hook inside the barn door. It's already near dark. Besides, this time o' year, ya never know when fog'll drift in."

Cad was surprised at the offer to use Acorn. Though he had ventured out on only a few occasions since moving to Freilings', he'd never been loaned a horse. He'd either walked, or ridden aboard the wagon or sleigh while Mr. Freiling drove. Cad interpreted the gesture as an indication of his new, trustworthy status.

"Thank you, Mr. Freiling. I'll go easy on Acorn, I promise." Cane in hand, Cad went to the barn, saddled Acorn, and rode out.

The sky had already turned dark gray with the onset of dusk, sending sparrows to the treetops where they chirped their evening lullaby. The scent of reawakening earth all but disappeared in the cold night air, but Cad was only mildly aware of such manifestations of early spring as the mare carried him toward the drive to the light station.

Foremost on his mind was the fact that with a horse, he could quickly get to the card game at the general store. He could play some hands, make his winnings, and still get home at a decent hour. How badly he wanted to show those ignorant island fellows a thing or two about gambling, and to get back for all the times they had ignored him, refusing to even extend a simple hello. He fingered the coins in his pocket.

When Acorn came to the south turn-off for the light station, Cad paused. He hated to betray Mr. Freiling's newfound trust. Surely he would inquire about his friend, Keeper Dixon, and delivery of the letter. A twinge of guilt tugged at his heart when he thought about lying.

Quickly, a new thought came. He wouldn't have to lie.

He would come home late, long after the Freilings had turned in, then rise early in the morning and visit Spunky at the light station. Surely she would be glad for a breakfast visitor once she realized he had come to pay off his debt. He tapped Acorn with the cane and headed her north, in the direction of the main road.

As he traveled the road he had been over time and again with Mr. Freiling, hauling logs to the dock, he began to have second thoughts. He shoved them aside, urged Acorn into a trot, and for the next three and a half miles, he mentally reviewed all the card tricks he could remember from his past. Tonight was his lucky night! Soon, he would be off this island, saying good bye forever to back-breaking hard work, overalls and a nine o'clock bedtime, and hello again to the life of leisure, silk smoking jackets, and all night card parties.

When he reached the edge of the village, he slowed Acorn to a walk. Bringing her past the life saving station and down the alley behind the store, he dismounted and tied her up. Approaching the rear entrance, he heard raucous laughter through a small back window that had been left open a crack, and saw Peter Anders, Max Carleton, and their cohorts, Slim and Jack, sitting around an old rough table sandwiched in amongst the crates, wooden boxes, kegs, and firkins stacked along the walls.

"Fifty cents says Mr. Chicago 'll show up here tonight!" Max Carleton announced confidently, plunking a coin on the table.

"I'll go ya one better 'n that," said Peter. "Seventy-five cents says he not only shows up, he goes home ten dollars poorer, and without no ticket to Chicago!"

"I object," said Jack, his bushy black brows coming

together above his bulbous nose. "It hardly seems fair to bet on somethin' we all know is a sure thing. Accordin' to you, Peter, Mr. Chicago never has passed up opportunity for a game. That pretty much guarantees he'll show, even if we ain't exactly the swank college boys he was accustomed to at the Monte Carlo cottage. And ain't we all agreed, no matter what the outcome o' *this* game, he'll be parted from his assets 'fore he leaves town? After all, it's four against one."

"Yeah! A little rough and tumble outside the back door oughta do the job," Slim suggested. When he flexed his biceps, Cad realized that, contrary to his name, he had thick muscles. Despite improvements in Cad's build, he sensed he was no match for this man, let alone the assistance he'd receive from the other three.

Swiftly, he mounted Acorn and urged her into a gallop, only slowing to a trot when he had put a mile between himself and the village. He stopped Acorn long enough to light the lantern. As he continued on his way, he realized he should have known better than to contemplate slipping into his old, bad habits.

A saying of Mr. Freiling's came to him. *People who can afford to gamble don't need money, and those who need money can't afford to gamble.* Cad could hear the words as if the old man were with him this very minute. He felt the coins in his pocket. He really *couldn't* afford to risk them, but he had forgotten that in the face of temptation.

*Opportunity knocks. Temptation kicks the door down.* Again, the words came to mind in the tone of Mr. Freiling's voice. He wished he'd remembered them before he'd ridden all the way up to the village. His desire to get back at Peter and the others for the way they had treated him these past few months had clouded his thinking.

*Vengeance is mine; I will repay, saith the Lord.*

How many times had Mr. Freiling quoted that Bible verse, and others in the last three months? But this, too, Cad had forgotten when he had let unhealthy emotions rule his head.

Good old Mr. Freiling—so wise, level-headed, and upright. He'd been half father, half grandfather to Cad since the first of the year. Cad checked his shirt pocket for the ticket. Once he left North Manitou, he'd lose touch with the Freilings. He'd have the buggy frame and those special bird's eye maple doors to remember Mr. Freiling by, but the camaraderie of working together in the shop, Cad's excitement at his first automobile taking shape, the satisfaction of executing his own design, or learning new principles in cabinet making as he had when helping to build the display case for the general store—those experiences, and opportunities for more like them, would be left behind.

He thought of his father, who had always been too busy at work in his office or on business trips across the state to pay much attention to him, except when he needed money. Then he had cut off funds, leaving Cad stranded on the island when his father had arbitrarily decided gambling losses had grown out of proportion, and Cad must earn his way home.

He jingled the coins in his pocket. He'd been accustomed to having ten dollars handed to him just for the asking. Earning it through six weeks of hard labor brought a satisfaction he hadn't experienced until he came to know Mr. Freiling. Now, he could appreciate his father's decision to leave him on North Manitou for the winter.

A wonderful new idea came to Cad.

He guided Acorn onto the path to the light station and nudged her with his heels, spurring her on until she broke into a trot. Cad could hardly wait to see Spunky, to pay off his debt, and tell her of his plan!

The light tower was shining brightly when Cad approached the light station. The drive brought him up at the rear of the reserve. Traversing the walk from the barn to the keeper's quarters was a lone figure on a crutch, and Cad wondered whether Stoney had been working on the parallel bars in the barn.

Involuntarily, he touched the scar on his left cheek, a reminder of his last encounter with the assistant keeper. A healthy measure of remorse had filled the three months since. He took a deep breath, rode silently across the sand, and quickly dismounted beside his former friend.

"Good evening, Stoney."

Harrison would have known the melodic baritone voice anywhere, but it startled him, coming unexpectedly out of the dark of night. The memory of whacking Cad with his crutch flashed to mind. His heartbeat quickened, recalling the anger he had felt for the smooth talker who had kissed Aurora. Being willing to use the parallel bars, and being truly able to forgive in his heart were two different things, Harrison realized, now that he was confronted by Cad in person. Eager to be rid of him, he started to limp away.

In the light of Mr. Freiling's lantern, Cad saw the set of Stoney's jaw and the look of dismissal in his eyes, but he was determined to deliver the gift he and Mr. Freiling had so carefully crafted. He stepped in Harrison's path and presented the cane.

"Mr. Freiling asked me to bring this by for you. It's a gift, sent with sincere wishes for a full recovery."

Harrison wanted to ignore Cad, to retreat to the sanctuary of the keeper's quarters, but he could tell the Chicago man wasn't about to let him pass. Reluctantly, he accepted the gift.

Taking advantage of the moment, Cad continued. "I want to apologize in person for my behavior with Mrs. Stone on Christmas Day. What I did was wrong, and I'm very sorry for any trouble I caused."

Cad's tone bespoke a sincerity Harrison hadn't heard in the past. Perhaps the city slicker really had changed, as Spunky had tried to tell him.

The anger Harrison had kept buried deep inside himself abated. Though he still wouldn't trust Cad alone with Aurora, no good could come in withholding forgiveness. He offered his right hand. "I accept your apology."

Their hands clasped firmly. Then Harrison traded the single crutch he'd been using for the cane, finding it just the right height. "Be sure to tell Mr. Freiling thanks for the gift. I'll make good use of it."

"I'll tell him," Cad promised. Eager to knock on Spunky's door, he quickly led Acorn toward the house.

Harrison limped along behind, thinking of all the hours he'd been spending in the barn, the improvements he'd made thanks to the parallel bars, and the man who was responsible.

"Cad, wait up."

The other man paused.

Harrison hurried to catch up. "Thanks for building the bars in the barn. They really made a difference."

Cad grinned. "You're welcome, Stoney." Feeling a

rare satisfaction within, he hurried on. Tying Acorn to the flagpole for lack of a hitching post, he pounded on Spunky's door.

As Harrison entered his back door, his gaze fell on the thread cabinet Cad had given Aurora on Christmas Day. It had been sitting there underfoot for months. Instead of going upstairs, Harrison took the lantern off its hook and headed for the basement in search of his toolbox. It was time to mount the thread cabinet above Aurora's sewing machine, where she could make use of it.

# CHAPTER

## 19

Cad's forceful knock quickly brought Spunky to the door, and the moment he laid eyes on her, he was certain she had lost weight. The results were becoming. Her cheekbones appeared more prominent, giving her face a regal look, and her waistline nipped in like the young ladies he'd known back in Chicago.

"Good evening, Miss Serilda."

For six weeks, Spunky had contemplated Cad's return, wondering how she would react. His greeting proved almost seductive, drawing her like a magnet. Her heart skipped a beat and she couldn't help breaking into a happy smile. Sensing her vulnerability to his charms, she warned herself to go cautiously, to maintain decorum. "Mr. Blackburn. What brings you out tonight?"

He could tell from the look of surprise on her face and the cordiality in her voice, she was delighted to see him. He grinned as he reached into his pocket and jingled the coins. "Ten silver dollars. All yours."

Her eyes widened, lighting her entire face. "Then come right in. I do hope you can stay awhile."

She was so preoccupied by the arrival of her caller, she almost didn't notice the faint noise penetrating the night air.

Stepping outside, she listened a moment, then closed the door and took his coat.

In the sitting room, Keeper Dixon occupied a chair strategically positioned by the front window where he was reading, and keeping watch on the tower light. "Keeper Dixon, Mr. Blackburn has come to deliver the balance of the money he owes me."

The head keep' rose, offering a hand. "Good evening, Cad. It's been awhile." To Spunky, he said, "Serilda, perhaps our company would enjoy a cup of that special tea, like you fixed last Sunday night."

"I'll set the tea kettle on to boil." She headed toward the kitchen. Remembering the noise she had heard outdoors, she paused. "And while I'm at it, you might want to step out to the fog signal building. The South Manitou whistle has just started blowing."

He set his book on his chair. "I'd better go out and light a fire under the boiler then, just in case their fog rolls in here."

Spunky put water on to boil, then joined Cad in the sitting room, realizing how easily he could kindle a flame in her heart just by his very presence. Feeling extremely susceptible, she took a seat on the sofa a couple of feet away from him.

How wonderful he looked, with his shirt collar open, revealing a neck grown thick and strong from his work in the woods. And his hands, no longer those of a manicured gentleman of leisure, bore the calloused mark of a working man when he opened them to show her the coins.

"Hold out your hands, Serilda. Today is payday." One by one, Cad counted the silver coins into her palms.

When he had finished, she closed her hands and hugged

them to her chest, a look of joy overspreading her features.

Thoughts of boarding the *Missouri* for Chicago made her so excited, she jumped up. "I can hardly believe it! All the money you took is back!" She spun about, dancing across the room like a child, then disappeared into the dining room, returning with a metal tea tin that rattled with coins. She smoothed the fabric of her skirt, popped the lid from the box, and dumped its contents into her lap. "Look! I've never had so much money in my life! Keeper Dixon paid me again today. Now I have more than enough for my trip!" Methodically, she counted every penny, then started over again, counting out sixteen dollars and setting them aside before tossing the remainder of the coins and bills back into the tin. "There. That's what I'll need for my tickets on the *Missouri*. All the rest, I can spend on my room, meals, and shopping. I'm going to have the best time ever!" She clapped her hands.

Despite the satisfaction Spunky's happiness brought Cad, he couldn't help feeling a little envious. He moved closer and picked up eight of the silver dollars she had set aside for passage, tossing them into the box. "You won't need those for a ticket."

"You aren't expectin' me to stay in Chicago the rest of my life, are you?" The unsettling thought made her diction slip.

He laughed. "Of course not, silly." From his shirt pocket, he took the ticket his father had sent and laid it atop the eight dollars she would need for her return.

Instantly she grabbed it up, then inspected it carefully, front and back. Old worries crept into her heart. "Where did you get this?" she queried skeptically.

"From my father. It came in today's mail."

"I don't believe you."

"You don't have to take my word for it." Cad smiled as he handed over his father's note. He watched her eyes as she read it, a word at a time. When they met his again, they set in a stubborn look. "You can't give me this. I don't know why you'd even want to. Besides, what would your father say?"

Cad chuckled. "He'd say, 'It's about time that son of mine thought of somebody other than himself for a change.'"

"But Cad, this is your ticket home! It's what you've been wantin' all these months!" She read the ticket again, her shoulders lifting in glee. "Oh, this is so excitin', I can hardly believe it! Now you and me, we can board the *Missouri* together, and when she docks down in Chicago, you can show me all around, and we'll just have a grand old time!"

How Cad wanted to show Spunky his town! His home, his family, the schools he attended, the streets jammed with people, the dining room at the Palmer House where he'd take her for a seven-course dinner—but it wasn't meant to be. Not this time.

"I'm not going home," he said solemnly.

"What?" His statement disrupted her scheme for only an instant. "Sure you are. Soon as the *Missouri* shows up, you'll be on her. With this ticket." She laid it on the sofa beside him.

"*You'll* be on her. I'm staying on North Manitou for a while longer, until I earn my passage to Chicago, the way you have."

His intentions showed he had changed far more than she had realized. "But how are you gonna do that?"

He answered without hesitation. "I'll run carriage rides for the summer visitors. Mr. Freiling and I have already got the buggy frame built. Later on, I'll convert it to an automobile, but for now, it's the start of a carriage. I haven't asked Mr. Freiling yet, but I'm sure he'll let me stay on at his place and help me finish it. Then I'll rent Acorn from him, and together, we'll provide the best carriage service this island has ever seen!" He picked up the ticket and dropped it into her tin box. "So you just keep that as recompense for the trouble I caused, and have yourself a good time in Chicago."

Spunky was shocked into silence. After a few thoughtful moments, she found her voice. "Cadwallader Blackburn, I never thought I'd see the day! You really *have* changed!"

Cad shrugged off her surprise, his mind whirling with additional plans. "First thing you'll have to do when you get to Chicago is pay a call on my folks. I'll write a letter introducing you and telling them my plans. They'll really like you. In fact, they'll insist you stay with them! I'll ask Father to take you to dinner at the Palmer House, and Mother will take you shopping in all the finest . . . "

Harrison squeezed his eyes shut, filled his lungs with the pure, balmy spring air that teased at his jacket collar, then looked again. At first, he had thought he was seeing things, but now he was certain. A boat was coming toward the light station dock! He hurried down the path from the barn to the house to tell Aurora the news, and get out the binoculars.

As he limped along, he realized how much easier he could get around with the use of the cane Cad had given him. Today, the second of April, was the first day he had been able to put all his weight on his left leg while exercising in the barn. He had left his crutches there for good.

Spring brought improvements in the weather, and in his leg as well. But as he entered the back door and headed toward the dining room where Aurora was working at her sewing machine, he ruefully acknowledged the chill that lingered.

He slipped his hand into his pants pocket and fingered the folded paper there. For a week and a half he'd been carrying around the words of poetry he'd copied, too self-conscious to give them to Aurora as an expression of his love for her.

She spent as much time as ever at her sewing. Sometimes, he wished he hadn't given her a sewing machine! Now, she didn't even look up when he entered the room and came to stand beside her.

"Aurora, where are the binoculars? A boat is coming in!"

Instantly, she rose. "Is it the lighthouse tender? Inspector Gordon?"

"I couldn't tell without the glasses."

"I'll get them." Aurora's heart thumped faster as she hurried to the front hall closet and retrieved the binoculars from the shelf. Her thoughts raced. *I must put away my sewing machine and supplies before Inspector Gordon gets to the keeper's quarters!*

She rushed back up the stairs to the sitting room and set the glasses on Harrison's bed while she moved it back from the east window far enough to gain access to a good view of the lighthouse dock.

Harrison raised the glasses to his eyes and adjusted the

focus. The boat was about seventy-five feet long—the right size for a light service tender, but the name on the bow didn't belong to Inspector Gordon's vessel.

"It's the *Manitou Lady*," he announced.

"Nat's and Seth's steamer!" Aurora cried. "Let me see!" As she located the boat through the binoculars, her heart swelled with emotion. She remembered coming to the island in November with her sisters, mother, and brothers. How she had missed her family!

She handed the glasses back to Harrison, sidestepping her way out from behind the bed. "I'm going down to meet them!"

Harrison started to follow. "We'll both go!"

Halfway to the door, Aurora turned and paused. "Are you sure you can make it down to the dock?"

"Sure as water is water."

At the front closet, she quickly donned her Mackintosh coat and held the door for Harrison. Keeper Dixon and Spunky came out of their house at the same time.

"Well, what do you know? We've got company coming in. That's a sure sign of spring," observed Keeper Dixon, pulling his jacket on as he went.

"Maybe the whole Richards family is coming for a visit," Spunky suggested.

"I hope so," Harrison declared, "for Aurora's sake. I'm sure she's missed them terribly." Switching the cane to his left hand, he reached for her as he limped along, pulling her close to his side.

Harrison's affectionate display took Aurora by surprise. Weeks had passed since they had touched, except for joining hands when asked to by Keeper Dixon during prayer at Sunday morning worship services. Even while courting,

Harrison had seldom shown affection in company of others. It seemed odd, being close to him after the weeks and months of limited contact. Aurora couldn't help wondering whether he was holding her only to put up good appearances for her family.

When they arrived at the sandy beach, she waited with Harrison at the shoreline while Keeper Dixon and Spunky went up on the dock to help Nat and Seth bring in the *Manitou Lady*.

As it neared the pier, several members of the Richards family congregated on the lower deck at the bow.

"Aurora!" Charlotte cried, her hand waving wildly in the air.

"Sis!" Dorin and Eli hollered, almost in unison.

Behind her sister and brothers stood Aurora's mother, waving just as enthusiastically.

Energetically, Aurora waved back.

The boat had barely nudged the pier when Eli and Dorin, now nine and ten years old and taller than when Aurora had last seen them, came bounding off the dock, wearing the flannel shirts she had made them for Christmas.

Somewhat reluctantly, Harrison released her as the boys rushed into his wife's arms.

"We missed ya, Sis!" Dorin exclaimed, hugging her so tightly about the neck, she could hardly breathe.

"Yeah!" concurred Eli, pushing Dorin aside to get in his hug. "When are ya comin' home to visit?"

"Soon, I hope!" Aurora replied, kissing them each on the forehead. How she had missed the boys' unlimited energy and happy voices.

Dorin quickly turned his attention to Harrison. "Will

you take us up to the tower?"

"Yeah, can we go up in the tower now?" Eli asked.

"Sure. I'll take you up. Come on, fellas."

Aurora reached for Harrison, a staying hand on his arm. "Do you think it's wise to put so much strain on your leg?"

He smiled confidently. "I'll be fine. I can go up and down those stairs on my right leg if my left one gets tired."

Reluctantly, Aurora let go, turning to Charlotte and her mother. They embraced her both at once, then Charlotte leaned back to eye her critically. "You look good, Aurora!"

Julia Richards caressed her daughter's cheek. "You do look good, but a little tired. Are you feeling all right?"

Aurora sensed her mother was hinting at the possibility of a grandchild on the way. She couldn't know Harrison's affection in all the months since November had amounted to no more than a few kisses.

"I'm fine, Mama. Truly." Eager to change the subject, she turned to Charlotte. "Where's Bridget?"

Charlotte's bright smile diminished. "She couldn't come. She sent a note explaining the reason." Charlotte pulled an envelope from her pocket.

"Bridget is with Meta, helping her look after Michael today," Julia said, referring to Nat and his wife and their young son. "Meta hasn't been well for several weeks. Nat plans to take her to Dr. Thurston in Glen Arbor now that the ice is breaking up."

Aurora tucked the letter in her own pocket. "I'm sorry to hear Meta isn't herself." Putting her arms about her mother on one side, and Charlotte on the other, she stepped off in the direction of the keeper's quarters. "I'm so glad at least the two of you are here! Come up to the house and tell me all the news since I left South Manitou."

"Charlotte has something important to tell you," Julia said.

Aurora paused, looking into her sister's brown eyes. "What is it, Little Sis?"

Charlotte grinned broadly, setting the gold flecks in her eyes to sparkling. "I can't say until Seth is with me."

Aurora glanced back at the dock. Seth, Nat, Keeper Dixon and Spunky were just stepping onshore. "Seth! Come tell me your news!" she beckoned.

He strode up beside Charlotte, his lopsided grin revealing his crooked front tooth. He wrapped his arm about Charlotte's shoulder. Nat, Keeper Dixon, and Spunky joined them.

"Charlotte and I are to be married on the twenty-fourth of June!" Seth announced.

Aurora had never seen him looking more pleased, nor her sister more proud. She tried to ignore the twinge of jealousy she felt over their obvious happiness. "Congratulations!" she said, hoping not to sound insincere.

"I'll have enough time after school is dismissed to make the final arrangements," Charlotte explained. "You'll be my matron of honor, won't you, Aurora?"

"Yes, of course!" Aurora hastily accepted.

"And may I wear your wedding dress?"

"If you like."

"Oh, thank you!"

As Charlotte hugged her, Aurora couldn't help the feelings of trepidation over her sister's wedding plans. What if something bad happened to Seth, the way it had to Harrison? She couldn't bear to think of the unhappiness Charlotte would suffer.

*Don't be silly!* a more rational inner voice told Aurora.

*Charlotte and Seth will be perfectly happy.*

"You'd better come inside and try on my wedding dress right now, in case I need to alter it for you," Aurora suggested.

"While you're fitting the wedding gown, I'll see to some coffee," Spunky offered.

Once inside, Aurora immediately took Charlotte upstairs to her room. As the petticoat that went with the wedding gown settled at Charlotte's waist, the need for alterations became evident. "I'll have to let this out about an inch," she told Charlotte.

"That means your dress will be too tight, too," Charlotte concluded with obvious disappointment.

"I can alter it to fit," Aurora assured her, lifting the pearl-studded satin gown over her sister's head. But as the dress fell into place and she studied Charlotte's reflection in the mirror, Aurora couldn't prevent the dark feelings which stole into her heart, reminders of the difficulties that had begun with Harrison's failure to arrive on South Manitou on her own wedding day, and had brought such discontent in the months since. She knew she shouldn't be superstitious, but she didn't want to risk the happiness of Charlotte's wedding. "Maybe I should make you a new gown," Aurora cheerfully suggested.

"Oh, no! I wouldn't think of it! I've dreamed of wearing this one since I first saw it on you!" Charlotte insisted. "Seth will love this dress on me. He's already told me so."

How Aurora wished Harrison were as communicative as Seth seemed to be. In the months since his accident he'd told her only once how nice she looked, though he had frequently done so before their marriage. And he hadn't yet told her he loved her.

"Charlotte," Aurora began thoughtfully, "I realize you and Seth have known each other quite awhile, but has he ever told you how he feels about you?"

"Of course!" Charlotte responded quickly, as if the question were pure nonsense. "He tells me he loves me every day. I imagine, now that you're married, you hear the same from Harrison both day and night."

Aurora only smiled, trying to shove aside a pang of jealousy.

As Charlotte took off the gown and donned again the blue serge skirt Aurora had given her for Christmas, she chattered. "Mama, Bridget, and I are all making good use of the skirts you made. They fit perfectly!"

"I'm glad you like them." Aurora slipped her gown onto its rose-scented padded hanger.

"I have something exciting to tell you! The Garritys are coming from Detroit for my wedding. Seth wired the invitation from Frankfort when he and Nat went over to get the *Manitou Lady* this past week. His old boss wired back immediately with an acceptance, and the news that he and Helen were wed just before Christmas!"

"So your former teacher married her brother-in-law after all. How nice," Aurora commented. As she hung up the wedding dress, she pushed aside the new lavender gown with the lacy collar she had recently completed, all but the hem. A whole bolt of the exquisite fabric had been given her by a customer who had bought it for bridesmaids' gowns, then called off her wedding.

Still in her undergarments, Charlotte reached for the dress, holding it up to herself in front of the mirror. "How lovely!" She ran her fingers over the lace that covered the collar and bodice. "It's the perfect dress for you to wear at my wedding! I wish you had enough material to make one like it for Bridget."

"But I *do*."

"Then it will be just the thing!" Charlotte held the new dress up to her sister. "If your wedding gown weren't so fancy, all eyes would be on you, wearing such a pretty costume as this."

"I'm glad you like it." The compliment meant more than Charlotte could know. Aurora had never before realized how much she depended on the approval of others to keep her satisfied with her sewing since Harrison had grown too withdrawn to even notice her efforts.

As Charlotte changed back into her blouse waist and skirt, a commotion developed outside the bedroom. "I'm going to find out the cause of all the noise," Aurora said, stepping out her door.

In the hallway, Nat and Seth were carrying Harrison's mattress into the bedroom across from Aurora's. Behind them came Dorin and Eli, each with an armload of sheets and blankets, while Harrison supervised.

"I thought it would be a good time to move my bed upstairs, with four strong men available to help," Harrison explained to Aurora. "If my leg is strong enough to take Dorin and Eli to the top of the light tower, it's certainly strong enough to manage the stairs in the house."

Amazed by Harrison's sudden talkativeness, and the unexpected modification in furniture arrangement, Aurora was still trying to adjust to the changes when Charlotte emerged from her room.

Harrison turned to her. "If you ladies are done with the dress fitting, we'll move Aurora's dresser across the hall and put her sewing machine in there."

"We're finished. You fellows go right ahead and put the furniture where you want it," Charlotte replied.

Aurora wanted to protest, but Charlotte went on, "The new arrangement will be so much more convenient for you both, now that Harrison's leg has healed."

Unable to argue her sister's logic, Aurora urged Charlotte toward the stairs. "Maybe we'd better get out of the way of the movers and go down to the kitchen. You can help me get out some cookies to go with Spunky's coffee."

As Aurora followed her sister down the stairs, she tried to put aside her keen apprehension at the prospect of sleeping in the same bed with Harrison tonight.

# CHAPTER

## 20

"Your leg seems nearly back to normal," Seth commented to Harrison.

Now that the furniture had been moved, everyone had somehow managed to fit around Aurora's dining table for coffee, milk, cookies, and conversation.

"I don't know what I'd have done without Aurora to take care of me these last four months," Harrison said, squeezing his wife's shoulder.

Aurora couldn't get over his continued affectionate, talkative nature, concluding it was only for show. No doubt, once their company left, he would withdraw, and the coolness between them would set in as before.

"Seems I told ya back on your wedding day Aurora could help ya get through a tough time," Nat recalled.

"I'm ashamed I took so long to recognize the wisdom of your advice," Harrison admitted. "This has been a difficult winter for us, but now that I'm on my feet again, everything will be fine."

Aurora bit back a retort. After weeks and months of

difficulties leading her to question Harrison's love for her, and hers for him, he showed incredible pluck making such a prediction. Once again, she reminded herself it was just for show.

"In fact," Harrison continued, "I feel so good, I've even talked Keeper Dixon into letting me put the light in the tower tonight!"

"That's wonderful, Harrison!" Charlotte exclaimed. "You really *are* better!"

Nearly choking on her cookie, Aurora took several sips of coffee to wash down the crumbs, and the words of protest that still threatened to spring off her tongue.

"Just remember, I'm taking watch duty once the light is on," Keeper Dixon reminded him. "I only agreed to let you do it because you promised me that afterward you'd stay off your feet."

"I'll keep my promise," Harrison assured his boss.

The conversation headed off on other topics. Nat and Seth told of the work that had been recently completed on the *Manitou Lady*, replacing dry rot at the water line, and their plans for the shipping season which was about to get underway. They spoke of Keeper Trevelyn and his wife, who was recovering from a bout with pneumonia; the Schroeders—Nat's in-laws; and other South Manitou Islanders familiar to Harrison and Aurora. Too quickly, the afternoon evaporated.

"We'd best get started back now if we're to get in before dusk," Nat suggested. "I don't like runnin' at night if I don't have to, not here in the Manitou Passage anyway."

Aurora hated to see the visit end. If only she could stop the hands of time!

230

Harrison kept his arm about her as they walked their guests to the dock. She wished his show of affection were genuine, rather than for the benefit of their guests.

Only reluctantly, did Harrison let go of Aurora when she said good bye to her family. Her little brothers offered quick hugs, then hurried to join Nat and Seth on the boat.

Aurora reached for her mother, kissing her on the cheek. "Thanks for coming, Mama." Then she hugged Charlotte. "You too, little Sis. I've missed you both so much. Give my love to Bridget."

"Don't forget her note," Charlotte reminded Aurora.

She searched her coat pocket. "I have it right here."

"Come visit us when you can," her mother said, stepping onto the dock.

"I will!"

How Aurora wished she, too, were boarding the *Manitou Lady!* Time with her mother and sister had proved far too short.

Then Harrison drew her beside him, and she was reminded her place now was with him. Together, they watched the boat steam away, until it became a small dot against the horizon.

Keeping her close against him, Harrison walked her to the house. His silence left her free to think—to realize how much she had missed having him by her side during the previous four months. She recognized, too, that the affection he was giving her now was not for the benefit of her family. Could he really be sincere in this tenderness he was showing?

But as she entered the sitting room with Bridget's note in hand, she was reminded of the new furniture arrangements, and her apprehension mounted. Thankfully, bedtime was still several hours away. She simply wasn't ready to face the night in the same room with Harrison!

She could hear him in the kitchen, filling the service lamp in preparation to carrying it to the tower. He was humming "Beautiful Isle of Somewhere," and as she opened the envelope from Bridget, she realized many weeks had passed since she had felt like singing.

The thought passed from her mind as she concentrated on the words from her sister.

*Dear Aurora,*

*The keeper's quarters haven't been the same since you left. I no longer have to help you clear your sewing from the dining table before every meal! But oh, how I miss our little routine!*

*I trust by now that both Harrison's leg, and his spirits, have recovered from the accident last fall. Time and healing have probably changed him from a reluctant bridegroom to a doting husband.*

*On the subject of bridegrooms, Seth is looking forward to his turn, and I sense it's all Charlotte can do to keep her mind on her teaching while she plans for her wedding!*

*I have written my measurements on a separate scrap of paper in case you need them, so you will be able to start right away on my dress for Charlotte's wedding. I know you have the correct skirt measurements, because the blue serge you made me for Christmas fits perfectly and I love it! Thank you!*

*Now for a bit of sad news. Undoubtedly, Mother and Charlotte have told you Meta has been ill. I would be with you today if not for her sick-*

ness, and Nat's need to pilot the <u>Manitou Lady</u> to bring the others for a visit.

Nat has been beside himself this winter, not knowing from one day to the next whether she will feel well, or take to her bed. Of late, she has spent part of every day in bed.

He is very good at playing with little Michael. Their precious son is two years old already! He's a joy to care for, but a challenge. Add to this the other household chores, and Nat soon felt overwhelmed, unaccustomed as he is to a woman's work.

On the days when Meta was first ill, either her mother would tend her, or Nat and Michael would come to fetch his mother. As Meta's condition worsened, his needs became a daily problem. Mrs. Schroeder came every day until her gout put a stop to it. That left more work for Mrs. Trevelyn. She eventually wore herself out and contracted pneumonia, from which she has nearly recovered.

In the meantime, I have stepped in to help at Nat's and Meta's home. Together, Nat and I manage to tend Meta, keep Michael from mischief, prepare the meals, and keep their little house in order.

Meta's affliction troubles me deeply. In the course of my days helping at her home, Nat has confided in me his fear that she may never recover. I pray Dr. Thurston will be able to prescribe a cure when they visit him this coming week.

I must close now. Charlotte and Seth are waiting to take me to Meta's, and fetch Nat for

*the trip to your island. God bless!*
*Affectionately,*
*Bridget*

Aurora folded the note and put it back in the envelope. Praying silently for Meta's healing, she thanked the Lord that Harrison's health problem had been easily diagnosed and successfully treated. At least they had not suffered the frustration of some unknown disease.

Her thoughts turned to Charlotte's wedding, eager to finish the hem on the dress she would wear. First, however, she should put the leftover soup on the back burner to warm.

In the kitchen, Harrison had already lit the service lamp, and it was burning with a perfectly adjusted flame. When he picked it up and turned to her, his beaming smile touched her in a way she hadn't expected. Without words, his face told her that the pain, the darkness, the doubts plaguing him for months were now past. Tonight he was making a bright, new beginning. The realization of how far he had come since the Thanksgiving Day tragedy put a lump in her throat.

He paused beside her on his way to the front door. "I'm going out to the tower now."

Harrison's quiet words, and the significance beneath their superficial message, stirred long-forgotten feelings within Aurora. Afraid to acknowledge them, she focused on the pragmatic.

"I'll start supper."

He nodded. She was tempted to reach out to him. But a tiny voice in a corner of her mind whispered doubt. *He hurt you before. He can do it again.* Her hands and her feet seemed carved of marble.

He stepped past her, limping only slightly with the help of his cane. The sound of the door closing behind him released her from inertia.

From the icebox, she took the pan of soup and set it on the stove to heat, rekindled the flame, then hurried upstairs. Though she had intended to go straight to work in her sewing room, she couldn't resist slipping into the bedroom which now held her dresser and the bed she would share with Harrison.

Opening the muslin curtains, she gazed out the only upstairs room with a window looking directly out on the light tower, monitoring her husband's every step. Softly into her heart and mind stole the realization that she was proud of the changes he had made in himself, both body and spirit, though they had come at so great a price.

When he disappeared inside the tower door, she went to her former bedroom to fetch her new gown. There, on her sewing machine, lay a folded note, her name on the outside in Harrison's handwriting. She picked it up along with her gown and sewing basket, returning to light a bedside lamp and make herself comfortable in a chair by the window where she could easily keep her eye on the tower. Dusk had only begun to set in, yet she recognized the soft glow of the lamp in the lower tower window as Harrison progressed on his climb.

Eager to read his note, she unfolded the missive, wondering whether the handwriting was truly Harrison's, or one of Cad's forgeries.

*Dear Aurora,*
*You needn't spend a moment worrying that this*

*is another of Cad's tricks. The handwriting is mine, but words too often fail me in expressing my feelings for you, so I have borrowed sentiments of some very fine poets to tell you what is truly in my heart. Please forgive the imperfections of rhythm and rhyme. As you well know, I am but an imperfect man.*

*When we first met, we did not guess*
*That love would prove so hard a master*
*Of more than common friendliness*

*So sweet love seemed that April morn*
*When we first kissed beside the thorn.*
*So strangely sweet, it was not strange*
*We thought that love could never change.*
*But troubles came, and now they go,*
*And one thing you must always know.*
*In my heart I love but you alone.*

*Deeper than speech*
*Stronger than life*
*Our tether.*
*Be it fair or cloudy weather.*

*Always remember the wisdom of Shakespeare:*
*The course of true love never did run smooth.*
*And remember these words of Harrison Stone: I*
*will always love you!*
*Harrison.*

Wiping away a tear, Aurora read the letter a second

time before she folded it and tucked it into her sewing basket. She picked up her work and began taking tiny stitches to complete the last few inches of the hem, but her thoughts remained on Harrison. Finally, her hands fell into her lap and she pondered.

For so long, she had yearned to know of his feelings. She no longer needed to wonder. Relief flooded her heart and she took solace in the assurance of his love. Still, she couldn't help thinking this letter seemed so unlike him. The old Harrison had been quiet, steady, and predictable.

Then she remembered some of the other things he'd done—popcorn popping, offers of a checker game, open affection in front of her family. From one moment to the next, she hadn't known what to expect. A new Harrison had emerged, and if his letter was the proof, the new Harrison was a far different man from the old. And, so he claimed, he loved her.

Inside the tower, Harrison put down his cane and took hold of the handrail. The familiar smell of burning oil masked a mild odor of damp wood as the lamp brightened the lower portion of the stairwell, playing his shadow against the wall.

Leaning on the railing, he placed his right foot on the first tread, then drew his left foot up beside it. Step, pull up. Step, pull up. He repeated the process nearly twenty times until he had carried the lamp up the first of five flights.

As he turned and faced the second flight, he realized that the muscles in his left thigh were sorely out of shape. His previous trip to the top with Aurora's brothers had taken a greater toll than he was willing to admit. Then, in order to prove his recovery to them and himself, he had taken the steps one after the other. But not tonight.

Step, pull up. Step, pull up. Halfway up the flight, he rested, looking out the window facing the keeper's quarters. At the sight of Aurora watching from the upstairs window, he paused briefly to wonder whether she had discovered his note to her, then resumed his progress. He must make it to the top in good time, or surely she would doubt the strength of his recovery. At last he stood on the next landing.

Above him rose the two flights of stairs leading to the watch room. There, he would face the greatest challenge of all, the ladder to the lantern deck. He set down the lamp and massaged his left thigh above the knee, then continued on his way. Step, pull up. Step, pull up.

Feeling a warm glow inside from the knowledge that Harrison loved her, Aurora knotted her thread and snipped it, slid the needle into the spool, and held up the finished dress, anxious to put it on before he returned.

She peered out at the tower. No light had appeared at the top yet, but the upper window, located about two-thirds of the way to the lantern deck, was starting to take on a faint glow. She watched as it gradually grew brighter, then dimmed. Judging from Harrison's progress thus far, he wouldn't reach the top for a few more minutes, just enough time for her to change.

Pulling the curtains closed, she hastily unbuttoned her shirtwaist and stepped out of it and into the lavender silk gown.

The skirt floated down over her petticoat, falling in soft folds. As she walked across the room, the gown made her feel as new and beautiful on the outside as Harrison's letter had made her feel on the inside. All her hours of hard work at the sewing machine had been worth the effort!

Then a dark thought came to her. Would Harrison even notice her new dress? In all the weeks she had labored over it, he had never said a word about it. But surely now, seeing the garment completed, he would notice. Wouldn't he?

She returned to the window and drew back the curtain. The top of the tower remained dark. Naturally, it would take Harrison longer to climb the stairs than before his accident, but it seemed *too* long since he had walked out the door carrying the lamp. She couldn't help worrying about him.

Harrison pushed open the door to the watch room, set the lamp on the cleaning table, pulled out the stool and sat down. The muscles in both thighs throbbed with fatigue. He gently massaged his left leg, then his right, which had started to knot from the strain. His shoulders, too, took on a steady ache, and he slowly rotated  them to relieve the tension. Staring up at the ladder leading to the lantern deck, he counted thirteen steps separating him from the top. They could prove much more difficult than when he had climbed them this afternoon without the lamp.

He reached in his coat pocket and pulled out a coil of wire and an s hook wide enough to fit over the broad rungs of the ladder, then he turned to the counter to study the Fourth Order lamp which had no wire handle, only a broad metal loop off to the side. "This won't exactly be by the book, but I don't think Keeper Dixon will mind," he muttered to himself.

Winding the wire snugly about the base of the lamp, he looped it over the chimney and twisted it about the s hook. Satisfied his temporary alterations would serve his purpose, he again eyed the steep ladder.

"Time to face the challenge," he told himself, procrastinating long enough to consult his grandfather's watch. Only a few minutes remained before the designated time to start the light, which must be in operation half an hour before sunset. A vision of his grandfather flashed before his eyes, of the healthy man he had been on Harrison's eighth birthday. Fond memory made Harrison smile. A second remembrance quickly followed, of the old man falling drunk into the bushes. Harrison's jaw set in determination. Tucking the timepiece back into his pocket, he stepped off the stool.

"This is for you, Grandpa."

Picking up the lantern, he hung it at the left side of the ladder and with both hands, grasped a rung high above his head. Pulling himself up by the arms, he rested his right foot on a rung below while raising the lantern to a higher position.

Again, he grasped a rung above his head, grunting at the strain of pulling up his full weight. Again, he moved the lantern to a higher rung. Sweat dampened his forehead and his palms as he struggled to raise himself higher still. Feeling his arms growing weaker, he reached down for the lantern. The s hook started to slip free of the wire. Harrison clamped his thumb over it just in time to keep it from falling to the floor.  At that  exact moment, his right foot slipped off the ladder, leaving him dangling by one sweaty hand!

Before his eyes flashed the sight of his grandfather falling from his ladder, breaking his leg!

# CHAPTER

## 21

Harrison hung by little more than his fingernails, finally managing to find a rung with his right foot. He hugged the ladder, struggling to catch his breath.

When his pounding heart stopped racing, he set his focus on the rungs above. Hooking the lantern at the top of the ladder, he reached for the highest step, pulled himself up, and pressed open the door to the lantern deck.

Cooler air welcomed him, drying the beads of moisture on his forehead. He pulled himself up through the hatch, then leaned down to retrieve the lamp.

Removing the wire and hook, he stood up, lantern in hand. His knees wanted to buckle, but he willed them to bear up. Glancing back at the keeper's quarters, he could plainly see Aurora watching from the upstairs bedroom window. A warmth surged through him, bringing with it renewed strength.

He turned to the Fourth Order lens and opened the chamber. "Aurora, my darling, this is for you!"

He set the light in place. As the lens took on a glow, he turned his face heavenward. "Thank you, Lord!"

Concentrating on his task once more, he released the brass finger that allowed the clock works to rotate the lens, and with his grandfather's watch, he timed the rotation. Ten seconds red, ten seconds white. Smoothly and quietly, the works turned on the ball bearings in perfect time.

Harrison stepped outdoors, onto the lantern deck, his heart overflowing with gladness that tonight he was making a new beginning as a lightkeeper. His gaze traveled across the water, four miles to the southwest. There, a steady white light began to glow from the South Manitou tower, reminding him of his beginnings in the light service, the year he had begun courting Aurora.

He leaned against the lantern deck rail and reminisced about the young girl he had fallen in love with so long ago. For five years, Aurora Richards had been the happy, beautiful person who put the brightness in his life, the one around whom his world centered, and for whom he planned his future.

He thought of how he had begun saving for Aurora's sewing machine from the first year he courted her, believing she would never be happy when they married unless she could continue to sew. Now, she spent nearly all her time sewing, yet she seemed miserable.

A daunting thought settled heavy on his heart—in four months' time, he had squelched Aurora's bright spirit. Through his own misery and pain he had extinguished the joy they once shared.

He remembered how, when he had broken his leg, he had not wanted to marry. He had not even wanted to live! He had been brutal to Aurora, telling her he didn't need

243

her. For months, he had filled her world with ill temper and gloom. Nevertheless, she refused to give up on him. She had taken care of his every need. He prayed she had found and read his love letter to her. Then he realized even if she had, it was terribly insufficient. He had not done nearly enough to show how much he really cared!

As the lens behind him continued its flashing pattern, and the beacon across the water grew brighter with the onset of darkness, a new light began to dawn in his heart, revealing an appreciation and love for Aurora far greater than he had ever known before, far greater than the words he had set down on paper.

He fixed his eyes on the figure in the window. "Aurora, I love you!" he shouted, wishing she could hear. "Without you, I wouldn't be standing here!"

How he longed to hold her close, to speak to her of his feelings, and kiss her as a husband kisses his wife!

Burning with the desire to close the distance between them, he lowered himself through the hatch. "Father in heaven, take me safely and quickly to Aurora's arms," he prayed, finding his way down the ladder.

Aurora paced the sitting room, the sweep of her silk lavender dress brushing the floor behind her. Nearly half an hour had passed since Harrison's figure disappeared from the lantern deck of the tower. For a long while after he set the light, she had seen him by the deck rail, looking out over the Manitou Passage, but he should have been back by now, despite the fact that his leg was still recovering its strength.

She returned to the window. Still no sign of him on the walk from the tower.

*He's fallen on his way down the steps!*
The fear nagged at her. Then she dismissed it as a worried wife's foolishness.

She wandered into the kitchen. The aroma of her chicken vegetable soup would have been enticing under normal circumstances, but anxiety had chased away her appetite. She stirred the soup and checked the fire in the stove. The glowing embers would keep supper warm for some time.

Returning to the front sitting room window, she pulled up a chair and stared out. As night fell, the beams of red and white became more distinct. Perhaps it was a silly thought, but their alternating colors seemed to parallel her relationship with Harrison, the pure white representing the glad times before their marriage, the bright red a symbol of the trouble they had faced since.

For months, she had been hoping time and healing would restore the Harrison she had known before his accident, and revive the happiness in their lives. She had longed for the past, for those days when his attention had been so readily given.

But the calendar couldn't be turned back. Harrison would never be the man he once was. Life's experiences had changed him forever.

As she continued to stare at the white and red beams, truths were revealed to her like the tower light illuminating the waters below. When she first came to North Manitou, she had tried to lift Harrison from his doldrums. In the process, her own spirits had sunk, and for a long time now, she had retreated into her own world, using sewing as a fortress in which to shut herself away from him.

Yet while she was imprisoned in her seamstress's

world, Harrison had been trying to reach her. She had paid little notice at the time, but he must have had more than checkers in mind the day he set out the board game and invited her to play. And what about the night he made popcorn? The quiet man who had never been much with words tried to make conversation, but she had been so walled up with resentment, she hadn't heard.

For weeks, she wondered if he really loved her. Had he been trying to show his feelings while she was too blind to see?

*I don't need you. I don't want your help!*

His hurtful words on their wedding day still haunted her, but they had come from a man rendered helpless, dependent, and scared for the first time in his life.

"I mustn't look back!" Aurora told herself. The tough times were in the past. Harrison's leg had healed. If only she could look ahead, she would see that the best was yet to come.

Into her mind slipped the words Keeper Dixon had read from the Bible during worship that morning. *. . . be ye all of one mind, having compassion one of another . . . that ye should inherit a blessing.*

"Dear Lord, I believe in the blessings you promise," Aurora prayed, "I know now, Harrison loves me, but I can't help wanting to hear him speak the words!"

Too fidgety to sit any longer, she began to pace the room, and as she walked, she reflected on the Harrison she had known. Even in his best days before his accident, he was a quiet man, letting her do most of the talking. She couldn't expect him to change into a conversationalist, unless she helped.

She returned to the window and peered out at the

pathway from the tower.  Harrison was nowhere in sight. *Lord, please bring him safely down from the tower!*

Harrison found his cane where he had left it just inside the tower door, then stepped onto the walk.  It seemed much longer than the hundred and sixty-some feet he had traversed in the opposite direction earlier.

Leaning heavily on his cane, he limped toward the keeper's quarters.  A twinge in his stomach caused a moment's apprehension over facing Aurora, but he dared not lose his nerve.

In the distance, a gull cried and its mate answered.  God had given those birds each other, and voices to communicate.  Surely He would not abandon Harrison in expressing the most important words he would ever say to Aurora.

He took the front steps carefully, one at a time, his heart pounding as he let himself in.

From the sitting room, Aurora could hear Harrison entering the door.  She had watched him coming down the walk.  His legs were badly fatigued, she could tell by the slowness of his pace, but thankfully, he was all right!

She wanted to run to him, but she forced herself to wait for him to come to her.

Harrison listened for the sound of the sewing machine as he climbed the steps to the front hallway.  The house was silent.

"Aurora!"  The instant he called her name, he regretted the tone so reminiscent of those days when he had been bedridden.

Aurora was so pleased to have him back, she didn't care that he sounded a bid demanding.  But now that he was on his feet, she would not rush to him when he called, as she had when he was laid up. "In the sitting room, Harrison."

He paused at the doorway, his gaze fixed on the attractive woman he had married. Tonight, she seemed more beautiful than ever, in a dress he had never before seen on her. He couldn't have kept from smiling if he'd wanted to for the love that bubbled up inside him at the sight of her.

The expression on Harrison's face radiated across the room to her, a look so full of affection she could almost feel its embrace. The way his eyes roved her dress from neckline to hemline told her without words he had noticed her new creation and approved overwhelmingly. Tentatively, she smiled.

Harrison took a deep breath, resolute in his intention to speak of his feelings.

"Aurora, darling . . . " The moment felt frozen in time, and so did he.

She moved a step forward. "Harrison . . . "

"I love you, Aurora!" His words tumbled out. Closing the distance between them, he crushed her against him.

"And I love *you*, with all my heart," she murmured.

His mouth found hers, covering her lips with a kiss that spoke more than words, leaving no doubt how he had felt about her for the last five years, assuring her of his feelings for the many years yet to come.

Long minutes passed before their lips finally parted. Aurora hated for the kiss to end, and kept her arms about his neck.

He inhaled deeply, then gazed down at her, eyes smoky with desire. "I know you've got soup ready, but I'm too tired for supper right now. Do you suppose you could help me up to bed?"

Aurora felt her face coloring deeply, but she didn't care. Putting her arm snugly about his waist, she turned in the direction of the front stairs.

Spunky drew in a deep breath of moist woodland air. Familiar spring odors of mud and rotting leaves helped to calm her nervous anticipation about boarding the *Missouri*. A mid-April mist ran in droplets from the roof of the carriage Cad had borrowed from Mr. Freiling to deliver her to the pier, but it would take much more than wet weather to dampen the anticipation she felt within, knowing only a few minutes separated her from the start of the most exciting adventure of her island-sheltered life!

Cad drove carefully through the puddles near the village. A thin fog veiled the island and kept the fog signal blowing on the point five miles away. But when Cad brought the carriage close to the dock, a gentle breeze pushed away the shroud, allowing a spot of sunlight through to glisten off the white M on the huge black stack.

The sight of the massive steamer was even more impressive than Spunky remembered. For a minute, she simply stared at the dark hull with its wide band of white at the gunwale, the swarms of people at the rails, the long row of portholes indicating cabins just below the main deck, and lifeboats hanging from davits just above it. In the open pilothouse near the bow, she could clearly see the captain. She would make her acquaintance with him soon, and let him know she was counting on him to bring her safely to her destination and back again, to her island and Cad.

"Having second thoughts?"

Cad realized the question he posed was a revelation of his own inward struggle. Giving away his ticket had seemed right at the time, but the hard work that lay ahead of him brought occasional twinges of regret. To earn his keep until his carriage was finished and his island tour service became profitable, he was helping Mr. Freiling build a summer home for a Chicago family. The contract had been let last year, and with the ground newly thawed, his work with the old man had already begun—backbreaking work digging a basement. He ached from his efforts of the past few days.

Worse than the hard work would be Spunky's absence from the island. He had visited her every other day since the night he had given her the ticket. Their time together had brought welcome diversion from the toil, and more. He didn't dare admit even to himself the feelings she stirred inside him when she was near. The skies could clear up tomorrow, but the next two weeks would seem cloudy every day without her to spread some sunshine in his life.

Spunky turned to Cad, studying the center part in his untrimmed hair, the faint scar on his left cheek, and the thoughtful look in his blue-as-sapphire eyes. "I only wish you were going, too."

"I'll get back to Chicago soon enough," he replied, his grin hiding his true sentiments. "Right now, we'd better get you and your trunk on board." He leaped down, lifted her out and handed her a little valise, then hoisted her small trunk onto his shoulder, carrying it to the dock where one of the crewmen tagged it and loaded it onto the cargo deck. Then he walked Spunky to the gangway outside the main lobby and pulled an envelope from his jacket pocket. "Here's the letter for my folks. Call them the minute you get in. Mother will send Arthur to fetch you. And most important, enjoy shopping and spending the money you've saved!"

She took the envelope and tucked it deep inside the small bag she carried, near the drawstring pouch containing her money, then she took out the ticket he had given her. "There's still time to change your mind." She held it out to him.

He shoved his hands into his pockets. "You go on, now. Get your cabin assignment. And be sure to ask for dining accommodations near the window."

Her heart in her throat, she walked up the gangway and into the lobby. By the time she looked back, Cad was already on his way to the carriage. She felt a pang of disappointment that he hadn't waited until the ship got underway before leaving, but she supposed he was eager to return to the Freilings'. With the rainy weather making it impossible to work on the new house today, he'd probably get a lot accomplished on his buggy.

Since paying off his debt to her, he had paid many calls on her, telling her of his progress on his carriage, and little details he had considered to distinguish himself in the carriage tour business, such as putting a plume on Acorn's head and a sign on his carriage door. Sometimes a lull developed in the conversation. Just when she sensed he might say something about the new friendship developing between them, he would start in again on business talk. She was pleased that his scheming was now directed toward more honest pursuits than in the past, and that he was putting his time to good use to succeed in business, but she couldn't help wondering. Would he take any time to think of her while she was gone? Would he miss her?

# CHAPTER

## 22

Aurora knew from the gentle knock and the sound of the rear door opening that Mrs. Dixon was letting herself in. When she had returned to the island, just prior to Spunky's departure a week ago, she had suggested this system of quiet comings and goings between the two households to prevent awakening lightkeeper husbands who needed part of each day to sleep. Aurora was at the stove, cooking herself some oatmeal for a very late breakfast, wondering why her stomach felt too touchy to eat earlier, when her neighbor tripped lightly up the steps to the kitchen.

"Good morning, Aurora!" The quiet greeting lacked none of the vitality that marked the petite woman's every move. "I wouldn't have bothered you, but I've just come back from the village and Mr. Cherryman asked if I'd bring this letter by." Before Aurora could even get a look at the handwriting on the envelope, Mrs. Dixon added, "It's postmarked Chicago—from Spunky. We received a letter as well. I must say, for someone who could barely spell her name when I left this island last fall, Spunky has done well under Mr. Dixon's tutelage."

Aurora poured the oatmeal into a dish and set the pan aside before taking the ivory vellum envelope in hand. It was of a heavy, lined stock with a deckle edge—the kind of paper she imagined a well-to-do woman might use. It was sealed with a drop of gold wax impressed with a floral design. Eager as Aurora was to read its contents, she set the letter aside, propping it against the coffee grinder on the shelf. "Thank you, Mrs. Dixon. I'll wait until Harrison gets up to read it." Apologetically, she added, "I'd invite you to stay for coffee, but my pot is empty. I thought it best to wait until Harrison comes down to make a fresh one."

Mrs. Dixon sidestepped toward the door. "I can't stay anyway. Goodness knows I've plenty of work waiting for me at home. I'll be on my way now and let myself out. Your oatmeal is getting cold. You'd best sit down and eat it. You look as though you need it. You're a bit peaked this morning. Do you feel all right?"

"A little tired, is all. I'll be fine."

"If there's anything I can do, just say so. I've had plenty of nursing experience, tending my sister all winter." She gave Aurora a critical eye. "Don't try to do too much."

Aurora set herself a tray with oatmeal, brown sugar, cream, and a glass of warm milk. She eyed the letter standing on the shelf. On impulse, she grabbed it and took it with her to the dining room.

When she was half finished with her cereal, she could

stand the anticipation no longer, and carefully loosened the wax seal on the letter.

*Dear Aurora and Stoney,*
*    All is better than I dreamed!*
*    Mrs. Blackburn came to get me off the boat. I'm glad. There are 100's of streets and 1000's of people, all crowded close at this end of the lake! I never would have found my way to the Blackburn place alone. Arther, the hired man, drove us there in a carrage with silver handles, and fancy glass, and velvet seats the color of midnite.*
*    Cad's folks live in a house bigger than the life saving station on our island. Just think! Only one family lives in it! (And their maids and cook and Arther. He works in the garden when he isn't driving us around the city.)*
*    My room is bee-you-tea-full. (Spelling not good.) It is big. Very big. Big as half the house at the light station. My bed has tall posts and a can-a-pea of pink silk. I never saw such a bed as this. The hed bord goes near to the seeling. All mahogi-knee. Carved real nice.*
*    I could write many pages about the other rooms of this house. It is all as nice as my room. When we eat, the cook puts on a fancy light over the long table. It has hundreds of glass pieces the shape of tear drops. I am glad I do not have to clean them or I would shed some tear drops myself!*
*    The parlor has a big fireplace. Also two blue velvet chairs and a love seat and a long sofa in dark red mohair. The Oriental rug matches. There are other chairs in that room. Mrs. Blackburn said some look like*

*the ones used by a French king, Louis something.*

*Mrs. Blackburn took me shopping. We went to the famous stores. Sears and Roebuck. Montgomery Ward. Marshall Field. I walked every floor of them. They are huge!*

*I spent a lot of money. I bought a fancy dress. Mrs. Blackburn said I needed one to wear to dinner. My dress is the color of a cabbage rose. It has lace sleeves, lace in front, and silk from the waist down. I have a hat and a parasol to match it. I never wore silk before. Mr. Blackburn said I look very nice in the dress and I should wear it all the time. He does not know a thing about work on a farm!*

*Mr. Blackburn took us to the Palmer House. I never ate so much at one meal before. Lobster. The best roast beef in the world. Real good gravy. Wine. It tasted awful. Mr. Blackburn paid a lot for it. I told him he wasted his money. Now I know why Cad liked my cherry wine so much!*

*At the end of the meal, a waiter brought out a dish and set it on fire! I jumped up from the table. I wanted to run for the door. Mrs. Blackburn laughed and told me to sit down.*

*Cad's folks took me to visit his sister. Violet and her husband live in a big house two blocks away. All the houses on this street and Violet's street and the street in between are big.*

*Folks around here have lots of money. I look at their faces when I take a walk each day. Some of them don't look happy. I only have a little money to spend but I am having the best time of my life!*

*I miss the woods on our island. The trillium are*

*everywhere this time of year. I miss our quiet end of the lake and the sound of little waves licking sand. And I will tell you a little secret.*

*I miss Cad.*

*I like his family. I like this house. But I will be glad to come home to my island. So keep the light burning for me and the* Missouri, *Stoney.*

*Your friend, Spunky*

Aurora smiled to herself as she put the missive back in its envelope. Her oatmeal was a little cool, but she managed to finish it. When she heard Harrison stirring upstairs, she filled his ewer with warm water and carried it up.

Still in his nightshirt and bare feet, he was laying his clothes out on the unmade bed when she entered the room.

He greeted her with a smile, taking the pitcher from her and setting it in the washbasin so he could take her in his arms. "Good morning, my sunshine!" He kissed her briefly, then held her close, whispering into her hair. "I love you!"

Aurora pressed her cheek against his chest, thankful for the tender words and affections Harrison had been quickly and regularly offering since the night they first shared his bed. The consummation of their marriage marked a wonderful new beginning, making him much more open with her, and she thanked God every day for the change.

Holding Aurora so close, smelling the familiar essence of her apple blossom toilet water stirred feelings within Harrison that made him want to go back to bed and take her with him. In this room of white plaster and oak, where he had once suffered so much pain, he now experienced the most joyous, ecstatic moments of his life, thanks to Aurora.

Reluctantly, he loosed his embrace. Still smiling, he cradled her face in his hands and gazed into her blue eyes. "Do you love me?"

"You know I do."

Despite the quick honesty in Aurora's reply, Harrison's question came at her like a two-pronged meat fork. Secretly, she anguished over the possibility that Harrison would someday hurt her deeply again. And she suffered knowing that she was holding back, afraid to trust him and love him as completely as she was able. Wishing to escape those thoughts, and the unsettling effects of Harrison's touch, she slipped her hands over his, smiling as she pulled them away, then broke contact.

"There's a letter waiting for you downstairs, from Spunky. Mrs. Dixon brought it over earlier this morning."

Harrison sensed an uneasiness in Aurora. Though she had been warm and giving every night in the marriage bed, she seemed restrained in discussing her feelings, and unprepared to be pressed on the issue.

"I'll be down in a few minutes to read it. Why don't you go to the kitchen now and fry up some bacon and cook me a stack of your delicious flapjacks. I just realized how hungry I am."

"Flapjacks and bacon and fresh coffee. I'll get started on it."

Harrison saw an eagerness in the way Aurora whirled out of the room that bothered him. He listened to the click of her heels as she hurriedly descended the stairs, and couldn't believe it resulted from any great desire to begin her cooking chores.

Turning to the mirror, he addressed his image. "Love, affection, kindness, patience. Offer those generously each

257

day, and the time will come when she won't be so quick to scat away."

"Cad!" Leaning against the deck rail, Spunky waved her handkerchief the moment she saw him at the dock. The sight of his tall form made her realize anew just how much she had missed him.

His enthusiastic wave and broad smile sent her dashing for the stairs to the lobby. Remembering Mrs. Blackburn's advice never to rush, but to carry herself always with dignity, she paused at the top of the gangway to gain composure. Shoulders straight, head held high beneath the plumed and beribboned sailor hat Cad's sister gave her, she moderated her pace, letting her hips sway just a little with each step. All the while, the farm girl inside her wanted to bolt off the dock to his side.

Cad could have confused Spunky for his sister, the way she elegantly stepped onto the dock. One thing he couldn't mistake was her smile. The sight of her beaming face lit him up inside, making him want to pull her into his arms and kiss her long and hard right on the mouth, in full view of everyone! Instead, he took her small bag from her and offered his arm, unable to stop grinning. "Welcome home, Serilda!" He wanted to add that the island had been weeping all the while she had been away, but he knew the time hadn't yet come for poetry.

"Thank you, Mr. Blackburn." She wanted to tell Cad barely a minute had gone by in Chicago but what she had wished he were there, how she had filtered every moment, every experience, through her longing to have him beside her. But she would not give away her heart to a man who was destined to seek his future in another place with a more suitable woman.

Those unpleasant thoughts took flight when Cad escorted her toward the carriages parked near the dock. Even from several yards away, she noticed the burgundy plume atop Acorn's head and the spiffy new buggy to which she was rigged. On the black door, above and below a handsome bird's eye maple panel, two lines were elegantly lettered in burgundy and outlined in white.

*Island Carriage Tours*

*C. Blackburn, Prop. and Guide*

"You finished your rig while I was gone!" Forgetting Mrs. Blackburn's advice on proper conduct, Spunky ran ahead, peering inside at the rich-looking maroon velvet seats.

Cad caught up. "What do you think?"

She ran her hand over the fancy maple inset. "It's prettier than anything I saw in Chicago." She turned to gaze into his bluer-than-blue eyes. They glimmered with pride. She was so pleased for him, she felt her own eyes begin to water. Set on avoiding sentimentality, she addressed him brusquely. "How many fares have you collected so far?"

Cad was tempted to exaggerate, but he replied honestly. "None. This is my first time out."

Spunky reached into her skirt pocket, coming up with a quarter. She held it out to him. "Then I'm your first."

"I don't want your money." Cad pushed her hand away.

"Nonsense. It's my privilege, being your first paying

passenger." She tucked the coin into his jacket pocket. "Now, Mr. Blackburn, if you'll kindly assist me into your rig and fetch my trunks, I'm eager to be on my way home." When Cad had helped her up and set her small bag at her feet, she added, "I have two trunks now, mind you. The small one I took with me, and a new larger one for all the clothes I bought, and the ones your sister gave me. Both trunks are well-marked."

Within minutes, Cad had loaded her trunks and set out on the road home, and for the first two miles, words flowed in a constant stream, Spunky telling of Cad's family, her shopping and dining experiences, and the clothes his sister had sent home with her; Cad sharing what little news came to mind of the island, the rainy weather, and his efforts to finish his carriage.

When there was at last a lull in the conversation, Spunky noticed the changes spring had brought to her island. The forest was alive with the music of songbirds—the *ick, chink* of the rose-breasted grosbeak, the trill and jumbled notes of the song sparrow, and the buzzy trills, twitters and *su-weets* of the goldfinch. Beneath the hardwoods, showy trilliums put down the welcome-home carpet she had known would be waiting for her.

She was sorry for the ride to end when Cad drove up to her father's farm. Somehow, the weathered gray siding of the clapboard house, the sagging roof of the barn, and the tilt of the wind-battered chicken coop presented a more humble appearance than she remembered. The smoke rising from the sugar shack and the essence of the boiling maple sap drifted her way, reminding her of the chore she had left behind. Her father and brothers had promised to finish making the syrup in her absence, but like so many

260

tasks, it evidently required her organization.

Cad jumped down and lifted Spunky out just as Peter came from the shack. She was unprepared for the tired, worn look on her brother's face, but he welcomed her with a half smile. "Spring chores didn't get done the way they shoulda with you gone, Sis. How 'bout changin' outa those fancy duds? Sure could use a hand around here."

In all Spunky's years of working on the family farm, she couldn't remember a time when Peter had admitted needing her help. His words welcomed her home in a way no others could have. She threw her arms about him and kissed him on the cheek—something she hadn't done since he was a very small boy.

He stepped out of her embrace, rosy patches blossoming on his cheeks. "Ain't no call to get sentimental," he scolded. As if eager to change the subject, he stepped up to Cad's rig, running his hand over the bird's eye maple panel, then making his way to the back. "That's some outfit ya got there, Blackburn. I hope ya prosper." He reached for one of Spunky's trunks. "Ya sure came home with a lot more'n ya took, Sis." Hoisting the trunk to his shoulder, he added, "Don't dawdle too long, now. Y'r work is waitin'."

When he turned to go, Spunky exchanged grins with Cad.

He stepped close, his smile fading, his gaze fixed tenderly on her. "Peter has a funny way of saying he missed you," he quietly observed, "but I'll say it right out. I missed you, Serilda. I'm glad you're back." Taking her hands in his, he tenderly kissed each of them, sending a thrill through her, making her wish the work would go away, at least until tomorrow.

Cad wanted to take Spunky into his arms and kiss her,

then kiss her some more. But he knew if he did, he wouldn't want to stop. Being with her now made him hate the thought of leaving. He forced himself to release her. "You've got work to do, and so have I. I'll call on you later."

Leaping into his rig, he gently slapped the reins against Acorn, not daring to look back as he drove away.

Spunky stepped out of Mr. Cherryman's general store, closed her eyes, and turned her face to the mid-June sunshine that had just peeked out from behind the bank of storm clouds scudding off to the northeast. She welcomed the brightness and warmth, pausing a few minutes, soaking it in, hoping it would act to dispel the gloominess that had settled deep within.

Setting out for home, she realized she was looking forward to the official start of summer only five days off, hoping it would usher in a more favorable climate. Spring on North Manitou had been cool and damp in more ways than one. Every Saturday morning since her return from Chicago, rain or shine, she had walked from the farm with her basket of goods to sell at the store, and each time, Cad had passed her on the road with a carriage full of pretty young ladies, fare-paying visitors to the island, charmed into gay laughter by his wit and humor.

He always made a point of tipping his hat and greeting her cheerfully and respectfully with a "Good day, Miss Anders," and the girls beside him never failed to offer a polite wave of their gloved hands, but the brief encounters rankled, knowing he had not once called on her as promised since her return from Chicago.

Seven weeks had passed since—seven lonely, work-filled weeks, each seemingly endless in its drudgery. She rarely strayed from home except for her Saturday morning excursions, and even those had become painful reminders that the one man she cared about, the man who had told her he'd missed her and had given her every reason to believe he cared about her, would never settle his attentions on her alone. She had been a fool to ever think it possible—a twenty-five-year-old unmarriageable fool. She tried to content herself with the memories of the times she had spent with him, of her visit with his family in Chicago, and the trunk full of pretty things she would never find reason to wear. But in her heart was an empty, lonely place that Cad alone could fill.

Her disturbing thoughts were interrupted by the sound of a carriage coming up behind her. She stepped off the road to leave room for it to pass, dreading the encounter. A part of her was tempted to ignore Cad completely this time. She kept her eyes on the ground, waiting for the telltale sound of laughter as the rig approached, but all was quiet except for the clip-clop of the horse's hooves, which slowed to a halt beside her.

# CHAPTER

## 23

"Spunky, climb aboard. I'll drive you home."

"Stoney!" She hadn't seen him for weeks, and then the encounter had been made in passing at the store, not an opportunity for conversation. She settled herself on the seat beside him. "How have you been, Stoney? And Aurora?"

Harrison's smile told more than words, making her covet the happiness he had obviously found. "We're just fine. And you? I haven't heard much since you wrote from Chicago and said the Blackburns were treating you kindly."

"I'm fine," she said half-heartedly.

"I see Cad now and again. He sometimes brings his customers around to the light station to see the sights." Harrison delighted in the opportunities Cad was bringing his way to share with others about the lightkeeping service. It had opened a new rapport between himself and the erstwhile city slicker. From the changes in Cad, especially since establishing his tour service, Harrison had developed a sincere respect for his former nemesis, and an honest friendship had resulted. Although Cad hadn't discussed his courting of Spunky, he *had* shared in confidence his surprising intentions toward her.

"You've seen more of Cad than I have, then," Spunky admitted with a sigh.

Her statement troubled Harrison. He'd spoken with Cad just last week, and hadn't heard of anything amiss. "Did you two have a falling out recently?"

"A falling out? How could we have a falling out? We've evidently never had a falling *in!* At least, *he* hasn't. Not once has he come to see me since I got home from Chicago, even though he promised he would." Her throat tightened, and tears began to collect in her eyes, but she couldn't refrain from pouring out the disappointment she'd kept locked inside. "I thought he'd changed, but it's the same old Cad—the great pretender! What a fool I've been!" She swiped at a tear with the back of her hand.

Harrison pulled out his handkerchief and dropped it in her lap. Somehow the pieces weren't fitting together, and he intended to let Cad know Spunky was suffering because of him. Giving the matter more thought, an idea came to him, an opportunity to change to a brighter topic. "Say, Charlotte's wedding is next Saturday. It's sure to be a wonderful affair," he claimed enthusiastically. "You're going, aren't you?"

"I didn't even know I was invited."

"Sure you are. Charlotte specifically asked if you would be coming when she was over to visit Aurora last week, and I've had in mind ever since to take the matter up with you. The ceremony is to take place on the beach in front of the lighthouse on South Manitou if the weather holds up. Everybody on that island will be there, including all the children Charlotte has been teaching at the school.

"The reception will be quite grand. The Garritys, Charlotte's rich friends from Detroit, are putting it on for her. They're pitching a big tent on the light station grounds. Their French chef is baking the cake and all sorts of special pastries. It will be the finest spread between Chicago and Grand Hotel on Mackinac Island! You can't miss it!"

Though Stoney had made the event sound appealing, Spunky wasn't in the right frame of mind to give her best wishes to a young bride. "I don't want to go, Stoney."

Harrison let a few moments pass before taking up his case anew. "It would do you a world of good to forget the work on your father's farm and the trouble with Cad and enjoy yourself for the day, Spunky. Besides, you could wear that nice dress you bought in Chicago. Aurora's been wanting to see it on you ever since you described it in your letter."

The thought of wearing the dress began to spark her interest. She had been longing for a reason to take it out of her trunk and put it on. Certainly Cad hadn't provided one, nor was he about to. She saw herself on the beach by the South Manitou tower, looking on while Charlotte and Seth exchanged vows. For once, she wouldn't feel out of place among the fancier folks. She could thank the Blackburns in Chicago for teaching her to be at ease, no matter what company she found herself in. "Oh, all right, Stoney. I'll go."

"Good!" Harrison slapped the reins, urging his horse to a slightly faster pace. He was eager to deliver Spunky home and chase down Cad. With the first half of his plan in place, he was impatient to proceed with the second, less challenging part.

He pulled up in Anders's drive and helped Spunky down. Peter was in the barnyard, and started toward them. Harrison hadn't seen Spunky's brother since last winter when he'd predicted Harrison's demise. He had no need of an encounter with the disagreeable fellow now. Quickly, he told Spunky of the plans for getting to Charlotte's wedding.

"Be at the light station at ten o'clock next Saturday morning. Nat and Seth are coming on the *Manitou Lady* to pick us up after they've fetched Preacher Mulder from Glen Arbor."

Spunky returned his handkerchief. "Thanks for the ride, Stoney. See you next week."

Peter approached Harrison as he climbed aboard his rig. "Y're gettin' about just as if nothin' ever happened to y'r leg," he observed with a scowl. "I s'pose y're up and down the light tower like there's nothin' to it, too."

Harrison nodded, eager to get away before Peter found something nasty to say. Then a grin spread wide across the farmer's face.

"Good! I just knew if I told ya y'd never get up that tower again, ya wouldn't quit tryin' till ya proved me wrong!"

Begrudgingly, Harrison smiled. "It's nice seeing you again, Peter."

As he drove off, he realized Peter was far more calculating and complex than he ever would have imagined. Splashing somewhat recklessly through a puddle left over from the early morning thunderstorm, his thoughts turned to another man who had proved himself complex, and he went in search of him for the sake of their mutual friend, Spunky.

Thanks to the magic Mrs. Freiling had worked with needle and thread, Cad's too-tight shirt and jacket now fit. As he straightened his tie in the front hall mirror, he realized he wasn't wild about missing an entire Saturday of driving his paying customers around North Manitou, especially now that the summer visitors were coming in greater numbers, but he had neglected Spunky too long. And to think Stoney, of all people, had brought the problem to his attention!

He hadn't intended to ignore her at all. He had planned many times to visit her. But, instead, his plans had been put aside. On several occasions, paying customers requested evening rides around the island. Other times, his tack or buggy needed repair or polishing. Once, he had actually been on his way to her place, then turned back, deciding that being with her, he wouldn't be able to leave, and it would be wiser not to flirt with temptation.

The clock on the mantel in the sitting room chimed a quarter till nine. He picked his hat off the hall tree and headed out the front door, stepping up into the buggy he had thoroughly cleaned and rigged just before going inside to change his clothes.

Driving down the road toward the Anders's place, he realized if he were going to take a day off from work, at least he had chosen a day fit for a king. The turquoise sky held a few fluffy clouds and plenty of pure gold sunlight—a heavenly treasure chest! And he was on his way to collect a real gem of a woman. Spunky would be surprised when he arrived to drive her to the light station, and even more amazed to learn he would be her escort for the entire day!

Standing on a podium on the beach, Aurora glanced out across the company of wedding guests gathered in front of the South Manitou light tower, then up at Harrison who stood close beside her in the charcoal gray pinstripe suit and striped tie he had purchased for his own wedding many months ago. How handsome he was, standing as tall and strong as he had before his accident.

She squeezed his hand, her signal that she was ready to begin the duet Charlotte had asked them to sing before the ceremony would begin. Her heartbeat quickened when she gazed into her husband's eyes and realized how blessed she was to have him near at this moment, and how very thankful she was for the seemingly unending patience and understanding he displayed when she was feeling tired or sick to her stomach.

He had been full of conversation, no longer shy in expressing his devotion in words, and generous in sharing his affections. The constancy of his love had assuaged the sting of the earlier, difficult months of their marriage, and nearly wiped away lingering doubts that he could ever hurt her like before. The new openness she saw in him had even improved the music they made together at home. Now, when they performed duets, he sang the words rather than humming or substituting "la, la, la."

In her mind, she could hear the message they would soon sing, and prayed it was not only a song, but a true promise between herself and the man she loved.

Harrison squeezed Aurora's hand, indicating he, too was ready, then he nodded to the accordion player. When the notes of the introduction sounded, he took up his wife's other hand, also, and held them both to his chest, hoping the pounding of his heart wouldn't be as distracting to her as the charming glow on her cheeks was to him. He drew a deep breath and began singing bass harmony to her delicate soprano melody.

*Oh promise me that some day you and I*
*will take our love together to some sky,*
*where we can be alone and faith renew,*
*and find the hollows where those flowers grew,*
*those first sweet violets of early spring,*
*Which come in whispers thrill us both, and sing*
*of love unspeakable that is to be;*
*Oh promise me, oh promise me!*

*Oh promise me, that you will take my hand,*
*the most unworthy in this lonely land,*
*and let me sit beside you, in your eyes*
*Seeing the vision of our paradise,*
*Hearing God's message while the organ rolls,*
*its mighty music to our very souls,*
*no love less perfect than a life with thee:*
*Oh promise me, oh promise me!*

Aurora's knees were so weak by the time the accompanist had finished the final notes of the piece, she was certain she would have fallen off the podium without Harrison to help her down. Somehow, she found the strength to walk to the back of the congregation. There, she joined Bridget, Charlotte, and Mr. Trevelyn for the bridal procession, while Seth and Nat Trevelyn and George Garrity took their places beside Preacher Mulder at the front.

Aurora's heart went out to Nat. Though he had put on a brave face for his brother's sake, he couldn't completely hide his concern for his wife, Meta, who was now gravely ill with an incurable disease. Bridget, too, seemed to be struggling to keep a smiling face.

But Charlotte had never looked prettier, or happier.

The bridal gown Aurora had made and worn herself seven months ago appeared even more attractive on her youngest sister today. And the golden flecks in her warm brown eyes absolutely sparkled with joy!

The procession began to the tune of the accordion player, and within moments, Aurora found herself at the front of the congregation again, this time listening to Pastor Mulder read the solemnization of matrimony from the church discipline. Harrison stood only a few feet away, an expression of total adoration on his face as he looked at her. She tried to keep her mind on Charlotte and Seth as they exchanged their vows, but instead, her gaze drifted to Harrison.

Harrison couldn't keep his eyes off Aurora. He had never seen her looking more beautiful. The elegant lace overlay of the fancy lavender dress she had made several weeks ago, contrasted nicely with the intense blue of her eyes, and the bright sun made the pin at her neckline—the gold pin his grandmother had worn years ago—shimmer with a warmth that only enhanced the natural brightness for which Aurora was named. He found her more appealing today than on the day of their own wedding!

But deep inside, he was a little troubled. Though she was his wife, he couldn't help feeling she was somehow not completely his, but was holding back a little piece of her heart, not quite ready to give herself totally to him. He prayed it would not always be so, that he would find a way to win her completely.

Then Preacher Mulder spoke to Seth, and it was as if Harrison were being given a chance to take his vows all over again, to rededicate himself to the promises he had made on his own wedding day in November when he had been too crippled physically and emotionally to fully grasp their meaning.

"Wilt thou have this woman to be thy wedded wife, to live together after God's ordinance in the holy estate of Matrimony? Wilt thou love her, comfort her, honor and keep her, in sickness and in health: and forsaking all other, keep thee only unto her, so long as ye both shall live?"

"I will."

Aurora saw Harrison's lips move, forming the words "I will." A warmth flooded over her, from the top of her head, into even the hidden corner of her heart. The feeling descended through knees still weak with emotion, to the tips of her toes. Inside, she sensed the most blessed, precious, complete feeling of love she had ever known. She need no longer wonder whether to trust again. No matter what life brought, Harrison's love for her, and hers for him would be sufficient to see them through.

Now, Preacher Mulder was leading Charlotte through her vows, and Aurora said them in her heart. The words brought tears to her eyes, and she couldn't keep from whispering the final phrase, "and thereto I plight thee my faith."

From the look on Aurora's radiant face, Harrison knew instinctively this day was the first day of a marriage given a new start. The union that had marked its beginnings in the storms of November had weathered the winter of illness, emotional strife, and frigid relations, and had finally healed itself beneath the warmth of a summer sun. He wanted to take her in his arms this very minute and kiss her even as Seth was now kissing Charlotte. But Harrison's kiss would not be a polite ceremonial peck.

Somehow, Harrison managed to restrain himself, waiting patiently for the wedding to end. When guests began to make their way to the reception beneath the huge canvas tent near the keeper's quarters, he put his arm about Aurora's waist and separated her from the others.

Aurora didn't need to ask why Harrison was taking her away from the wedding party. She, too, felt the need to be with her husband.

Finding a quiet place near the water's edge, Harrison wasted no time in pulling her close and placing his mouth over hers, offering a kiss that conveyed more than love. In it, she sensed a vibrant joy pulsing through him that sealed a new and greater commitment of sharing as husband and wife. When their kiss ended, he kept his arms tightly about her.

"Aurora, maybe that kiss has told you all you need to know . . . that I love you with all my heart—"

Her face, upturned to his, was radiant. "And *I* love *you* . . . more now than ever—"

He bent to touch her warm lips again, but she pulled slightly away.

Seeing the furrow in his brow, she hastened to reassure him. "Harrison . . . I have some news—" When he paled at this, she smiled encouragingly and hurried on. "Oh, it's quite wonderful news, really. I've just been waiting for the proper time to tell you . . . that we're going to have a baby—"

The look on his face was pure happiness mingled with awe. "A baby?"

She nodded. "I hope it will be a boy, just like you!"

"Aurora . . . darling . . . you've made me the proudest man in the Islands!" Resisting the urge to sweep her off her feet and whirl her about, he settled for a gentle kiss on the forehead. "Remind me to treat you much more tenderly from now on!"

"Oh, that's not necessary," she countered affectionately, "at least not until later." Rising on her toes, she claimed the kiss she had forestalled moments earlier.

In the middle of Cad's conversation with George Garrity in the open-sided tent where Charlotte's wedding reception was underway, his mind strayed to Harrison and Aurora. He was probably the only guest who was paying the least bit of attention, but he couldn't help noticing the scene unfolding on the beach several yards away, the loving exchange of affections. He had long admired the couple's devotion to one another. Being with Spunky again and attending this wedding made him want more than ever the commitment only marriage could provide.

Keeping his mind on his favorite subject—the automobile—shouldn't be a struggle at all, but Cad found he had to force himself to pay attention to what Mr. Garrity was saying.

"This idea you have to build extra strong frames on North Manitou intrigues me, but there's one thing I don't understand. Why take them to Chicago? Why not Detroit? I've got a warehouse, or at least part of one, where you could assemble ... "

Cad's mind and eyes strayed again, this time to Spunky. She was talking with George's wife and his mother, and to his surprise, she even made the uppity old woman laugh! Seeing Spunky at ease in such fancy company made him realize how much she had changed over the winter, and through her experience in Chicago, from the uneducated, untraveled, plain-talking island farm girl to a woman with knowledge, schooling, and social graces that far exceeded her upbringing.

And how beautiful she looked in the deep rose lace and silk gown she had brought home from Chicago! Never before had he seen her in such fancy costume, with her hair pulled up on her head, Gibson girl style, exposing her elegant neck. When she had been away in Chicago, he had come to terms with the fact that he loved her. He had been wise enough, too, to know he had nothing to offer her until he earned his own self-respect. Being here with her only sharpened his desire to make her his, and his determination to focus on his fledgling business in order to be a success in his own right. But once the summer was through, then what?

" . . . and some capital to invest to get you started. What do you think, Mr. Blackburn? Are you willing to come to work for me in Detroit to start up an automobile business?"

Mr. Garrity's questions recaptured Cad's attention in short order, making him realize that the three things he wanted most in life seemed to be coming into focus in the same picture—his need to make something of himself, his strong interest in developing an automobile, and most importantly, his ardent desire to make a lasting promise to Spunky. He scratched his chin, taking time with his reply so as not to appear too eager. "I'm a Chicago man, myself, Mr. Garrity, but I'm more than willing to entertain the possibility for a change, if the terms are to my liking . . ."

Spunky had heard more than enough of the elder Mrs. Garrity's boastfulness concerning Detroit society to last a lifetime, but she dared not be rude. She sipped her cup of punch as she listened politely, and looked right past the old woman's shoulder to the handsome fellow across the way, the man who had dominated her thoughts day and night for months, and whose companionship today would only make her unable to forget the happiness he could put in her life. Only with a great measure of reluctance, and self-discipline, would she be able to return to her dull existence without him tomorrow.

She knew she was a fool for him. He could charm any lady. But over the winter, he had become much more than a charmer. He had become a man with a sense of right and wrong, a man willing to help a fellow man. Most importantly, he had become a man with a heart, and in so doing, had captured her own heart without even knowing it.

She loved him. Surely he felt *something* for her, too, or he wouldn't have shown up early this morning to be her escort for the day. She was tired of keeping her feelings for him a secret, tired of waiting for him to reveal his heart to her, and most of all, she was tired of spending her time with the ladies at this reception while he spent his with the men.

Now, Mr. Garrity was offering his hand and Cad was shaking it. Perhaps their discussion was coming to a close. But she sensed the old woman was far from finished talking to her.

" . . . these islands are so remote, so removed from civilized society. Don't you agree, Miss Anders?"

Unable to bear the city talk any longer, Spunky politely inched away. "You'll have to excuse me, ma'am. There's someone I must see just now." She had taken one step in the direction of Cad when he headed straight for her.

"Miss Serilda, I would like a word with you in private, if you don't mind." His hand at her elbow, he began to usher her out of the tent with urgency.

Thankful, but puzzled over her rescue, Spunky spoke her mind. "And I would like a word with *you*, Mr. Blackburn." When they were several feet from the nearest guest, she stopped to face him, her heart aflutter, her finger raised. "Mr. Blackburn—"

Cad placed a finger to her lips. Taking her by the shoulders with gentle firmness, he looked straight into the warmest brown eyes he had ever seen, the only ones that could melt his heart even in a Manitou blizzard, and took a deep breath. "Miss Serilda, listen carefully, because I'm only going to say this once. I love you and I want to marry you. Will you have me?"

The question nearly knocked the wind out of her, but she looked into the most uncommonly blue eyes she had ever known, eyes blue enough to brighten a gray Manitou sky, and drew a long breath. "Mr. Blackburn, listen carefully, because I'm only going to say this once. If you don't marry me, I just might run away to Chicago and find someone who will!"

Cad swiftly captured her face in his hands and pressed his lips to hers. The sweet urgency of his kiss left no doubt of his feelings.

Long moments later, they parted. A little breathless, Cad said, "I hope you're willing to wed when the summer is over, then move to Detroit for the winter. I've agreed to help Mr. Garrity start up in the automobile business, but I made him promise I could spend my summers on North Manitou . . . that is, of course, if you're agreeable."

Spunky kissed him briefly, her heart overflowing with joy. "Jumpin' junipers, Cadwallader Blackburn! I'd marry you even if it meant never seein' North Manitou again!"

# ABOUT DONNA WINTERS

Donna adopted Michigan as her home state in 1971 when she moved from a small town outside of Rochester, New York. She began penning novels in 1982 while working full time for an electronics firm in Grand Rapids.

She resigned from her job in 1984 following a contract offer for her first book. Since then, she has written several romance novels for various publishers, including Thomas Nelson Publishers and Zondervan Publishing House.

Her husband, Fred, an American History teacher, shares her enthusiasm for history. Together, they visit historical sites, restored villages, museums, and lake ports, purchasing books and reference materials for use in Donna's research and Fred's classroom.

Research for *Aurora of North Manitou Island* sent the couple on their first wilderness camping trip. On North Manitou Island, they pitched their tent two miles from the former lighthouse grounds and ventured forth on foot each day with camera, notebook, and pen, to visit the settings described in the book.

Donna has lived all of her life in states bordering on the Great Lakes. Her familiarity and fascination with these remarkable inland waters and her residence in the heart of Great Lakes Country make her the perfect candidate for writing *Great Lakes Romances*.

*Photos opposite show Donna Winters on her research trip to North Manitou Island during the summer of 1992.*

# ABOUT THE ARTIST

Patrick Kelley has been an artist since childhood. Nurturing his dream of one day seeing his work in print, he attended art school in his hometown of Grand Rapids, Michigan, completing his Bachelor of Fine Arts Degree at Kendall College of Art and Design in 1987.

A freelance artist since 1985, his creative ability has served clients such as American Greetings, Butterworth Hospital, and Zondervan Publishing House. In addition, his illustrations have been published in the Michigan Sports Gazette, Grand Rapids Magazine, and West Michigan Magazine.

Mr. Kelley's proficient use of airbrush, colored pencils, and stabilo pencils, along with his excellent draftsmanship and innate ability to interpret rough concepts into engaging designs, make him popular with his clients, and a winner at art shows. Over the years, he has earned first place awards for his work in pastels, photography, and watercolor.

Bigwater Publishing is pleased to feature the work of this talented Michigan artist on the covers of many of the books in the *Great Lakes Romances* series.

***More Great Lakes Romances***
For prices and availability, contact:
Bigwater Publishing
P.O. Box 177
Caledonia, MI 49316

***Mackinac***
by
Donna Winters
**First in the series of *Great Lakes Romances***
(Set at Grand Hotel, Mackinac Island, 1895)

*Her name bespeaks the age in which she lives* . . .but **Victoria Whitmore** is no shy, retiring Victorian miss. She finds herself aboard the *Algomah*, traveling from staid Grand Rapids to Michigan's fashionable Mackinac Island resort. Her journey is not one of pleasure; a restful holiday does not await her. Mackinac's Grand Hotel owes the Whitmores money—enough to save the furniture manufactory from certain financial ruin. It becomes Victoria's mission to venture to the island to collect the payment. At Mackinac, however, her task is anything but easy, and she finds more than she bargained for.

**Rand Bartlett**, the hotel manager, is part of that bargain. Accustomed to challenges and bent on making the struggling Grand a success, he has not counted on the challenge of Victoria—and he certainly has not counted on losing his heart to her.

### *The Captain and the Widow*
by
Donna Winters
**Second in the series of *Great Lakes Romances***
(Set in Chicago, South Haven, and
Mackinac Island, 1897)

*Lily Atwood Haynes is beautiful, intelligent, and ahead of her time . . .* but even her grit and determination have not prepared her for the cruel event on Lake Michigan that leaves her widowed at age twenty. It is the lake—with its fathomless depths and unpredictable forces—that has provided her livelihood. Now it is the lake that challenges her newfound happiness.

When **Captain Hoyt Curtiss**, her husband's best friend, steps in to offer assistance in navigating the choppy waters of Lily's widowhood, she can only guess at the dark secret that shrouds his past and chokes his speech. What kind of miracle will it take to forge a new beginning for *The Captain and the Widow? Note:* The Captain and the Widow *is a spin-off from* Mackinac.

## Sweethearts of Sleeping Bear Bay
by
Donna Winters

**Third in the series of *Great Lakes Romances***

(Set in the Sleeping Bear Dune region of
northern Michigan, 1898)

*Mary Ellen Jenkins is a woman of rare courage and experience . . .* One of only four females licensed as navigators and steamboat masters on the Western Rivers, she is accustomed to finding her way through dense fog on the Mississippi. But when she travels North for the first time in her twenty-nine years, she discovers herself unprepared for the havoc caused by a vaporous shroud off Sleeping Bear Point. And navigating the misty shoals of her own uncertain future poses an even greater threat to her peace of mind.

Self-confident, skilled, and devoted to his duties as Second Mate aboard the Lake Michigan sidewheeler, *Lily Belle,* **Thad Grant** regrets his promise to play escort to the petticoat navigator the instant he lays eyes on her plain face. Then his career runs aground. Can he trust this woman to guide him to safe harbor, or will the Lady Reb ever be able to overcome the great gulf between them? *Note:* Sweethearts of Sleeping Bear Bay *is a spin-off from* The Captain and the Widow.

## *Charlotte of South Manitou Island*
by
### Donna Winters
**Fourth in the series of *Great Lakes Romances***

(Set on South Manitou Island, Michigan, 1891-1898)

**Charlotte Richards' carefree world turns upside down on her eleventh birthday . . .** the day her beloved papa dies in a spring storm on Lake Michigan. Without the persistence of fifteen-year-old **Seth Trevelyn**, son of South Manitou Island's lightkeeper, she might never have smiled again. He shows her that life goes on, and so does true friendship.

When Charlotte's teacher invites her to the World's Columbian Exposition of 1893, Seth signs as crewman on the *Martha G.,* carrying them to Chicago. Together, Seth and Charlotte sail the waters of the Great Lake to the very portal of the Fair, and an adventure they will never forget. While there, Seth saves Charlotte from a near fatal accident. Now, seventeen and a man, he realizes his friendship has become something more. Will his feelings be returned when Charlotte grows to womanhood?

*Jenny of L'Anse Bay*
by
Donna Winters
**Special Edition in the series of**
*Great Lakes Romances*

(Set in the Keweenaw Peninsula of Upper Michigan in 1867)

**A raging fire destroys more than Jennifer Crawford's new home . . .** it also burns a black hole into her future. To soothe Jennifer's resentful spirit, her parents send her on a trip with their pastor and his wife to the Indian mission at L'Anse Bay. In the wilderness of Michigan's Upper Peninsula, Jennifer soon moves from tourist to teacher, taking over the education of the Ojibway children. Without knowing their language, she must teach them English, learn their customs, and live in harmony with them.

**Hawk**, son of the Ojibway chief, teaches Jennifer the ways of his tribe. Often discouraged by seemingly insurmountable cultural barriers, Jennifer must also battle danger, death, and the fears that threaten to come between her and the man she loves.

## *Sweet Clover: A Romance of the White City*
## Centennial Edition in the series of
## *Great Lakes Romances*

**The World's Columbian Exposition of 1893** brought unmatched excitement and wonder to Chicago, thus inspiring this innocent tale by Clara Louise Burnham, first published in 1894.

A Chicago resident from age nine, Burnham penned her novels in an apartment overlooking Lake Michigan. Her romance books contain plots imbued with the customs and morals of a bygone era—stories that garnered a sizable, loyal readership in their day.

In *Sweet Clover*, a destitute heroine of twenty enters a marriage of convenience to ensure the security and well-being of her fatherless family. Widowed soon after, Clover Bryant Van Tassel strives to rebuild a lifelong friendship with her late husband's son. Jack Van Tassel had been her childhood playmate, and might well have become her suitor. Believing himself betrayed by both his father and the girl he once admired, Jack moves far away from his native city. Then the World's Columbian Exposition opens, luring him once again to his old family home.

Hearts warmed by friendship blossom with affection—in some most surprising ways. Will true love come to all who seek it in the Fair's fabulous White City? The author will keep you guessing till the very end!

READER SURVEY—*Aurora of North Manitou Island*

Your opinion counts! Please fill out and mail this form to:
Reader Survey
Bigwater Publishing
P.O. Box 177
Caledonia, MI 49316

Your
Name:_____

Street:_____

City,State,Zip:_____ _____

In return for your completed survey, we will send you a bookmark and
the latest issue of our *Great Lakes Romances®Newsletter*. If your name
is not currently on our mailing list, we will also include four note
papers and envelopes, two each of the North Manitou keeper's quarters
and light tower (while supplies last—see pages 6 and 7 of this book).

1. Please rate the following elements from A (excellent) to E (poor).

_____Heroine    _____Hero    _____Setting    _____Plot

Comments:_____

_____

2. What setting (time and place) would you like to see in a future book?

_____

(Survey questions continue on next page.)

3. Where did you purchase this book?

_____

4. What influenced your decision to purchase this book?

_____Front Cover  _____First Page  _____Back Cover Copy

_____Title  _____Friends

_____Publicity (Please describe)_____

_____

5. Please indicate your age range:

_____Under 18  _____25-34  _____46-55

_____18-24  _____35-45  _____Over 55

If desired, include additional comments below.